ROAD TO GOLD

LT. COMMANDER
WILLIAM H. LABARGE,
USN (RET.)

HarperPaperbacks
A Division of HarperCollinsPublishers

Dedicated to my Mother.
The extraordinary woman who was always by my side,
and to my two beautiful daughters, Jennifer Anne and
Julie Marie, who inspire me daily.

This book is published by HarperPaperbacks, a private company in no way connected with the Department of Defense or the U.S. Navy. The characters and events portrayed in this novel are of the author's invention and are in no way sponsored by the U.S. Navy.
All characters in this book are fictitious, and any resemblance to actual persons, living or dead, is purely coincidental. The names, incidents, dialogue, and opinions expressed are of the author's imagination and subsequent editing, and should not be construed as real. Nothing is intended or should be interpreted as expressing or representing the view of any branch of the United States Armed Forces or any department or agency of any government body.

HarperPaperbacks   *A Division of* HarperCollins*Publishers*
                   10 East 53rd Street, New York, N.Y. 10022

Cover illustration by John Berkey

First printing: September 1993

Printed in the United States of America

HarperPaperbacks and colophon are trademarks of HarperCollins*Publishers*

❖ 10 9 8 7 6 5 4 3 2

ACKNOWLEDGMENTS

The author wishes to express his gratitude to the following persons who have helped in the preparation of this book:

•RADM Raymond W. Burk, USN (Ret.), who helped open some welcome doors;

•Capt. Tom Leonard, USNR, for personal recollections and gathering of research material;

•Capt. Dale M. Doorly, USN, for providing key technical material;

•CDR James H. Oliver, USN (Ret.), for his support and encouragement throughout the writing of this story;

•LCDR Gary Watts, USN (Ret.), for a valuable critique of the manuscript;

•Capt. James D. Scott, USMC, for firsthand information and editing of the manuscript.

CONTENTS

PROLOGUE

From the streets of Hometown, USA, to the body-numbing pace of the Pensacola pressure cooker, men, and most recently women, put their integrity on the line to see if they are worthy of wearing the famed "wings of gold." Not all that try prevail, but those who survive are of a special breed and truly have the right stuff to be a navy pilot.

On Florida's Gulf Coast, just south of the Alabama line, lies Pensacola. It is here that the "Cradle of Naval Aviation" was established, with Saufley Field being the first taste of naval aviation for the fledgling aviator. Ask any naval aviator what the hairiest flying in the navy is and you will probably get answers like "night carrier landings, all-weather terrain following low levels or test and evaluation flights." While these are undoubtedly challenging events, I contend that for pure terror, accident potential, and premature grayness, nothing can exceed being a student going through the Navy's flight program.

Primary flight training is where you develop basic airwork techniques that are the building blocks for further training. Basic and advanced flight training is where you sharpen mission-required skills and strive to obtain the pride in performance that makes a naval aviator. While an aviator's training never really ceases, the formal training received before you earn your "wings of gold" is probably the most significant, because here you learn the basics that you must build on for the rest of your aviation career.

Road to Gold will give you an appreciation of what it takes to become a naval aviator. When I left my hometown for navy flight school, I took many things: a naive enthusiasm; a love of family and country; hopes of becoming a naval aviator; a will to live; a sense of adventure; a fear of the unknown and a doubt in my ability to perform adequately under extreme stress.

Upon successful completion of flight training, if indeed you are able to do so, you will go to the fleet with many new values. A sense of pride and professionalism second to none; a level of technology and experience that will allow you to handle the physical and mental pressures of day-in and day-out tasking. You will be prepared for combat if asked to fight. But most of all, you will have measured up to the highest standards of any flight training the military has to offer and those coveted "wings of gold" will put you in an elite group of a select few.

Do you have the right stuff to become a naval aviator!

William H. LaBarge
LaJolla, California

GHOST OF CROW HILL

It was quarter to five in the morning when I rolled over and focused on the alarm clock next to my bed; it was set to go off at 5:00 A.M. As I waited for the alarm to sound I started to think about my future and to wonder if I was doing the right thing by joining the navy flight program. I wasn't worried about the physical part of the rigorous program. At six-feet-two, and with an athletic build, I figured I was ready for that part of it. I'd played baseball and basketball in college and was used to making demands on my body. But I was still scared.

As I lay in bed I recalled the first time my dad took me to see the Blue Angels perform at an air show. I was fourteen years old. The excitement of the show really made me want to fly navy jets, and I especially wanted to be among that elite group that landed on aircraft carriers. I thought anyone could land on 12,000 feet of runway, but to land a 60,000-pound aircraft on a pitching deck in the South China Sea at night was something else again. That's the team I wanted to be a part of and why I chose the Navy over the Air Force. Now, after four years of college and a half year of playing baseball, my dream of becoming a navy pilot was about to become a reality in four short weeks. I had my starting class date, I was to report to the Naval Air Station Pensacola, Florida, Building 699, on Monday, November 15, 1970.

Just as the alarm sounded my dad knocked on the door to see if I was up. We were going bear trapping, something he and I had been doing every fall for years. It was my dad's hobby, and as soon as I got old enough to go along, he started teaching me the art of trapping the black bear in Maine.

My father, Dr. Howard Sullivan, was a small man in his early fifties who stood five-feet-ten and weighed only 165 pounds, but he was as tough as they come. He had been an All-American football player at Syracuse University. He'd been born and raised in upstate New York, but after completing medical school, he moved to Dexter, Maine, to start his medical practice, raise a family, and secretly, I think, to hunt and fish.

Dexter is a small rural town in the center of Maine, and is world famous for Dexter Shoes. Because this part of Maine was so sparsely populated, doctors were few and several of Dad's patients lived hours away. Many of them were farmers whose cattle and sheep fell prey to bears during the fall months. The bears would often destroy a lot of livestock as they prepared for winter's hibernation. Most of his patients knew Dad's passion for hunting, so he and I would occasionally be called to trap these varmints.

While my father was still a newcomer to the pine-tree state in the early forties, two of his patients were trappers, and they taught him the art. The bears were trapped because they were killing cattle and sheep, and not just for the pleasure of catching a trophy. My dad always made it clear to me that we hunted and fished for a purpose and not just for the sake of killing.

I knew this would probably be my last hunt for a while because I had no idea where I might be in a year. Dad realized this and wanted us to spend some time together before I left for flight school. My mother was also uneasy. The Vietnam War was very real, and since I was the only son out of four children, she didn't want to lose me. But worried or not, they were both proud that I was joining the Navy.

I rolled out of bed and headed for the bathroom. The smell of freshly brewed coffee and bacon was filling the upstairs hallways. I knew it was hunting season, because the scene was the same one I had experienced every fall for the last ten years. Don't get me wrong, I loved to go on these hunts. It was fun to be out in the woods learning how to trap and live off the land. But this year we would be spoiled: we got to use a hunting camp. The farmer we were trapping the bear for had a cabin nearby, so he offered my dad its use. The camp would make the hunt much easier.

After a hearty breakfast, we checked to be sure we had all our gear, then loaded it into the Jeep and car. The barbed wire and bear bait went into the Jeep due to the bulk and smell. The rifles, food, and sleeping equipment went into the car. Once we got to the hunting camp, we'd leave the car and the Jeep would become our primary vehicle. We would be using two new bear sets and each set would take about two hours to build. Because it was a new location and we had to provide more equipment than usual for this hunt, we had a lot more bulk than usual. The hunting area was about two hours northwest of Dexter, and I wasn't looking forward to the drive because the roads were unpaved and poorly maintained.

I bounced along in the Jeep and Dad followed me in the car. Once we got to the campsite, we each had chores to perform. As usual, Dad handled the camp setup and I got the bait and traps primed and tested. Checking the traps was the most tedious job, because they had to be set and tripped to ensure that their closure speed and strength were acceptable. By law, each trap had to be able to sever an eight-inch circular log on closing. This required a closing speed of about 120 pounds. If the trap did not perform to these specifications, it could not be used.

We used steers' head for bait. Holes had to be punched through the skulls so that we could drive stakes through them and on into the ground at the base of a tree. "Cubby" was what we called the V- like entrance. It was built out of brush and ferns and stood about three-and-a-half feet high. The entrance V was four feet wide and six feet long. Its function was to guide the bear into the trap. The cubby was always built at the base of a large tree, with the V flaring out away from the trunk.

After the bait had been prepared and placed at the base of the tree, the trap was then set and positioned in the center of the V. A four-foot-long chain was attached to the trap and a log, six feet long and twelve inches in diameter, was attached to the opposite end of the chain. This allowed the bear to run free once he was trapped, but he wouldn't get far before he got tangled in brush. The log and chain would lie along the inside of the cubby once the trap was set.

A bear trap is not like a fox or beaver trap. You can't stand on the legs to open the jaws, you have to use C clamps. When we went bear trapping, we always worked in pairs, because if you got caught in a trap, you'd need the assistance of your partner to get out, otherwise you could bleed to death before you found help. This season we planned to stay up on the trap line due to the distance we had to travel. The law requires you to check the traps every twenty-four hours, once they have been set. It would be to difficult to travel back and forth each day, so we stayed on location.

Barbed wire is used because it is required by law. You must have two strands around the whole set. The first strand is two feet above the ground and the second is four feet. Signs must be posted on all four corners, in both French and English, reading BEAR TRAP. The wire keeps hunters from accidentally walking into the trap. Of course, if the bear you're after can read, then you're in for a long hunt.

After the equipment had been tested and the camp set up, Dad and I loaded up the Jeep and headed over to the farmer's house. He showed us the area where the bear had killed his livestock. The farmer, Eric Frost, lived two miles from the one-store town of Parkman, population eighty-two. His sheep and cattle grazed on Crow Hill, which was two miles behind his farm. Mr. Frost had found twenty-six of his sheep ripped apart and stacked in the back of a little weather shelter he had built for his livestock to get in out of the elements. This is a typical pattern that a black bear will follow. He does not like freshly killed meat; he likes it cold and rotten, so he kills and stacks the carcasses of his prey and returns later to feed on them. The bears usually do this just before winter, to bulk up for hibernation.

As we approached the shelter the smell was enough to gag a maggot. It was an unbelievable sight. All the dead sheep were neatly stacked in the back of this small hut. After dad surveyed the area, he told Mr. Frost that we were ready to go to work and that with any luck by the following week we would have a bear to show for our efforts.

It was obvious that this was the work of a bear. There were tracks everywhere and this bear was not a cub. My dad estimated by the size of the footprint that he was between four and five hundred pounds. We followed the tracks and bear droppings back into the woods about a half mile and located an ideal area to set our first trap.

There was a logging road close by, so we drove the Jeep to the area. While I unloaded the Jeep Dad cut boughs and small trees to build the cubby. Once all the materials were gathered for the bear set, Dad started constructing the cubby at the base of a sizable pine tree. I tied a loop through the steer's head and dragged it along the ground away from the set, in order to leave a scent to lure the bear to the bait once it was staked at the base of the tree.

After the cubby was constructed, Dad drove a wooden tree branch through the steer's head and anchored it to the ground at the base of the tree. As the wooden support went through the skull Dad said, "It sure would take a big aspirin to cure that headache." Once the head was in place, I took bailing wire and secured the bait to the base of the tree. This would keep other animals from stealing it.

While Dad prepared the trap, I cut the toggal pole, the six-foot log that was attached to the trap. This would allow the bear to run once caught and prevent him from smashing the trap or chewing his leg off to get free. The bear would get tangled up in brush and nine times out of ten we would find him close by.

Before Dad handled the trap, he put on gloves that were covered with bear scent. He wiped the trap down with a rag to remove as much human scent as possible before setting it. A bear's smell is its best sense and masking the human presence improved our chances of luring him into the set. Dad bought this nasty fragrance from an old trapper who swore by it. The ingredients, as near as we could figure it, were bear urine and beaver carcass. We called it Chanel No. 5.

After the trap was set, Dad put a wooden matchstick

under the pan to keep small animals from tripping it. With the matchstick in place, it took at least fifty-five pounds of pressure to set the trap off. We then positioned the toggal pole along the left side of the cubby. A piece of green moss was put on the trip pan, to indicate where the center of the trap was located, then we covered the trap with leaves and twigs. Several logs were placed at the opening of the cubby and along the sides of the entrance. This would force the bear to lift his paw over the hazards and place it into the center of the trap. The final chore was to string the barbed wire and post the signs.

We cleaned up around the set and made it look as natural as possible, then headed back to camp for lunch. During our break, we discussed the best location for the next trap. Dad had a feeling that this was an old, crafty bear and it was going to take some clever stunts to catch him.

After lunch Dad surprised me when he said, "Matt, I want you to go home and bring back all eleven bear traps. Stop at the grocery store on the way out of town and pick up a box full of meat scraps."

Of course I asked what he had in mind. "Why in the world do we need eleven more traps?"

"Well, son, if we plan on catching this bear, we're going to have to outfox him. I think the only way this bear will be caught is by using live bait."

"Live bait?"

"Yes, Matt, live bait. If Mr. Frost will let us use four live sheep, we'll pen them up down by the swamp and put all of our traps around the pen. Then we'll take the meat scraps and hang them on trees back in the swamp. If we're lucky, this will lure the bear to the livestock. While you're getting the traps I'll try to sell our plan to Frost."

After lunch I jumped into the car and headed out. By six that evening I had returned with everything on Dad's shopping list. Mr. Frost was more than willing to go along with the plan and had gathered up four sheep and penned them In his barn overnight. That evening, after dinner, Dad and I checked all the traps and made sure they were in good working order. We got to bed before midnight, knowing that the next day would be a busy one.

By six o'clock Dad and I were up and getting ready for a long day. After breakfast we headed down to check the first trap to see if we had gotten lucky. When checking the bear set, the lead man carries a rifle in case he runs into the trapped bear. The backup man has a pistol for protection and uses it to kill any small animal that might be caught in the trap. As we approached the set we could see that things were normal—the trap was still set and the bait had not been disturbed by smaller animals. It's evident when you have a hit. The cubby and surrounding area are completely destroyed. There is a trail of broken branches and turned up underbrush that a bear leaves behind him as he drags the toggal pole to the point where he finally gets entangled.

After the first set was checked, Dad and I gathered our traps, collected the materials necessary to build the pen for Mr. Frost, and started in on our new project. Four hours later, the live enticement was completed. This was the most dangerous work we had ever attempted. With twelve bear traps set in a very small area, we had to be very careful not to step in the wrong place. There were no cubbies built. All the traps were positioned around the penned-in sheep and covered with leaves and dirt.

We then strung the required strands of barbed wire around the whole site and posted the signs. As we walked back to the Jeep the stench from the decomposed carcasses was almost overwhelming. Frost would have to bury them soon, so we hoped for a quick hit.

We ate a late lunch and then drove into Parkman to get some more meat scraps and honeycomb. The Parkman General Store was unique. It had a little something for everyone. As we entered there were several old boys smoking corncob pipes sitting around a potbelly stove in the middle of the floor telling stories. The owner greeted us at the counter and a large German shepherd circled around our legs as we explained what we needed. After the proprietor got all the latest gossip on what we were up to, we paid for our goods and headed back to Crow Hill. There were only a few hours of daylight left, so we had to hustle to finish up before dark.

My job was to wire the chunks of meat to trees a mile or so from the bear sets while Dad cooked the honeycomb with birchbark. This mixture created a lot of smoke and the aroma could bring a bear out of hibernation. This was an old trick that a trapper taught my dad, one he used when he had to draw a bear out of a swampy bog.

As darkness started to fall I had completed my

job and headed back to the area where Dad was working. As I approached the field I could smell the fire. Dad saw me coming and gave a wave.

I waved back and yelled, "You've mixed a great batch, I could smell it a mile away."

"It should get some attention," Dad replied. "Did you have any trouble stringing the meat, Matt?"

"Not really, but I had the feeling I was being watched, especially on the back side of the ridge near Crow Hill."

Dad laughed and said, "Bears are pretty crafty. You probably *were* being watched. I'm all done here. Let's get back to the cabin and fry up those steaks we brought."

"Sounds good, Dad. I'm so hungry I could eat the asshole out of a dead skunk."

Dad laughed and said, "I don't think I'm that starved yet, son."

After dinner Dad and I sat in a couple of old rocking chairs in front of the potbelly stove that heated the cabin, and did a little reminiscing. Dad lit up his favorite pipe and started telling stories about me that I had forgotten or wanted to forget. One saga I particulalry wanted to erase from my childhood was resurrected. "Matt, remember the time you hopped the freight train and got your leg caught?"

"How could I ever forget that stunt? You grounded me for three months. If Mr. Kite hadn't seen me on the back of the caboose, I might have pulled it off."

"I don't think so, son. That two hours it took you to walk home after you jumped off would have given you away. And besides, you would have come clean eventually."

"I learned my lesson that day, believe me. Say, Dad, remember when we were ice fishing on Moose River up near Moosehead Lake and you fell through the ice?"

"You bet I do. If I hadn't got my arms out to break my fall as quick as I did, I probably would have been swept downstream. The current under the ice was strong and I was almost a goner."

"I never saw you go through the ice, but I'll never forget that two-mile hike across the river to get to our Jeep. I was afraid you were going to freeze to death; it was about five below zero that day, wasn't it?"

"Something like that and I've never been so bone-chilled cold as I was that day. I never would have made it off the ice if you hadn't been there to help me, Matt."

After a few more stories, Dad started to get a little philosophical. He was beginning to realize that I really was leaving the nest soon and the type of career that I had chosen was very dangerous and there was a strong possibility that I could get killed. But he was very positive in his lecture on goal setting. He told me to be aggressive, professional, and always to remember my limitations.

He said, "Don't allow yourself to be put in a situation that you can't recover or escape from. Take that with you, son, and you'll be a survivor."

I started to get a little teary-eyed, but recovered when Dad asked me to get some more wood for the stove.

These hunting trips that Dad and I spent together were very special, because when I was growing up, I hardly had time to see him. Being one of two doctors within a hundred-mile radius, he was always on the go taking care of his patients. His hospital was over an hour from our home, so it was difficult to make our cycles match. As I got older and more physicians came to Maine, we got more prime time together.

The next day we planned to do a little grouse hunting after we checked the bear sets and the bait in the trees. Dad wanted to stop by the shelter to see if any of the carcasses had been moved or eaten on our way to the apple orchard where we would hunt the birds. Once the traps were set, it became a waiting game and we had time to play. If a stream or lake was near, we would wet a line or look for birds while we waited.

The weather was warm and that was to our disadvantage. Bears move better when it's cold, wet, and damp, but a front was scheduled to pass through midweek and we hoped it would stir up some action. We cleaned and oiled our shotguns for the next day's hunt and went to bed.

I didn't sleep very well during the night, tossing and turning as the hours ticked away toward morning. My subconscious must have been reviewing Dad's lecture. When I finally fell asleep in the early morning, I was having some wild dreams. In one dream I was dogfighting with Russian MiGs, then I was shot down in Vietnam and tortured in a Vietnamese prison camp. When Dad came over to stir me, I awoke with a start and was soaked with perspiration.

He asked if I was all right and I said, "It was a rough night killing communists."

He said, "There aren't many communists up here, but we do have some bears to kill."

I got cleaned up, put on my hunting clothes, and sat down to a wholesome breakfast Dad had prepared. He made the best pancakes, and I was so hungry from working the day before that I had a dozen. The bacon was done just right, crisp but still bubbled and clear.

After breakfast we cleaned up the camp, gathered our hunting gear, and headed out the door. The weather was turning in our favor—an overcast had settled in and the temperature was dropping.

Before we did any pleasure hunting, we had to check the traps and bait. Things looked normal at both sets. The sheep in the pen were lying down resting, so Dad and I split up to check the chunks of meat I had wired to the trees. I scouted out the back side of Crow Hill and Dad checked the ridge line.

I backtracked the logging road that I had used to wire the bait. As I approached the first chunk of meat I saw a big northern shrike sitting on the meat having a feast. A shrike looks a lot like a blue jay, but is much larger and has a prominent blue-and-white-feather crown on its head. I hadn't seen one of these birds for years. They were on the endangered-species list, and according to the game wardens, there were only a few hundred remaining.

As I walked deeper into the woods I couldn't see any more meat hanging. My heart started to race. As I examined the trees where the meat scraps had been wired, I could see claw marks gouged into the bark and bone remnants lying at the base of the tree. Our plan was working.

I decided to take a shortcut to intercept my father on the other ridge line. I had a mile or so to hike before I could catch him. By the time I reached the top of the first ridge, mother nature called and I had to go to the bathroom. I looked around, found a suitable fallen tree to squat over, and did my thing. Not carrying any suitable toilet paper, I had to use some leaves. As I pulled my pants up I saw movement down at the bottom of the ridge near a big brush pile. I froze. The next thing I saw I couldn't believe. Out of the ground came a man who had a white beard down to his waist.

I didn't move an inch. This strange creature slowly worked his way along the ridge line to a stream that was flowing down the hillside. He filled a bucket with water and headed back to his hole in the ground. Once he disappeared, I zipped up my trousers and headed for Dad on a dead run.

By the time I reached my father, I was out of breath and speechless. "Slow down, son," Dad said, "slow down. What's the matter? You're acting like you've seen a bear."

"Dad, you won't believe what I saw."

"Well, what was it?"

"I saw a man come out of the ground. He had a white beard down to his waist; he walked several hundred feet to a stream, got some water in a bucket he was carrying, and walked back to his hole and disappeared into the ground."

"Come on, son . . ."

"No, I'm not shitting you. I was up on the next ridge taking a dump and the old bastard came out of the ground. He looked like Rip Van Winkle. Oh, by the way," I added, "a bear has ripped most of the meat out of the trees I baited."

"Boy, it sounds like you've had an exciting morning. Let's get some more chunks of meat and take a hike back to where you saw this man come out of the ground, then we'll plant some more bait."

"You think I'm bullshitting you, don't you, Dad?"

"No, son, I believe you. It's your mother we're going to have trouble selling that story to."

As we headed back toward the ridge it started to sprinkle. Dad was pleased because he knew this would get the bears on the move, and if the temperature dropped another ten to fifteen degrees, we would really be in business. I showed Dad where I saw the old man and we waited around for a half hour, hoping to see him, but to no avail.

I asked Dad if he wanted to walk around down by the brush pile where I had seen him.

He said, "Let's wait until tomorrow."

The rain was coming down steadily by now and we were both pretty wet, so we finished wiring the bait and headed for the Jeep. On the way back to the cabin, Dad wanted to stop by Mr. Frost's house to find out when he planned to bury the sheep and ask him about this mysterious being on Crow Hill.

By the time we got to the farmhouse, it was pouring and we both had a good chill. Mr. Frost saw us coming and invited us in. "You guys look a little cold, how about some homemade soup? Mother has a warm pot on the stove."

"Sounds good," we replied simultaneously.

We all sat around the kitchen table near the Franklin stove.

"Well, Doc," he said, "how's it going?"

"I think we have one on the move," Dad answered. "If the weather stays like this and the temperature drops, we should see some action within the next few days. We have a bear eating the scraps that we planted in the woods. With luck he's on his way back to finish what he started. The reason we stopped by was to find out how much longer we had before you planned on burying those decaying carcasses."

"The smell hasn't got to the missus or me yet, so let them lie if it will help catch that bear. I can't afford to lose any more livestock."

"My only concern is that we don't want him to start eating the dead carcasses. We want him to get good and hungry so he'll go to our baited sets."

"I can close up that shelter if you want."

"It might be the best thing to do. We'll help you."

"Don't worry, I can take care of it tomorrow. You fellas get some dry clothes on."

Dad nodded and started to get up. I tugged on his sleeve, and he stopped, looked at me, and said, "Oh yeah, what do you know about a man who lives on the back side of Crow Hill, underground."

"Why, that's Old Man Hall. Didn't I tell you about him?"

"No," we both replied.

"Hell, that old hermit has been homesteading on

my land for nearly sixty-five years. I got tired of fighting with him and let him be. Why do you ask?"

"Well, Matt saw him come out of the ground this
afternoon, and it gave him a start."

"I guess it would." Frost laughed. "He's harmless,
but I'm surprised you got an eye on him. Nobody, and
I do mean nobody, has seen that old bastard for years.
He usually spots you first and goes underground. He
has quite a maze of tunnels under the hill."

"Mr. Frost, how old do you think he is?" I asked.

"We figure he's almost a hundred."

"How do you know that?" asked my dad.

"Well, he used to live up in these parts with his
family, and one day he went off the deep end and they
put him in an institution down in Boston. Within six
months he was back up on Crow Hill. I didn't know for
a year that anyone was back there until I saw some
wood cuttings. I caught him out of his hole one day
and we had a hell of an argument and he told me he
would burn my house down if I didn't leave him alone.
I got the sheriff after him and that didn't work, so I
just let him be. He's become sort of a legend up here, I
guess. Everyone calls him the ghost of Crow Hill."

Dad and I finished our soup, paid our respects,
and headed for the camp. After we got into some dry
clothes and cleaned our guns, we fixed dinner. As we
sat around the dinner table talking Dad began to
show some interest in this old hermit. He wanted to
make friends with him and find out what drove him to
give up society and live in the ground.

I said, "He probably wanted peace and quiet."

Dad laughed. "He sure as hell will find it up on

Crow Hill. I'm going to check this guy out after we finish trapping season."

Dad had promised me the bear hide if we caught one this year. I wanted a bear rug made, and if he was big enough I would get my wish. By the looks of his paw prints, he would be the right size for a rug. Every bear we ever caught was always spoken for. Usually one of Dad's patients wanted the meat and someone else got the hide. I had waited ten years for this opportunity and prayed we would bag one.

We were awakened early by someone beating on the cabin door. It was still dark out and we hadn't heard anyone drive up. Dad hopped out of bed first since his bed was close to the door and opened it. It was Mr. Frost. He was all in a pant.

"What's up?" Dad asked.

"The sheep are going crazy in the pen. I was on my way to feed my cows and I could hear them making all kinds of noise. I'm afraid they're going to hurt themselves."

"Sounds like we got a bear close by. We'll get dressed, and head down there. Don't go near the set, Mr. Frost, you could step in one of the traps."

"Thanks for the warning."

Dad was hurrying like he does when he has a maternity case and has to get to the hospital. As we got dressed he said he was sure that a bear was close by. "Get the rifle, son. I'll get the Jeep started."

The rain had stopped, but it was still overcast and cold. Dad had known what he was talking about when he said we needed some weather to get these bears on the move.

By the time we got to the shelter, dawn had broken. We looked inside at the carcasses and could see right away that they had been disturbed. We could see bear prints in the dirt and parts of sheep that had been eaten.

The penned-in sheep were at the end of the field. Dad loaded the .30-06 and took the lead down across the field. The sheep were in a frenzy, running into the wire around the pen and making all kinds of noise. As we got close to the pen it appeared none of the traps had been tripped. We walked around the outside of the barbed wire and all the traps were still set.

"Hey, Dad, look here," I said. I had spotted some bear droppings and prints close to the set.

"A bear was down here all right, Matt, and he's a clever son of a bitch. Something spooked him and he moved on. But we've got his attention, he'll be back. We have to get this shelter closed up today so that bear doesn't get a gutful and leave the area."

We stayed around the penned sheep until they settled down, then headed over to the other trap. As we approached the bear set our hearts started to pound. The area was destroyed. We had a bear!

Now all we had to do was follow his path through the woods and find where he was hung up. The cubby was completely flattened and the first strand of barbed wire had been ripped from the tree. This bear was big.

The trail was easy to follow and we found our victim about two hundred yards away. The toggal pole was wedged between to trees and the bear was lying still, ready to spring when we arrived on the scene.

The first thing you do is to check to see how well you have him caught. The ideal location to snag a bear is the front paw up by the wrist. This ensures he can't get away. You must be very cautious as you survey the animal because he can come at you at any moment. Dad had gotten too close one time and a bear took a cuff at him. He had to have twenty stitches in his leg. Bears are powerful animals and they can hurt you, especially after being trapped.

This bear weighed close to six hundred pounds and had the most beautiful fur we had ever seen. It was bluish black in color. I wanted to stare at him but Dad reminded me that the time had come to put the bear out of his misery. Since it was my bear, I got to shoot him. I tripped the safety off the .30-06, took careful aim just below the right shoulder so as not to damage the pelt, and squeezed the trigger.

It was a direct hit and the bear died instantly. Dad stayed with the bear and I got the Jeep and our equipment to reset the trap. We took the trap off the bear, gutted him out and tied him to the Jeep's hood, and headed back to Dexter to get the bear tagged by the game warden and set up a date to ship him for tanning.

As we headed down the road a lot of heads were turning. The bear covered the whole hood of the Jeep and then some. It was one of the biggest black bears Dad or the game warden had seen.

And I had a trophy and a hunting trip that would stay with me for a lifetime.

2
PENSACOLA
PRESSURE
COOKER

I had ten days before I had to report to Pensacola for flight training. My orders and plane ticket had arrived while I was hunting. There was a welcome-aboard packet with some do's and don'ts prior to arriving in Pensacola. We were advised to get into some sort of shape, not to be late checking in and to review the enclosed study guides on math, physics, and aerodynamics.

Don't bring a suitcase, the letter warned, *just a small duffel bag for personal items and make sure you have your orders.*

I spent my last few days of freedom working out and visiting my close friends. One day David Sailsbury and I took a ten-mile canoe trip down Main Stream and did some duck hunting. The stream ran through North Dexter about six miles from my house. Dad dropped us off at the stream's edge and Dave's father picked us up downstream in Harmony, a small town southwest of Dexter. The trip was enjoyable and we shot several wood ducks. Dave was my closest friend. We had grown up together and had done a lot of hunting over the years. As the days before my departure dwindled I also made a few courtesy calls on friends of the family.

The introduction package that was sent to me gave a breakdown on what to expect while attending the Naval Aviation Schools Command. The Aviation Officer Candidate, or AOC, program was thirteen weeks long. This was the recruiting plan I had signed up for prior to graduating from college. The AOC training schedule included two weeks of indoctrination, nine weeks of classroom academics/training, one week of survival training, one week as a candidate officer supervising the regiment, and, finally, commissioning day, when we became officers in the United States Navy. Once this program was completed, we'd start our flight training.

Everything in the packet seemed pretty straightforward, except for the math, physics, and aero. I had been an economics major in college and these subjects made me break out in hives, but I tried not to worry about what was coming, until I had to face it. I had heard horror stories about navy flight training and how tough it was, but I was determined to get through it, because I wanted to fly off aircraft carriers.

The Monday morning I was to leave started off quietly, but got pretty emotional before I left for the airport. Everyone had a little advice. "Don't worry, you can do it." "Call if you get homesick." "Always be prepared." And so on. It was starting to get to me, and I couldn't wait to get on the road. Dad had to work, so Mom and my sisters drove me to the airport. Dad and I were both tearful as we hugged each other and said our good-byes.

The trip to Bangor, where the nearest sizable airport was located, took about an hour by car. As the time to board the plane got closer, I could feel the tension building. I wasn't good at saying good-bye, so I cracked a few jokes to my sisters to break the stress.

"Hey, Mary-Ellen," I asked, "did you hear the one about the two bums walking down the railroad tracks?"

She wrinkled her nose and shook her head. I guess maybe she knew what was coming, but didn't want to let on. I didn't let that stop me.

"One bum says to the other, 'Did you shit your pants?' The other bum says, 'No.' They walk for a while and the first bum asked the other bum again, 'Say, did you shit your pants?'" I was laughing now, and it was hard to get the words out. Mom didn't look too happy at my language, but under the circumstances she wasn't about to make a fuss. I pushed on. "The other bum says, 'No.' 'Okay,' the first one says, 'the next time I have to ask you, we're taking a look.' They walk down the tracks for twenty minutes or so and the smell got to be overwhelming, so the first bum tells the other to drop his pants. Well, sure enough, there was a big load in his drawers. The first bum said, 'I thought you said you didn't go in your pants?' The other bum says, 'Oh! You mean today!'"

By the time my sisters stopped hitting me and telling me how gross I was, the announcement to board came over the loudspeaker. I gave each of them a hug and a kiss and went over to my mother, who was standing near the window. She had started to cry, which got me going. I tried to hold back the tears as best I could, but it was no use. After hugging my mother, I headed for the jetway and Mom called me back.

"Matt, I want you to take this with you," she said, reaching into her pocketbook and pulling out my baptismal scapular medal. "Wear this or have it with you when you fly. Our lord will protect you." Mom handed it to me as I gave her one last hug. I put the scapular medal in my pocket and walked to the jet way, turned, and waved one more time to everyone, then boarded the plane.

The flight to Boston was uneventful. I had an hour layover, then caught a plane to Atlanta. From Atlanta I had a direct flight into Pensacola, which arrived at 2:45. I had never been as far south as Atlanta, so the Navy had already given me the opportunity to travel.

The Atlanta airport was much larger than most airports I had been to and it took me a while to figure out where my next gate was located. I got directions, then found an empty seat in the waiting area and watched people come and go until it was time to board. As the time drew closer to my flight I began to see a familiar sight. There were at least five passengers carrying a small duffel bag and a brown manila envelope. I put two and two together and assumed they were also headed to flight training.

The plane took off on schedule and we had an hour flight to Pensacola. The weather was warm and clear when we got off the plane. This airport was more my style: it was small like the one at Bangor and easy to find your way around. I headed over to the information booth and asked the charming attendant if there was a bus to the naval base. At that moment an announcement came over the PA. "All aviation officer candidates assemble outside. A bus will be by to take you to the naval air station in thirty minutes."

I made some small talk with the young lady, then walked over to a large picture of the Blue Angels hanging on the wall. Under the picture was information about Pensacola. The article said that Pensacola was the "cradle of naval aviation" and that it was the country's first naval aviation station. Pensacola is on Florida's Gulf Coast, just south of the Alabama line.

In 1910, the first naval officers were ordered to learn to fly under the instruction of the Wright brothers and Glenn Curtiss. With that kind of history behind the program, I broke out in goose bumps as I walked outside to meet the bus.

By the time the bus arrived, fifteen of us were waiting. The bus was white and the windows were tinted over so you couldn't see in. As it came to a stop in front of the terminal, a large man wearing a Smokey the Bear hat got out and asked, "Are you gentlemen all reporting to flight training? If you are, please have a seat on the bus, and welcome to Pensacola, home of naval aviation."

As I climbed onto the bus and took my seat halfway down the aisle, I thought what a nice greeting it was.

The doors slammed shut and the bus jerked away from the curb. Within two minutes the nice man with the Smokey the Bear hat turned into a goddamn wild man. He stood up in the aisle and said, "Okay, sweet-hearts, the fun and games are over. My name is Staff Sergeant Varney and I am going to be one of your drill instructors—your mother, your father, your baby-sitter, and your worst fucking enemy—for the next thirteen weeks—that is, if you last that long.

"From this moment on, you are lower than whale shit at the bottom of the ocean. You will only speak when spoken to, and you will answer, 'Yes, sir' and 'No, sir' when spoken to, do you understand me?"

We whimpered a weak "Yes, sir."

But Varney wasn't satisfied. "I can't hear you, sweethearts."

We tried again, this time louder. "Yes, sir."

"Take a good look outside, sweethearts. It's going to be the last of your eyeballing around. Once we pass through those gates at the base, you fuckers are all mine and I am going to do everything possible to make you quit. DOR, remember that term. DOR. That means 'dropout on request,' and when you can't hack it any-more, just request to DOR and you will be gone so fast you'll think lightning has struck you in the ass."

After Hitler sat down I wondered what in the hell I had gotten myself into.

The ride to the base took almost thirty minutes. The scenery along the way was quite pleasant and Pensacola looked like a nice town. Once on the base, we drove to the southwest corner and stopped in front of Building 699, an old wooden barracks.

Staff Sergeant Varney stood up and told us to get out of the bus. "All right, sweethearts, I want you to line up in single file, nut to butt, and face the building."

As we were getting off the bus I was trying to figure out what he meant by "nut to butt." It became apparent once we were in line. If things weren't bad enough already, within minutes two more drill instructors arrived on the scene.

I was the seventh body in line when the order came from Varney to file into the building. Most of the candidates looked pretty clean-cut, but there were a few who had long hair and mustaches. Once we were through the doors, the DIs started in on the long-hairs and the shit hit the fan. While we stood in line to get our orders stamped by the candidate officers who were in their final week before commissioning, the DIs started trimming the long-hairs with a pair of scissors, and once that was accomplished, they shaved off one side of the mustache on those who had them. It wasn't a pretty sight.

Building 699 had two stories and was horseshoe-shaped. After our orders were stamped, we were sent to the second floor to get our bedding, towels, and green coveralls. As we filed up the stairs we ran smack into a big eyeball painted on the wall at the head of the stairwell. In front of it, a DI started barking out orders. "Don't be looking around or shooting the shit with your neighbor. Get your arms outstretched and square your corners."

As we entered a space on our right we filed past several more candidate officers lined up. They filled our arms with sheets, a pillow and a pillowcase, a heavy blanket, a washcloth and towels, and a green flight suit. At the end of the line we were instructed to find a room, select a bed, and await further instructions.

After receiving my gear, I shuffled down the hall to a room that had three men in it, unloaded my stuff onto the only remaining bed, and introduced myself.

"Hi, I'm Matt Sullivan, how're you doing?"

"Okay. I'm Dale Morely."

"Hi, I'm Mark Sasson."

The last guy said, "And I'm Bob McFadden."

"Glad to meet you," I replied.

Once the introductions were out of the way, we stood by for the next surprise. Just as I started to catch my breath, a DI started pacing up and down the passageway, yelling at the top of his lungs. "Thirty minutes to make your racks. By the way, ladies, they had better have hospital corners and be tight enough to bounce a quarter off. After your racks have been made, get into your green 'poopie suits,' put your civilian clothes in your duffel bags, and stand by for evening chow. Your duffel bags will be collected while you are at chow and placed in a personal storage locker. Make sure your name is on your bag. That's all."

As I looked around the room I realized everyone had the same look on his face—total bewilderment.

At precisely 5:00 P.M. a drill instructor ordered everyone out into the passageway. He started barking, "When you hear me say get out in the hall, I want you all standing like wedding cocks with your heels and asses locked up against the bulkheads in front of your rooms. Do you hear me?"

"Yes, sir!" rang up the passageway.

"You are class 34-70 and from what I have seen in the last couple of hours, you are the hoggiest bunch of whale shit I have seen come through here in years. Look at you!"

Some of the guys started to look up and down the ranks and the DI went nuts. "Quit eyeballing around down there," he yelled.

Another guy had a smirk on his face and the shit hit the fan all over again. The DI screamed, "Push-up position. Everybody!"

We all hit the floor.

"So, you sweethearts think this goddamn program is a joke? Let's see how many push-ups you lowlifes can handle. Everybody up! Begin! Down, up, down, up, down, up, down, up." This went on until everyone was laid out. "Now get your fat asses outside."

There was a fire-escape ladder at the end of the passageway that we had been instructed to use when told to get outside. The ladder brought us out on the back side of Building 699. After we spent five minutes standing around, three DIs appeared from nowhere.

"All right, herd, listen up!" one of them barked. He appeared to be the most senior drill instructor. "My name is Gunnery Sergeant Fisher and along with Staff Sergeants Varney and Bergman, I am going to teach you how to march. I want five men across the front and the rest of you fall in behind them. Move! Hurry up! Hurry up!"

Once we were all in some sort of order, Fisher said, "When I give the order to march, I want this herd to start off on your left foot, understood?"

We all replied, "Yes, sir!"

"Class 34-70—forward . . . march! Your left, your left, your left right left, your left, your left, your left right left," Fisher barked.

We got about fifty yards, when one of the DIs yelled out, "Whoa, herd."

"Hey, sweetheart," yelled another. No one dared to look around. I knew it was Varney because he always called us sweetheart. "Hey you, pretty boy, you with the half-ass haircut and harelip . . . yes, you—get over here."

I didn't move an inch, but I could see peripherally that the man he was singling out was to my left, three over. The DI was speaking loud enough for everyone's benefit.

"Your hair, candidate, is distracting the rest of the herd. They think they're marching behind a she-cow. Let's tie that rat's nest into a pretty little ponytail. Tomorrow you won't have to worry about this mess, because it will all be shaved off."

By this time the young man was back in ranks and we were off and marching again. As we marched forward, out of the corner of my eye, I could see one of the DIs goose-stepping in cadence with the barking. His swagger stick was neatly tucked under his right arm and he looked pretty sharp. I began to chuckle, and the more I listened to the marching cadence the more I began to laugh. The only thing I could think of was a scene when the DIs were trying to teach Gomer Pyle how to march, and the more we marched, the harder I began to laugh, until I heard, "Whoa—herd—whoa."

Within seconds I had a DIs mouth one inch from my face. It was Varney. It happened so fast, for a moment I didn't realize he was yelling at me. "You think this program is funny, sweetheart, well, I will show you what funny is. Get over here, hurry up."

He pulled me out in front of the formation and he wasn't worrying whether he ripped my arm out of its socket. "Assume the push-up position."

I did as I was told and waited. And waited. And waited. Nothing happened for about a minute. Then Varney said to the rest of the class, "Are you going to stand there and let your classmate do these push-ups alone?"

Before anyone could say a word, he told them all to assume the position. "Now, sweethearts . . . begin. Up, down, up, down . . ." Ten solid minutes. After everyone was completely exhausted and out of breath, Varney made me march the formation the rest of the way to the chow hall. Of course, I didn't know what I was doing and made a complete ass out of myself, but it taught me a valuable lesson. This program was for real.

We had duck for dinner. In navy parlance, as we learned, it meant we ducked in and ducked out. I think the DIs planned it that way. It took so long to march to the chow hall that we hardly had time to eat before they closed the serving lines. Half the class didn't get anything to eat, and once the line closed, the DIs made everyone line up outside for our march back to Building 699.

After an uneventful march back to our new home, we had the rest of the evening to get to know our roommates. Dale Morely was from Portland, Oregon. He was six feet tall and his shoulders were the size of a redwood. Mark Sasson was about five-ten and had the body of a swimmer. He was from South Bend, Indiana. Bob McFadden was short, slightly overweight, and lived in Lincoln, Nebraska.

There wasn't much to do but talk about ourselves, which I guess is what the DIs had in mind. As the evening progressed we found out that we had a lot of the same interests. Wake-up or reveille, as the DIs put it, would be at 0430 and lights out was scheduled for 2200. As I lay in bed that first night I wondered if I had bitten off more than I could chew. It was starting to look that way.

The next morning I was awakened with a start. A loud banging and rolling of something metallic jarred me from a deep sleep. A belligerent voice was yelling, "Get out in the hall, hurry up, hurry up!"

Once outside the room and standing at attention, I could see what all the racket was about: Staff Sergeant Varney had a huge trash can that he was rolling up and down the passageway and banging with a drumstick. After everyone was out in the hall, he told us we had five minutes to get into our poopie suits and line up out back.

As we recklessly ran back into our rooms, tripping over each other to find our coveralls, I took a glance at the time and it was 0405, and at that point I knew we were in for a long day.

After we got dressed and were standing around outside for several minutes in the dark, wondering what in hell was going to happen next, Varney showed up again, this time in physical-training gear. "All right, sweethearts," he said. "I want ten men in the front row and the rest of you maggots cover down behind them."

Once we shuffled around and got into place, Varney told us to fall into this formation whenever we were ordered outside. "Remember who is beside you and in front of you. Do you hear me?"

When we responded with a loud "Yes, sir!" he continued. "Now get on your backs, we're going to see who's out of shape."

We did sit-ups, push-ups, leg lifts, jumping jacks, and ran in place for fifteen minutes. After thirty minutes of calisthenics, we finished our workout with a little run. Most of us just had our street shoes on and we were hurting when we finished the short jog. I felt as though I had put in a whole day's work and it wasn't even 5:30 in the morning.

At the end of the run we all assembled behind Building 699. Varney, who was hardly out of breath, said, "Today you sweethearts will officially become 'poopies.' Your hair will be shaved off, and for you pretty boys who have half a harelip, it will also be history. You will be issued military clothing, and you will receive your book bags with all your textbooks. You are probably wondering what a poopie is. Well, sweethearts, a poopie is a name we give you candidates because you are lower than whale shit in the military ranking system and you will be treated accordingly until you prove otherwise. Do I have anyone who wants to DOR yet? It won't be long before some of you maggots will want to go home to Mommy. Now, get your filthy, skuzzy bodies back up to your rooms, get your racks squared away, and clean up for morning chow. Be outside and ready to march at 0600. Now move, move, move!"

As we hustled up to our rooms I wondered how

the son of a bitch expected us to do it all in less than thirty minutes. But adrenaline is the great equalizer. With minutes to spare, all but one made it. Fortunately the candidate officers were marching us to chow instead of the DIs. I could see the game they were playing—it was the good-cop, bad-cop routine. The candidate officers were kind and helpful, but the DIs were out to separate the men from the boys.

After morning chow we headed to the barbershop. The candidate officers lined us up outside. At seven, one of the five barbers opened the door and the first five in line entered and we continued until all of us had been skinned. The barbers shaved our heads with the speed Sherman displayed as he went through Atlanta. And the results were about as pretty.

It was hard to keep from laughing at your classmates when they returned after being scalped. You couldn't even recognize your own roommates. I had never seen so many bald heads assembled in one place. There were a lot of different shapes and sizes and it really was a funny sight. After our buzz job, we went to military issue and received our uniforms, sweat gear, swimsuits, and low quarter black shoes. After receiving the gear, we had to carry everything in our arms as we marched back to Building 699. The rest of the morning was spent removing the protective coating on our black leather shoes, shining brass, and learning how to wear our uniforms correctly.

After lunch the drill instructors had us behind the barracks, down on the seawall, and were attempting to teach us the art of marching. Four hours later many of us had blisters on our feet and our egos. As we formed up to march to evening chow, we had four empty slots. Four men had dropped out and there was no trying to talk them out of it. They were kept away from the rest of the class and we never saw them again.

The next two days were spent drilling, cleaning our brass and shoes, and studying for the math tests that would be administered that Saturday. The tests had to be passed before you could become a commissioned officer. If you failed any of the four, you had to go to "stupid studies" every afternoon for two hours until you passed the test or tests you failed. If you hadn't passed all the tests before your tenth week, you were washed out, so it behooved you to pass them on the first take. By Saturday morning, three more candidates had dropped out.

Each of the four tests was two hours long. The test results would be posted by noon on Monday. By Saturday evening I was a complete vegetable along with the rest of my classmates. I had never known I could pack an hour's worth of work into five minutes.

Each day I couldn't wait until 2200 rolled around. This was when the lights were turned out and the DIs were off our backs. At times I wanted a passing car to hit me while we were marching so I could leave with honor and not be labeled a quitter. Sunday was a day of rest and we were allowed to call home for the first time. Each candidate would have five minutes to talk.

After I went to mass and did my laundry, I called home. As the phone rang I tried to think positively so I wouldn't upset my folks. My mother answered, "Dr. Sullivan's residence. May I help you?"

"Mom, it's Matt."

"Matt, how have you been? We've been so worried."

"This is the first opportunity they've given us to call."

"What's the matter, son?"

"What do you mean?" I barked back.

"Your voice doesn't sound good, are you sick?"

"No, Mom, just beat. This Pensacola pressure cooker is getting to me." At that point I felt like having a good cry, but gathered my composure and explained to her what it was like. Before she turned the phone over to my dad, she told me how proud she was of me and to hang in there. Dad got on the phone and asked how I was doing. I told him some of the stuff I'd been through, and we had a few laughs. Just hearing his voice made me feel better and he explained how tough med school was for him and that nothing comes easy in this world. By the end of our conversation he had my battery recharged and I was ready for some more humiliation.

"Say, Matt, your sister wants to say hi."

Susie got on the phone and the first thing she said was, "What's the matter, big brother, can't you take what they're dishing out?"

This got my dander up and I was determined to make it through now. Little did Susie know how effective that ribbing was. I spoke with Mom and Dad once more before hanging up and told them I would call again soon.

Sunday night the candidate officers talked to us before they marched us to evening chow. They told us the upcoming week would be a real ballbuster and to help each other out. "If some of you are behind in cleaning your brass or squaring your rooms away, get some assistance from your classmates. The DIs are going to try to break as many of you as they can, so be prepared and work as a team. Only the strong will survive. After chow, class 34-70 will move to the west side of the upper deck to make room for the new class coming in tomorrow. Assume the same rooms you have on this side you'll have until 2200 to get the place squared away."

I thought, this is great, I must be a veteran of Poopieville now.

"Tomorrow you will have your physicals at the naval aeromedical facility. This will be a full day of testing and the DIs can't harass you until the following morning." A loud cheer came from the ranks. "On Friday, you will receive your final room, locker, and personnel inspection, and for those who pass, you will have your 'death march' to battalion. The ones who don't will remain here another week."

One candidate spoke up in the rear. "What's the death march?"

"This is a term the DIs use to finalize your indoctrination training. It's tough, because you must put everything you have accumulated over the past two weeks in your sheets and carry it all over your shoulder, while the DIs march you to battalion. The battalions are down by the chow hall and you know how long it takes to march to chow. The DIs will triple it for your final march. Every man must carry his own gear, and the physical-training sessions along the way are a bitch. So figure out your game plan early. There are three battalions which make up the regiment and I believe this class is scheduled to go to batt one."

After evening chow we spent the rest of our free time moving to the other side of the building. By the time 2200 rolled around, we were established in our new residences. As I lay in bed I began to see what trends were being set. Within a week you could see our class starting to work together as a unit and paying attention to detail. I think this was one of the DIs main objectives in their training plan. I knew the next day was a make-or-break day for myself and a lot of my classmates.

The physical we were to receive was probably the most extensive and thorough examination we would be given in our naval careers. Even though we all had to pass a recruiting physical, this was the one that went over you with a fine-tooth comb. If you were not physically qualified for the pilot program due to eye restrictions, you could pursue the naval flight officer program, which allowed your eyes to be correctable to 20/20. However, if they discovered something like diabetes or glaucoma, you were history and your aspirations of becoming a naval aviator were gone.

My night was a restless one, and when reveille sounded at 0600, I felt like I hadn't had any sleep at all. We couldn't eat before the exam and we had to be over at the hospital by 0630. The candidate officers marched us over and assembled us in a large classroom. Candidate officer Lar Stampe, the indoctrination battalion commander, had us fill out forms until 0730. The exam lasted all day and I was beat by the day's end. Although I had made the grade, eight had not.

By 1600 we had completed the physicals and were ready to march back to Splinterville, the name we had given to our barracks because of its design. As we lined up outside the hospital Varney was waiting for us.

The first words out of his mouth were, "Sweethearts, enjoy your freedom for the rest of the day, because tomorrow you're all mine. By the way, grades have been posted and I have never seen so many goddamn stupid college boys in my military career. There are only three of you who didn't make stupid studies, the rest of you dumb fuckers will be studying during your free time. Lock it up, cover down," he barked. "Class 34-70, forward march!"

When we got to the front of Splinterville, Varney dismissed us and we all bolted for the bulletin board to see the test results. I had failed two out of the four tests. The retake was on Thursday, and if I didn't pass the two I had failed, I would be studying while the rest of my friends were out playing. There always seemed to be a rope waiting to hang you if you didn't perform.

The rest of the week was devoted to getting prepared for the retake exam and the final inspection. If we weren't shining our brass, or cleaning our room, we were studying for the exams. This pressure made Dale, Mark, Bob, and me become close and we began to learn the team concept at an early stage in our naval careers. Any words of encouragement passed between us really helped.

Morely and I were slated for flight training. McFadden was an air intelligence type and Sasson qualified for the flight officer program. We all got along well and tried to help each other out.

McFadden was the oddball in the room. He was about three steps behind in everything he attempted, and we were always helping him get caught up. Morely was pretty sharp militarily. Being raised as a military brat, he knew all the proper techniques for shining brass and getting a good spit shine on our low quarter black shoes. Sasson was the smart one, and he tutored us when we needed academic help. Being a bookworm in college probably was what destroyed his 20/20 vision and disqualified him from the pilot program. I was the athlete in the room, and I tried to motivate McFadden and others who were having difficulty doing their physical training.

Late Tuesday afternoon Morely and I got tagged with dumping the trash. The Dumpster was in front of the building and we couldn't use our normal route because the new class was out back getting drilled. We had to go out the front door, which passed by the DIs office, and this was just asking for trouble. They would always find some excuse to PT us and make our lives miserable for several minutes.

Dale and I got close to the DIs office and slipped by without incident. But when I kicked the front door open, it hit Gunnery Sergeant Fisher square in the back and knocked him off the step. I just about shit my pants when Dale yelled, "By your leave, sir," which was a proper request.

Gunney said, "Carry on, candidates," in a gruff voice, followed by, "Watch where the fuck you're going next time."

As we got out of hearing range I said, "That was pretty slick. How did you know that term?"

"My dad taught it to me. You use it when you come up behind someone who is senior to you and you want to pass by him or her. It's proper military courtesy."

"Shit hot, Slick. Hey, that's a good nickname for you. 'Slick.'"

As we dumped the trash we could see that Gunney was waiting for something and that's why he didn't say much to us. Just then a van pulled up and a guy hopped out. "He looks like a new recruit, but they checked in yesterday," Slick said. "Unless this clown is late."

"Holy shit," I said. "If he's late, we're going to see some major fireworks. Let's get out of here before the shit hits the fan."

Slick said, "No, we better wait until he runs into the buzz saw before we make our move."

"Good idea."

The guy was either stupid or had brass balls. He went to the back of the van, hauled out a ten speed bike, a surfboard, and a set of golf clubs. He said good-bye to his buddy, picked everything up, and started walking toward Fisher.

We finished dumping the trash and started back. By now Fisher had this guy flat on his back doing sit-ups. "You think this is a goddamn country club, do you?" Gunney shouted.

We figured we'd better take our chances and return the back way. We made a right at the corner of the building and went up the back fire escape. Once upstairs, we spread the word about what had happened and everyone raced up front to take a look out the upper window at this guy.

Before it was over, Gunney had him take his bike

apart, put it back together, and PTed him until he could hardly walk.

As Thursday approached I spent every spare minute studying. I didn't want to give up any free time, especially for stupid studies. After lights were out Tuesday and Wednesday night, I studied in the toilet with a flashlight until I couldn't stay awake any longer.

But it paid off. I passed all the required exams, which they graded right after you turned them in. If you had failed more than two after the retake, they kept you behind a class, which meant another week in Splinterville. Five candidates failed three of the retake exams and they had to spend another week in hell.

By Friday morning our room was pretty squared away. The brass belt buckles were shining, our collar devices were tarnish free, you could use our shoes to shave by, and our closets and drawers had all the items arranged and hung as instructed. McFadden was the only one in our room who hadn't passed all the required tests.

We displayed our brass and collar devices on the center table, then formed up outside for morning chow. Since our room, locker, and personnel inspection was scheduled for 0900, we had an hour or so after chow to make last-minute changes. A marine officer and three drill instructors would do the inspecting. As we waited to be marched to morning chow, I felt good about myself for the first time in two weeks.

COMMISSIONING DAY

After a leisurely breakfast and a brisk morning march, the candidate officers returned us to the back of Splinterville and wished us luck before dismissing us to our rooms. We had a little over an hour before the inspection went down, and you could feel the tension building. This would be the first time we discarded our green poopie suits and put on our uniforms.

As we filed up the west-side fire escape the first men in the passageway went into shock. "What the fuck happened?" the lead man shouted.

Everybody on the fire escape started pressing forward to get inside to see what all the excitement was about. Once inside, I couldn't believe my eyes. The whole floor was a complete mess. Our room looked like a tornado had ripped through it. It was another pressure test to see how well we would react; I just knew it.

Slick and I gathered our wits and tried to motivate the rest of our classmates. "This is a ploy to see how well we'll work together in time of distress," I said.

I wasn't as calm about it as I tried to sound. There was no way we could have the rooms ready by 0900, but at least we could have ourselves and our lockers squared away by then. Each man busted his ass to make sure. For the next hour the building looked like a colony of ants, hard at work.

With fifteen minutes to go before the inspection was to start, Bobby McFadden's circuit breaker was about to pop. His locker was a mess, he wasn't dressed, and his brass looked like someone had shined it with a Brillo pad. Since he was our roommate, we all pitched in to help get him squared away.

A few minutes later Sergeant Varney yelled, "All right, sweethearts, lock it up by your racks. Now move, move, move!"

McFadden was a dead man. He still wasn't dressed and he started going in circles trying to decide what to do. To get him out of the way, Slick told him to get into the closet and close the door.

Mark Sasson, whose bed was closest to the door, started muttering, "We're fucked, we're absolutely, totally fucked."

A moment later Gunney Fisher stuck his head into the room on his way to inspect the candidates next to us and said, "This room looks like a goddamn pigpen! It looks like you maggots will get to stay with us another week."

Luckily he didn't notice that McFadden was missing. We looked at each other in dismay, wondering if this was another scare tactic or if he meant business.

Once we felt the coast was clear, we started to clean up the remaining mess. Then Varney walked in on us. "Get your filthy, slimy bodies locked up by your racks, candidates," he bellowed. He looked around the room, like he knew something was out of whack. "Where is the fat man?" he asked.

We all stood at attention, staring into the middle of the room. "Well, where is he, Morely? Has the cat got your tongue?"

Slick said nothing.

I couldn't stand the tension and yelled, "He's emptying the trash."

Varney did a 180, walked over to my rack, and stopped about an inch from my nose. "Who asked you, shit for brains? Get out in the hall."

I knew I was in for trouble, so I got my mind set for a good workout. I was right, I spent the next ten minutes doing mountain climbers, which just about did me in. For this torture, your body is in the push-up position and you move your feet and legs like you're running in place. Several minutes before the inspecting party was to enter our room, Varney told me to get back into my room.

My uniform looked like shit, I felt like a wet noodle, and I started to get pissed off. Sasson, who was standing next to me, said, "Relax, this is part of the game. They're trying to piss us off and see how far they can push us. Don't worry about Varney, he's just a mad dog."

And I knew immediately that we had a new nickname for Sergeant Varney—Mad Dog. Just then, the inspecting party entered our room.

Slick was the room captain, and he sounded off. "Candidates Morely, Sasson, and Sullivan ready for room, locker, and personnel inspection, sir." Captain Greaseman, the inspecting officer, asked where the other candidate was.

Slick said, "The last time we saw him, he went to empty the trash, sir."

The inspectors started looking over our gear when Mad Dog went nuts. "Whose fucking shoes are these?" he asked. Nobody acknowledged, knowing they were McFadden's.

"These shoes look like they were shined with a goddamn Hershey bar," he said, throwing them into the trash can. Then he ran out into the passageway and threw the can down the corridor. As it ricocheted off the walls while it bounced down the hall, I looked across the room at Slick and almost started laughing.

Gunny Fisher and Captain Greaseman were standing right in front of the closet where Bobby was hiding as they recorded data from Mad Dog's bellowing report. The anguish on our faces told the story and we prayed they would forget the closet. No such luck.

Greaseman said, "Gunney, I've seen enough. Check the closet and let's move on to the next room." Our hearts jumped into our mouths. Fisher opened the closet door and jumped back when he saw this half naked Pillsbury doughboy standing in front of him. Everyone's attention was directed toward the closet.

McFadden, standing at attention in his undershirt, white boxer shorts, and black knee socks, simply said, "Going up, sir." Everybody in the room broke up. Trying to keep his composure, Captain Greaseman told the inspecting party to meet him outside on the fire escape. As they walked outside we could hear them laughing hysterically. We thought we had dodged a bullet.

Wrong again. Once the inspecting party regained its composure, the shit hit the fan. Greaseman ordered our whole class out into the passageway and read us the riot act. He told us we were the most disorganized, unprofessional group he had ever seen come through flight training. He then turned us over to the drill instructors and we headed outside for the playpen, an area behind Building 699 where the public couldn't see what was going on.

They wore us down for one solid hour. We did sit-ups until we couldn't do any more, we did push-ups until we couldn't do any more, we did leg lifts until our guts gave out, and we ran in place until several guys passed out. Several of them were puking as the DIs watered us down with hoses. Once everyone was stable, Mad Dog told us we had two hours to get ready for another inspection.

The excitement of getting ready for the "big" inspection was gone. Everyone kind of moved in slow motion as they climbed the stairs to their rooms. Four more candidates dropped out after the session in the playpen and it looked as though we were going to spend another week in Splinterville.

Once in our room, we started to get back the spark that makes a winning team. McFadden was down, so I stayed in the room with him and got him fired up while Slick and Sasson went up and down the passageway motivating the rest of the class. Within twenty minutes most of the men were back on track and working toward what we hoped was our last inspection.

The light was starting to come on as I helped McFadden. I could see the psychological pattern that the drill instructors were guiding us toward. "Just hang on, Bobby," I told him, "and we'll be out of Splinterville and in battalion by nightfall."

"How do you know that, Matt?" he asked.

"Can't you see what the DIs are trying to pull? They're weeding out the weak, developing a bonding among the survivors, and teaching us to work together as a unit. Look up and down the passageway, Bob. See the team concept emerging? Everyone is working together to get ready. You wouldn't have seen this effort a week ago, would you?"

"I guess not," replied McFadden.

As I walked back from helping clean the bathroom, our two hours were about up, and by the looks of all the rooms, the upper west side of Building 699 was ready for inspection. We were all standing at attention in our rooms when the inspectors arrived for their second look. They stopped outside our door, had some small talk, and walked down the passageway to start.

While we anxiously awaited our turn we could hear yelling and things being thrown out into the passageway at the end of the hall. This wasn't normal and it sounded like the DIs were ripping the place apart again. Since Mark was next to the door, I asked him to take a look up the hall to see what in the hell was going on.

He gave me the finger. "Look yourself, if you feel lucky," he said.

Just as I started to reply Mad Dog jumped into our room like a goddamn gazelle. "Who told you sweethearts to speak?" he asked as he walked over to McFadden. "Well, fat boy, what cute remarks do you have for us this time?"

Bobby said, "I don't like being referred to as fat boy, sir."

"Oh, is that right? Well, if you got rid of that gut, you might be able to see how hoggie your shoes look." Just before walking out, he stepped on the toes of McFadden's newly shined shoes and scuffed them up.

I could see that Bob was frustrated and hurt, so I immediately told him to relax. "Varney's trying to break you, Bob, and make you fall into his trap. It's a game," I said. "You're going to make it or I'll kick your ass." That got a little smile out of him and he gave a thumbs-up to reassure me that he was hanging in there.

As the inspecting party got closer to our room, I figured out what was going down. They weren't spending much time in the rooms. I assumed the inspectors were looking at very few items, and if satisfied with the results, they instructed the men to pack their belongings, secure them into their sheets, and line up outside.

As my classmates filed past our room with their sheets slung over their shoulders like Santa's toy sack, I realized my theory was right. The time had finally come for the dreaded "death march" to battalion. Just then the inspecting team entered our room.

Mad Dog and Gunney Fisher looked over our brass and shoes. Greaseman checked our lockers and closet, then told us to pack our belongings in our sheets and get outside. "All except for McFadden," he added.

They told Bobby to stand fast. My stomach sank as I looked across the room at Bob. Within ten minutes we were all packed up and out of the room. As each of us left we told Bob to hang in there and we would see him in a week. I never heard what Greaseman told him, but I figured they were going to hold him back another week and slim him down before sending him to battalion.

As I struggled down the stairs with my sheets slung over my back, I could see why they referred to this jaunt as the "death march." It was going to be a miracle if I made it all the way to battalion without losing anything. As our classmates stood outside with bulging sheets at their sides, Varney walked out the door and announced that he would be our class drill instructor while we were at batallion.

I could hear some "oh shits" from the back and that was the start of what would be the longest death march in the history of naval aviation preflight training.

What was usually a couple of hours of harassment

on the march to battalion lasted five hours. Everybody's sheets eventually ripped and our personnel gear was spread all along the route. We couldn't get five yards without Mad Dog making us stop, put down our packs, and do some sort of physical exercise. It was almost ten o'clock in the evening before we all got our new room assignments in battalion one.

Morely, Sasson, and I got to room together again and the DIs put Bennie Nunn in with us to make up the fourth. He was from New Bern, North Carolina, and had a great sense of humor. Bennie stood five-foot-eight and had been an All-American wrestler at Duke University. His build fit the part and he was glad to have some roommates again, since all three of his bunkmates in Splinterville had gone the DOR route.

The DIs and class officers left us pretty much alone over the weekend so we could get our rooms and gear squared away. Classes would begin again on Monday and we knew our military training would become more intense as we got closer to commissioning.

Monday morning started off at O500 with PT and a half-mile run. After we got cleaned up, we marched to chow, then marched back. We had a half hour before our first class started. I spent my time arranging my book bag and making sure I had the right textbooks for the morning classes. The afternoon would be devoted to weapons issue and close order drill.

The morning went by relatively fast, like a typical college day. Meet the instructor, receive the course layout, get some homework, and on to the next class.

It felt good to be in a uniform and out of the DIs immediate reach. We were officer candidates now and not poopies, but we were still lower than whale shit in the eyes of the DIs.

At twelve noon we lined up in front of batt one for noon chow. The officer candidates from our battalion normally marched us, but we had a special treat in store. Mad Dog was waiting impatiently as we filed out. "All right, sweethearts," he barked, "I haven't seen you for a couple of days and I'm wondering how many bad habits you've picked up. Now lock it up and cover down. I can see we've weeded out the quitters. Now let's see how many of you can really hack it. Class 34-70, right face, forward march! Your left, your left, your left right left, your left, your left, your left right left, six to the front, three to the rear, left right left," he bellowed.

When we reached the mess hall, we got into single file and proceeded through the chow line. It was long and the hall was filled. As poopies, we were always the last to eat, so the mess hall would be almost empty by the time we arrived. Today the grills were not working right and the place was backed up. The DIs and officer candidates for all three battalions sat in the upper left corner of the mess hall, to watch what went on during the meals.

Only those candidates who had been in battalion for several weeks and performed up to the standards of their class drill instructor were allowed to talk. You could tell which class and battalion had been honored by the red, blue, or yellow tape on the candidates' name tags. The tape was the key, and if you were without one, you ate in silence. The red tape meant you were from batt one, blue was batt two's color, and batt three's color was yellow.

One mistake by anyone in the class could cause us to lose our tape, be it the third week or tenth week in battalion. Since we were the newcomers on the block, we had to eat in silence.

After getting my meal, I looked for a decent table, but the only two open were right next to the incoming chow line, so close you were always getting bumped as the candidates passed by.

Slick and Bennie sat across from me. As I filled my mouth full of hot soup, I heard someone say, "Hey, Sweetwater, how the hell are you?"

I snapped my head around to see who called but couldn't pinpoint the exact area. There were only a few people who knew my nickname and I couldn't believe any of them would be in flight training. I looked to see if Mad Dog or any of the other DIs saw me looking around, and when I felt the coast was clear, I started goosenecking again, trying to locate the culprit. Within a few seconds I narrowed the area down.

Looking over my left shoulder, I could see the new poopie class entering the chow hall. Once they picked up their trays and rounded the corner, they were visible to everyone seated. As a poopie you had to hold your tray in front of your face until you entered the serving line, so it was hard to see who was who. Then I spotted him. It was Cannonball Anderson, a pitcher I had played with.

Once we made eye contact, I started to make gestures with my hands until I got a kick under the table. By then it was too late. Mad Dog was on his way over and I could see we were going to have "duck" for lunch.

I was right. He didn't even get halfway to our table before he yelled, "Class 34, get outside. Move! Move! Move!" Some of my classmates had just sat down.

Once outside, Varney singled me out in front of the whole class. In a very loud voice, he said, "Thanks to Sullivan, some of you candidates aren't going to eat lunch today. Now all of you give me a hundred sit-ups."

As we were finishing up Varney said, "I knew I couldn't trust this herd. Leave you alone for two days and you forget what this program is all about. Well, we have many more weeks together and I don't give a shit if you ever get your tape. After your sit-ups, give me fifty push-ups, then get on your feet."

By the time we finished, our uniforms were all filthy. And my name was mud.

Mad Dog marched us back to the battalion and released us. We had thirty minutes before we were to be issued our weapons. Most of the class had to change their sweaty uniforms before filing in at the armory, which was located in the basement of our battalion. I went up and down the passageway apologizing to my classmates. One of them said, "Don't worry about it. He was looking for any excuse to yank us out of chow early anyway." Most of them said something similar.

They were probably right, but I still felt bad, and I was back in the limelight with the DIs, and that wasn't good.

After we received our M-1 rifles, Gunney Fisher drilled us for two hours. We were taught how to field-strip the weapon, put it back together, and how to execute the manual of arms. Fisher warned us about leaving our rifles unattended. If a DI or a class officer found an open locker with a rifle exposed, there would be hell to pay.

The rifles had not been used for several weeks and they needed some attention, so Gunney gave us the rest of the afternoon to get them cleaned up. The following morning would be our arms inspection.

By the time we were dismissed, it was 3:00 P.M. and we had the rest of the afternoon to ourselves. During free time we could relax or work out until evening meal, unless we had stupid studies. Fortunately everyone in my room was off remedial studies.

As we walked up to our room Bennie said, "Hey, Sweetwater, you want to play some b-ball with Slick and me?"

"Sure, but don't call me Sweetwater."

"Why not, it's your nickname, isn't it?"

"Not really."

"Bullshit! I heard that guy finger you at chow today. How'd you get pegged with that call sign anyway?"

"When I was playing minor-league baseball, I used to save all my near-empty bottles of cologne and mix them into one bottle. After application, the smell would last for hours, and when I hit the field, everyone knew Sweetwater Sullivan had arrived."

"I like it," Bennie said. "I think we have another man with a nickname."

* * *

That evening we did our homework and cleaned our weapons for the inspection in the morning. All candidate officers were required to participate in the commissioning-day parade, which took place on the parade grounds every Friday morning. Our class would be involved for the first time this week, so we needed to have our weapons inspected for cleanliness and to get a little practice marching with our rifles before Friday.

Everyone in the room had his weapon cleaned and locked away except for Bennie. He couldn't open the small butt plate on the bottom of his rifle to clean it out. This plate covered a hole where extra cleaning gear was stored when you were out in the field. We all tried to pry open the plate, but with no success. Slick and I had found used cleaning swabs stuck down inside our butt plates and we knew the DIs would be checking.

The following morning at 0730 we were ordered to fall into ranks and assembled in front of battalion one. At precisely 0745 Gunney Fisher and the battalion one commander approached the formation. The candidate officer brought the formation to attention and turned us over to the drill instructor.

Gunney Fisher put us at parade rest, then explained what we could expect over the next several months, regarding the Friday parades. He explained the point system used and told us how the points were figured into an overall grade during the pass-and-review part of the parade. These points were part of an ongoing competition between the three battalions. The battalion that accumulated the most points by the end of the quarter would become the honor battalion. This carried a lot of prestige and special privileges. It behooved every candidate to drill well and learn the manual of arms because one mistake could cost valuable points for the whole battalion.

The manual of arms was precision handling of your weapon while in close order formation. The drill could be executed while marching or standing in ranks.

After ten minutes of executing the manual of arms from right shoulder to left shoulder to parade rest, Gunney returned us to order arms, which was back to attention with our rifles on the ground at our right sides. Then he gave us the order, "Open ranks, march!"

The men in the first row lifted their rifle butts slightly and took two paces forward, the second row took one pace forward, the third row stood fast. As Gunney Fisher approached the first candidate in the front row, the candidate raised his weapon horizontally to waist level and went to port arms. He then brought the weapon's bolt to the rear, looked in the chamber for shells, and held the rifle at eye level until Gunney ripped it from his hands.

Fisher flipped the weapon around like a toy, then threw the rifle back. Once the candidate got his composure, he let the bolt go home, pulled the trigger, and went back to order arms, and Gunney moved on to the next candidate. I was in the second row and had plenty of time to watch and learn the procedure before I had to execute. It appeared that Gunny was checking every third butt plate for loose gear, so Bennie might be able to dodge a bullet.

Mark Sasson was standing at the end of the front row and everything appeared to go well until Fisher threw the weapon back at him. Mark dropped the rifle and the sideshow began. Gunny had him pick up his rifle and go to port arms. He then snatched the rifle out of Mark's hands again and threw it back at him. Mark dropped the weapon again.

Gunny went nuts and started calling him a sissy and a mommy's boy. I could see the smoke coming out of Mark's ears and I knew he was headed for trouble. He had a bad temper when he got pissed. Gunny yelled, "Hold that weapon like a virgin's titty and relax." He put him at port arms again and snatched the weapon and immediately threw it back at Mark. This time Mark caught the weapon and threw it back at Gunny. You could hear the whole class gasp.

Gunny said, "Get out of ranks, Sasson, and give me one hundred up-and-overs." This maneuver was a real ballbuster. You had to raise your weapon over your head to arm's length, then bring it behind your neck, and continue repeating this until you finished the assigned number given. While Mark was struggling on the side Gunny continued the inspection. By the time he got to me, I knew what to expect. He put me at port arms and snatched my weapon, flipped it around and opened the butt plate.

"Looks good, Sullivan," he said as he threw the weapon back at me and continued on. There was one row to go and I knew Bennie's heart had to be pounding. Bennie was locked up directly behind me and I could hear Gunny working his way down the ranks. When I thought he had finished inspecting Nunn's rifle, I realized my calculation was off by one.

Just then a loud wisecrack came from the rear. "Phantom gear, phantom gear. Look at this horseshit candidate." I was afraid to turn around, but I knew it had to be Bennie. I could hear rifle parts being disassembled as Fisher read Bennie the riot act.

Before he continued any further, Fisher ordered the class to fall out and gather around him, except for Mark. He told him to continue his up-and-overs. "All right, class, I want you to observe as I demonstrate how to field-strip an M-1 rifle." Within thirty seconds Fisher had Bennie's weapon in pieces. He gathered all the parts, walked over to the main street, and threw them into the oncoming traffic. He then ordered everyone, including Sasson, to fall into ranks. Once we were all standing at attention, Fisher started in on us.

"Gentlemen," he said, "what we have here is a failure to communicate. When I say I want your weapons cleaned, I mean I want them cleaned. Do you nipple heads read me?"

By this time the morning traffic had rifle parts flying everywhere. "Now, I want candidate Nunn and the remaining men whose weapons did not get inspected in my office at 1700 sharp. Dismissed!"

As Fisher and the candidate officers headed for the door, they observed what was the beginning of naval aviation teamwork; the whole class was out in the street helping Bennie find the parts to his weapon.

Within twenty minutes all the parts were found and it was just short of a miracle nothing came up missing. Bennie, Slick, and I carried the parts to his locker, Bennie locked them up, and we headed for class. Sasson had to do a complete uniform change, so he bolted as soon as we were dismissed. Mark showed up five minutes late for class and received two hours of extra military instruction on Saturday, which really meant marching on the seawall with his weapon.

After classes Bennie still had to get his weapon squared away for another inspection. Slick, Mark, and I helped clean the parts. Bennie said, "I never thought he would check that plate, but it was almost like he knew what to look for. After he snatched my weapon from my hands, he snapped that rifle around to the butt plate and opened it like it was a well-oiled hinge. I almost shit, because I knew I was on borrowed time." As Bennie finished putting his weapon together he had five minutes to get down to the DIs office on the first floor.

At the stroke of five Bennie headed down to see Fisher. Slick and I went to the edge of the steps to observe. The other five candidates were already in line when Bennie arrived. Just as Bennie got in line Staff Sergeant Bergman came out of the office and told the first five candidates to come with him, and Bennie was left in the hall alone.

Slick hissed to get Bennie's attention and motioned for him to go into the office. There was a set procedure for entering the DIs office. You squared off in front of the door and slapped the side of the wall three times. This was referred to as "pounding the pine." When acknowledged by a drill instructor, you entered. Once into the room, you walked directly to the desk of the DI who had requested your presence and sounded off. You gave the seated drill instructor your name and said, "Reporting as ordered, sir."

Bennie pounded the pine. When somebody inside said, "Enter," Bennie walked in and Slick and I moved down the stairs to a better vantage point. We could see Bennie squared off in front of Gunney Fisher's desk, but Mad Dog Varney was sitting in his chair and he looked pissed.

There was a "limit line" in front of all the DI desks. When you squared off to speak to them, you had to be two feet from the desk.

Before Varney said anything, he got up and walked in front of Gunney's desk and measured to see if Bennie was within limits. Bennie missed his mark by one inch, so it cost him fifty push-ups. Once our roommate was back up on his feet and somewhat composed, Varney proceeded to ream him a new asshole.

"You, Nunn, are an embarrassment to me and your whole class. Out of thirty-five men you were the only candidate that failed the inspection. What do you have to say for yourself?"

"Nothing, sir," Bennie said, which was probably the smartest thing to do.

"You will spend the next two weekends marching on the seawall and you better not drag this class down again, do you hear me?"

Bennie answered with a loud, "Yes, sir!"

At that point Mad Dog squared off in front of Bennie, inspected his weapon, and dismissed him. Just before Bennie exited, we headed for our room.

When Bennie returned to the room, he looked white as a sheet as he walked over to his locker. Slick and I were sitting at the study table in the middle of the room and pretended we hadn't seen anything. Mark was lying on his rack reading when Bennie opened his locker and put his rifle away.

Mark sat up and asked, "What did Gunney have to say?"

"Gunney, my ass," Bennie replied. "It was Mad Dog Varney who ripped me a new one."

"Well, what happened?"

"Two weekends of EMI."

"Shit, you got off easy; it could have been worse."

"Say, you two can march and play soldier together down on the seawall this weekend," Slick suggested.

"Fuck you," Bennie replied.

The following week was the beginning of our swim qualifications and probably one of the most intense weeks in the whole program. Swimming was part of my childhood and I enjoyed the water and its associated sports, but a lot of my classmates made it known they were uneasy. Especially about completing the mile swim with full flight gear on. This was probably the hardest qual to complete. If you had difficulty swimming some of the strokes or treading water, you had to take remedial swim lessons after classes, and practice until you passed the required maneuver.

The first day in the swim tank was pretty basic, but the training intensified as the week went on. The dreaded Dilbert Dunker was scheduled for Thursday. The dunker was a simulated aircraft cockpit, mounted on rails, positioned twenty feet above the pool. Once you were strapped in, the instructor tripped a lever and the cockpit started down the rails. After water impact, it would roll several more feet, then turn upside down. The student inside had to wait until all the bubbles cleared, then unstrap and swim to the surface. The hair-raising stories about this ride caused a lot of us to lose sleep the night before.

We knew we had an hour and a half to complete the swim. At no time could we touch the sides of the pool, and our flight suits and boots had to remain on throughout the test. Eight candidates failed, but they had several weeks to pass before commissioning day. Both of my armpits were raw and bloody from the rubbing of the flight suit and I had several bruises on my head and face from being kicked with flight boots by frustrated swimmers. It was probably the hardest phase of training so far.

As we reached the halfway mark of our training, we began to see the light at the end of the tunnel. Unfortunately the obstacle course, which encompassed running in sand, climbing, and jumping over and under man-made obstacles for time, was between us and that light. The sea course was a mile-and-a-half run through woods and sand; it also had a time limit to pass. Everyone qualified on both courses and a couple of candidates set new time records. That pleased Mad Dog.

The harassment from the DIs had subsided somewhat and our class was becoming one of the more senior classes in the regiment. As we watched the incoming classes it was quite apparent what the DIs were doing. But I remember being at the early stages of the program and feeling the world was caving in around me. I was now able to complete tasks in minimal time with 100-percent accuracy. The DIs had taught us how to pay attention to detail in a few short weeks.

Regimental weekend was our next big event and this function would probably be the highlight of our candidate officer training. It was almost like fall weekend in college. During the weekend the whole regiment competed in football, basketball, obstacle, and sea-course times. The parade points accumulated over the quarter could determine who would become the honor battalion; that's why it was so important to do well during Friday's parades. The regimental ball Saturday night was where the announcement was made as to who was the honor battalion.

As the big weekend drew closer, the basketball, football, and parade competition became fierce. Each battalion tried to achieve as many points as possible to have a healthy lead going into the final two days. On the Wednesday prior to the regimental weekend, the points were posted. Batt two had a sixty-point lead over batt one and a ninety point lead over batt three. The most points you could accumulate during the two days of competition was two hundred, so it still was anyone's ball game.

The days leading up to the weekend were very busy. Quarterly tests in military history and aerodynamics were being completed. Candidates who were still on stupid studies for academics and swim were spending every spare minute to complete the requirements. Uniforms were being tailored so they'd fit like gloves for the ball and our guest lists for commissioning day had to be finalized.

The weekend finally arrived and the competition was brutal. All of the top competitors from each battalion were chosen for each event. The final event was steal the flag, and the whole regiment had to participate. Steal the flag meant exactly that. Each battalion had its flag positioned in a tree at a separate location. A triangle that encompassed three square miles surrounding the football field was the field of play. Once a battalion's flag was captured, it had to be brought to the fifty-yard line.

The competition would last two hours and the winner of this event would receive one hundred points. The battalion that got the flag first would probably become the honor battalion, because we were within a few points of one another going into this final event. We all received maps as to where the other battalions' flags were located. The tactics used were basic and the most innovative battalion would win.

Sasson had a lot of problems with blisters early on in the program, so he spent a lot of time at sick call getting them treated. While there, he met a couple of nurses who took a liking to him and he was seeing one of them regularly. Prior to the regimental weekend, we knew the flag stealing would be the last event, so we got our game plan together days in advance.

Slick and I were slated to steal the flag. Bennie and a couple of former football players, big tight ends, would run interference for us if we ran into resistance. Mark and Carol, his girlfriend, were the decoy. After the maps were distributed and the event got underway, we had a runner get a map to Mark and "Operation Ambush" went into effect.

Batt two's flag was located down by the obstacle course near the water and that was our target. The plan was for Mark and Carol to use her car to get to the other end of the base and rent a fishing boat. They were to motor down to the obstacle course and beach the boat, then start rolling in the sand and playing grab-ass while making enough noise to get the guards' attention. Once they had caught the eye of the guards, the plan was to head behind a sand dune, making the guards think a little hanky-panky was about to begin.

We gave Mark and Carol a half hour to get into place before we made our advance on the flag. Carol was wearing a flesh-colored leotard under her clothes and Mark changed into civilian clothes. As Slick and I approached the target zone we could see that Carol was putting on an Academy Award performance, because the candidates who were guarding the flag were trying to get a look at what was going on.

When they were far enough away from the flag,

we snatched it and headed back. Before the candidates got close enough to identify Mark or Carol, one of them turned around and saw us running with the flag. But it was too late and the trap had worked. We were the first to return with a flag, won the competition, and became the honor battalion. The regimental ball was a huge success and we all had a grand time.

The final week before commissioning day, our class became candidate officers and at this point we really began to feel like somebody. We assisted the drill instructors and helped the new classes get squared away, as we were helped when we first arrived. The whole program finally came into perspective. Learning to pay attention to detail and having team spirit drilled into us were done for a reason and now it became clear. But I had my eye on an even bigger prize. I couldn't wait until I was a commissioned officer and received that first salute from Mad Dog Varney. That would be a moment to savor forever.

Friday morning finally rolled around and commissioning day had arrived. This would be our last parade. Of all my accomplishments through high school and college, this was my greatest—becoming an officer in the United States Navy.

WELCOME
ABOARD

It was a cloudy, overcast Monday morning as Slick, Bennie, and I walked toward Building 2434 at Naval Air Station Saufley Field. Saufley was named for Lieutenant J. G. Richard Caswell Saufley, naval aviator number 14, who had been killed in a crash on Santa Rosa Island in 1916. Saufley Field was first opened as a base field for NAS Pensacola, on August 26, 1940, and was offically commissioned March 1, 1943, as a naval auxiliary air station. On July 31, 1968, the "auxiliary" was dropped, and Saufley became a full-fledged naval air station.

The temperature was in the mid fifties and a cool breeze hustled across the base as we approached the entrance to the building. Just as I started to open the door we were stopped dead in our tracks by the loud popping and out-of-sync sound of a sick airplane engine. We all peered out over the airfield and saw an aircraft trailing black smoke as it circled the field like a hawk eyeballing its prey.

I closed the door and we rushed behind the building to get a better view of the airfield and the stricken airplane. By this time the crash alarm was sounding, the ambulance and crash trucks were rolling toward the active runway, and everyone was out in the back lot watching the emergency.

The pilot made one pass, but didn't have the right angle, and he had to circle again, the engine coughing and choking as he tried to avoid a stall. On her second pass, the engine died altogether, and our hearts were in our mouths as the nose dipped dangerously low, but the pilot knew what he was doing and managed to maintain enough airspeed and enough control to reach the end of the runway before the plane fell like a rock, its tires screeching and blowing off puffs of gray smoke as it lurched to a halt.

Once the aircraft was safely on the ground, we headed back to the building. As we entered the conference room for our first briefing, Bennie started making wisecracks about getting killed on your first hop.

"Sweetwater, if you buy the farm," he said, "can I have your TV and stereo?"

At that moment the comment didn't sit well with me and I glared at him. We found a seat and waited for the briefing officer to enter.

There were thirty-six officers in our preflight class. Twenty-nine ensigns, and seven second lieutenants. It was nice to have a little authority and be away from those wonderful men in the Smokey the Bear hats, better known as drill instructors. Even though we were the lowest ranking line officers in the Navy and Marine Corps, we were now one step above whale shit, which helped my ego a bit.

As I sat waiting for the brief to begin, I started to feel homesick and to miss my parents. I'd hardly had time to visit with them after I was commissioned, and they were gone before I knew it. It was starting to get to me when someone called, "Attention on deck!"

We all rose as the senior officer entered the room. "Please be seated," he said. "Good morning, gentlemen, I am Commander Mike Grocki, your training officer, and on behalf of the CO, Commander Jim Morris, who is out of town, I would like to welcome you aboard training squadron one, the world's busiest naval air station, which you will soon call VT-1 like the rest of us.

"Your next nine weeks are going to be very challenging. Give 110 percent and you will come out winners. The name of the game at VT-1 is 'procedures.' Gentlemen, you must know your flight procedures cold or your flight instructors cannot teach you how to fly. Flying is very stressful, and if you don't know your material on the ground, there is a good possibility you will forget it in the air.

"You will start your training with thirteen familiarization flights, during which you will learn how to conduct a proper preflight of an aircraft, learn to take off and land, do stalls and spin recoveries. Once the familiarization stage has been completed, you will be taught precision aerobatics and basic instruments. After successfully completing all of these requirements, you will then be introduced to radio instruments, which will teach you airway navigation and instrument approaches.

"Once you have successfully completed VT-1, you will be selected for future training in jets, propeller aircraft, or helicopters. The aircraft you are selected for will depend on your flight and academic grades and your class standing.

"Does anyone have any questions so far?"

Slick Morely raised his hand.

"Yes, sir," said Commander Grocki.

"What happens if you have a problem in one of these flight phases?"

"Good question, Ensign. If you have difficulty in an area, you could receive a SOD, which means signal of difficulty. If you receive a SOD, you will be debriefed by your flight instructor and most generally be awarded two extra flights to overcome the problem and then continue on in phase. Two SODs in one phase will constitute a review board at higher levels. If you get an 'up,' you will get two more reflys and continue on. If you get a 'down,' you will be washed out of the flight program. If you get a 'ready-room SOD,' you could go straight to a review board. A ready-room SOD would indicate that you haven't been studying and you don't know your procedures prior to your flight. Are there any more questions?"

The room was silent.

Grocki continued. "Gentlemen, your academic training will provide you with a solid foundation for this particular aircraft. Engineering, aerodynamics, and meteorology will be your main courses, with additional instruction in radio navigation and preflight planning. The rest of the morning will be devoted to lectures on course rules and regs pertaining to NAS Saufley Field. Now let's take a short break and be back in ten minutes."

During the break I asked Slick and Bennie if they learned anything. Bennie said, "Yeah, you best know your goddamn procedures."

We laughed, knowing very well that things were starting to get rough. Looking at my watch, I said, "It's time to head back in."

"Roger that," the two of them responded.

Grocki finished the morning session and broke for lunch. He instructed us to be down at hangar one by 1300 for flight gear issue, before letting us go.

During lunch you could feel the excitement in the air around the table. Slick was already talking about flying fighters and how he was going to burn up the program. I wanted fighters, too, but didn't say much for fear I might not get them. Bennie was undecided as to what aircraft he wanted to fly; he just wanted to be in the air and part of the navy team. The sweet taste of actually flying was about to become a reality. Everyone's major concern was on getting his hooks on a navy leather flight jacket.

At 1300 our preflight class was lined up outside flight-gear issue in hangar one. Slick and Bennie were in front of me and we were ten deep before we reached the flight-gear-issue door. At five after, the door opened and the line started to move almost immediately. There were four men passing out flight equipment and it seemed like forever before we reached the bench.

When we finally got there, they barked out our sizes as we moved down the table and for the most part they were right. These old salts had been there since Christ was a midshipman and probably saw a hundred flight crew personnel a month. They definitely knew their jobs.

By the time we reached the man who issued the jackets, we had so much goddamn flight gear we could hardly walk. With steel-toed boots slung around my neck, a large box with my helmet in it under one arm, survival gear under the other arm, gloves in my mouth, and long underwear over my shoulder, it was tough to carry anything else. The man who was passing them out was as classy as the flight jacket itself. Everyone called him Trader Vic. Trader was a midsize man sporting a big black handlebar mustache and a huge panama hat. His Oshkosh blue jeans were two sizes too large and the big Havana cigar he was smoking smelled almost as bad as he did. But he was a class act and I loved the way he ran his section. He was chanting, "Come on, sonny, move it or lose it, we only have a few left."

I knew there were plenty more, but the thought that I might not get my flight jacket made me play the game.

As I reached the end of the line and squared off in front of Trader Vic, he said, "You know, sonny, this jacket I am about to hand you wasn't made overnight. It takes five to six weeks of flushing to remove the hair and another week of soaking in tannic acid to soften the cowhide to fashion it into a jacket. After a week of staining and three weeks of sewing, I get the honor of issuing it to you. Don't lose it, sonny. You only get one."

As he laid the jacket and two flight suits on my already oversized mound, the added weight about put me to my knees. Looking around for Slick, I spotted him at the west end of the building and headed after him. Barely making it across the hangar floor, I unceremoniously dumped my gear into a pile and sat down.

As we talked I lifted my flight jacket from my pile and was surprised by its weight. The suede jacket I wore in college weighed less than half of what I was now holding in my outstretched arms. At nearly seven pounds, it actually weighed more than the rifle with which I had qualified on the range during AOC training. I turned the jacket around so its plain back faced me, then I brought the leather to my nose. The smell reminded me of the interior of a new Coupe de Ville my grandfather had bought many years ago.

I recalled an old saying my grandfather had told me when I was young. He used to say, "Matt, there are three commodities you can judge solely by smell. A good cigar, a fine woman, and a great car." I inhaled deeply and added a fourth to the list.

I turned the jacket around and felt the lamb-fleece collar, then I gave a cursory glance at the thin nylon liner and knitted cuff and waistband before throwing it on. It came on easy, due to the tapered three-inch-wide leather bands under the arms.

Supposedly these built-in inserts gave a flyer greater flexibilty in the air, but I knew most aviators didn't wear their leather jackets when they flew, because it was too uncomfortable.

Many of our friends in the civilian world would sell their souls in a New York minute for a navy flight jacket, if they could get their paws on one. So it behooved us to keep a close eye on our newly acquired treasure. One had to suffer in silent discomfort for several years until the bulky leather finally broke down sufficiently to be somewhat comfortable. Overall, a new leather flight jacket rated downright poor in the comfort department, but it was one helluva status symbol.

After we caught our breaths, we headed back to our bachelor officer quarters to change into our flight suits and assemble our flight helmets. At 1430 we had the bailout demonstration.

The bailout trainer was a modified T-34/B airframe, with the wings and wheels removed. The fuselage was bolted to a reinforced metal cage secured to four cement pilings in the ground. There was a large canvas netting around the starboard side of the fuselage, which we jumped into when we got the word to bail out.

The cockpit and power plant were both functional. A wooden staging was attached to the port side of the fuselage and we entered the front cockpit at that point. The aircraft was started by a mechanic to simulate the noise and wind blowing in your face when you opened the canopy and prepared to jump. After the aircraft was started, the mech jumped into the rear cockpit.

Once you got into the front cockpit, you strapped

into a four-point safety harness, plugged in your helmet cord to the intercom phones, and closed the canopy. When instructed over the headphones to bailout, you unplugged your helmet, slid open the canopy, jumped up into your seat, put both hands on the canopy rails, and made a diving roll out of the cockpit in front of where the wing would be attached. Everyone was cycled through at least twice or until they got it right.

After we finished the bailout trainer, the rest of the day belonged to us, to do as we pleased. Slick and I went back to our rooms to relax and Bennie and a friend went fishing. One of the advantages to being a commissioned officer was having your own room. We all lived one or two doors from each other, but it was nice to have privacy. The rooms at Saufley Bachelor Officer Quarters were very comfortable and within walking distance of everything on the base.

The next day we started ground school for the T-34/B aircraft. The "T" meant that it was a trainer and not a fleet airplane, the "34" was the model type, and the "B" signified that it was built by Beechcraft. Within five days we could be scheduled for our first flight, so Slick and I figured we best hit town for some liberty before the shit hit the fan. Slick was the only one who had a car, so I helped pay for the gas and he would let me use it on special occasions.

After dinner Slick and I went over some of the material that was to be covered in our engineering class the next day and started to make out some procedure cards for our first flight. As we started to rap up our studying there was a knock on the door and

Bennie walked in with four huge sea bass that he'd caught.

"Hey, you guys want to have some fish on the grill?" he asked.

"No thanks, we've already eaten and were just about ready to head to town," I said. "Want to come?"

"I'd better not. Earl and I need to fillet these fish and get them into the freezer before they spoil. I also need to study some before tomorrow. Where are you two headed?" Bennie asked.

"We're going down to Rosie O'Grady's."

"Fun place, if you can stay out of trouble," he said as he headed out the door.

Slick and I changed our clothes and met at the Blue Goose, the name we'd given to his car. It was an old police car that had about 200,000 miles on it and was on its last legs. Slick had only paid four hundred for the Goose and it was a beautiful thing.

We arrived at Servile Square about eight, and the place was hopping. This was Pensacola's tourist trap, and there were shops, restaurants, and small pubs all within the square, but the main attraction was Rosie O'Grady's. They had a sideshow on the hour, the beer was the coldest in town, and everyone seemed to end up there after touring the rest of the establishments.

There was a line outside Rosie's, so Slick and I figured we'd better get in before the place filled up. It was a good deal for servicemen. With an ID, you didn't have to pay the two-dollar cover charge. Once in the door, we looked for a table and spotted one with a couple of open seats. Rosie's was your basic bar; it had sawdust on the wooden floor and bench-like picnic tables to sit at. Beer and wine were the only spirits served and the sing-alongs were what made the place so popular.

Once we got squatters' rights at the table, we ordered a pitcher of beer, and started to live it up. As I did a combat sweep of the room, I spotted Cannonball Anderson over in the corner. In the International League, he'd gotten his nickname for his hard fastball.

"Hey, Slick," I said, "I see someone I know. I'll be right back, save my seat."

He gave me a thumbs-up.

As I approached Cannonball I noticed he didn't look so good. As a matter of fact he looked pretty drunk. I yelled at him from a distance, but he didn't recognize me at first.

"Hey, Sweetwater," he hollered, when he finally recognized me, "how the fuck are you?"

"Not bad. What's the matter, Cannonball? You don't look so hot."

"You got that right. I washed out today, one goddamn week before commissioning."

"Jesus, what happened?"

"I couldn't pass those fucking tests and they gave me the boot."

"Oh, man, I'm really sorry to hear it, Cannonball. Got any plans?"

"I'll try one more season with the minors, and if I don't make it to the bigs, I'll get a coaching job somewhere."

"Come on over to our table and we'll raise a little hell for old times."

"No, thanks. I've got a flight to Atlanta in an hour, so I have to run."

"Okay then, take care of yourself."

"Thanks, Sweetwater. Give 'em hell."

As I walked back to the table I was shaking my head and Slick asked what was wrong. I told him about Cannonball washing out, and to cheer me up, he said, "Say, Water, I want you to meet a couple of ladies. They were sitting across the table from us. This is Mary, Jean, and Alice. Ladies, this is Sweetwater, soon to be one of the hottest fighter pilots in the Navy."

I acknowledged the ladies' presence and immediately locked onto Alice, who had the best face and an even better figure. Slick explained that the women were from Atlanta and had come down to Pensacola for a week's vacation. He was already well under way, and I'd have to go some to catch up. He had just ordered another pitcher of beer and the show was about to begin.

While the barbershop quartet sang I made small talk with Alice and asked her what she did for a living. She said that she and her friends were all in the field of education, so I left it at that. It was too difficult to carry on a conversation with all the noise.

By the time the show was over, I had a pretty good buzz on and I was ready to dance. Mary appeared to be the designated driver and chaperon of the group. She was quiet and was keeping a close eye on Slick and me, almost to the point where I was becoming uncomfortable. Since Slick seemed to take a liking to Jean, I swapped sides of the table so I could be close to Alice, and Jean could sit next to Slick.

When the floor opened, I asked Alice to dance
and she kind of hesitated for a moment, as if looking
over at Mary for approval before she accepted. It
seemed a bit odd, but since I was feeling no pain, I
didn't think much about it. The first few dances were
fast and Alice could cut a pretty nice rug. During the
slow dances she snuggled up close and I started to
kiss her neck. She seemed to enjoy it, but asked me
to stop because it got her too excited.

After a half hour of dancing, we went back to the
table and sat down. Slick was dancing with Jean and I
felt sorry for Mary, so I asked her to dance. She
declined and said that they would have to be going
soon. That was my cue, so I figured I better make my
move.

I asked Alice, "Would you like to go out again
Friday night?"

"I really can't," she said, "but thank you."

"Then how about if I come up and see you in
Atlanta?"

"I don't think it would be a good idea."

Now I was really confused, because the initial signal from her seemed to be positive, but any attempt I
made to further the relationship only got me a cold
shoulder. By this time Slick had returned to the table
with Jean.

As Slick sat down Mary said, "Come on, girls, we
have to be going."

"We'd be happy to drive you ladies to your hotel
later," I suggested.

"No, thank you. That won't be necessary," Mary
said.

I was starting to get pissed off. "Mary, what are you, their mother?" I demanded.

"No, but I *am* their mother superior, and we must be going, gentlemen."

Slick and I looked at each other and I almost lost it. I said, "Come on, Mary, you're joking." I looked at Alice, and she shook her head as if to say, no, she wasn't. Things were starting to fall into place, but I was still a little fuzzy from the booze, and said, "Why aren't you wearing your habits?"

Alice said, "Our order doesn't require us to wear them anymore. We teach school in Atlanta and are attending a conference at St. Joseph's this week."

"Christ Almighty . . ." I said, then realizing that wasn't the best opener, tried again. "What I mean is, I'm sorry for being so forward."

She smiled. "I don't mind," she said, "I enjoyed it as much as you did, Sweetwater. We *are* human, you know."

I looked at Mary then and she had a big smile on her face, as if to say welcome aboard, boys, you're in the real world now.

We said our good-byes and thanked them for a nice evening. After getting shot out of the sky, we sat down and had another beer to recoup. As I looked around to see if anyone was watching, I said, "Slick, we've got to swear an oath right now, never to admit putting the moves on a couple of penguins. If this ever gets back to the base, we'd never live it down. Finish your beer and let's get the hell out of here before someone spots us."

We made a quiet exit and headed back to Saufley.

5

AIRSICK AND SCARED

At seven the next morning Slick and I met for breakfast and looked over the day's activities. The morning was dedicated to ground school and after lunch we would be assigned to our flights. There were four of them at VT-1; flight 12, flight 13, flight 14, and flight 18. The word was out to stay away from flights 12 and 18. The flight leader in 12 was a mean son of a bitch and flight 18 was an all-marine flight.

After a full morning of electrical-wiring diagrams, fuel-flow charts, and hydraulic valves, we were ready for lunch. At 1300 we had to be back in class for a briefing on course rules, then we were broken up into our individual flights. A student from each flight escorted us to our respective training spaces and we received a brief from the flight leader. Slick and I went to flight 14 and Bennie went to 13.

Flight 14 was in a large room that had a blackboard that ran the length of the front wall. Eight feet behind the blackboard were three long tables, all connected. Two instructors sat at one end and a student duty officer sat at the other end. Behind them were twenty chairs evenly spaced on each side of an aisle that led to the entrance. As we walked in, the heads of students in the flight turned and then quickly returned to business, knowing that a new class was checking in.

We took our seats on the left side of the aisle and waited for the senior flight instructor, who was the flight leader for flight 14, to give us a short brief. Within a few minutes he entered and introduced himself. "Good afternoon, gentlemen. My name is Lieutenant Commander Tim Tuck and I will be your flight leader while you're here at VT-1. As you know by now, the name of the game around here is this—know your procedures and be on time. If you live by these rules, you will not see my bad side.

"However, if you violate them, we will have some words. Feel free to come see me if you can't get a straight answer from your instructor. Have fun while you're here, and remember, your naval aviation career begins today. Don't accept anything less than perfection. Does anyone have any questions?"

No one raised a hand. "Okay, then I'll turn the show over to Lieutenant Bobby 'Big Hands' Johnson. He's my scheduling officer and he will brief you on this monster of a blackboard."

Lieutenant Johnson stood up and said, "Yes, gentlemen" as he held his hands high in the air, "they are big and I can write a mean schedule. Good afternoon and welcome to flight 14. This board looks intimidating, but once you know how to read it, it's a piece of cake. If you look up to the far left and read down, you'll see your names. To the right of your name will be your instructor and brief time for your flight. I haven't gotten that far yet, but will have you all assigned by this evening, and some of you will have a brief time to boot.

"The next block will tell which flight you're on and you'll need to fill in the time that you checked out to go fly. When you return, write in your time and indicate whether you completed or incompleted the flight in the next space. Pretty simple, isn't it? You need to call in each day between five and six P.M. and ask the duty officer if you're flying tomorrow, and if so, what your brief time is.

"If something should come up and you can't fly, contact the duty officer or the schedules officer and let him know what's up. We start writing the next day's schedule at two, so get your inputs in early."

Once Johnson had explained what everything meant, the board didn't seem so awesome. After some questions were answered about leave and sick call, a knot began to gather in my stomach. The pressure to perform was beginning to build and the journey down the "road to gold" was about to get a little rougher.

*   *   *

After dinner we walked over to our flight to see if we were scheduled to fly the next day. Before we got ten feet into the building, a watch officer stopped us and asked for some identification. Once we were cleared, we headed down the passageway to our flight and entered the room just as Lieutenant Johnson was putting the final touches on the following day's schedule.

Big Hands looked up, the marker still in his fist. "Can I help you gentlemen?"

"We're just checking to see if we have an instructor assigned, Lieutenant," I said.

"Well, let's see if you learned anything in my lecture. What're your names?"

"Sullivan and Morely," I replied.

"Okay, find your name on the board and look to the right, as I showed you this afternoon."

We both gasped when we saw that we not only had an instructor but were scheduled for our first flight. I had a seven o'clock brief, with an 8:30 go, and Slick had a 12:30 brief with a 1400 go.

"Don't look so surprised," Big Hands said. "I told you some of you would be flying tomorrow."

Lieutenant Miller's name was next to mine and Lieutenant Warrington was next to Slick's name.

"Anything you can tell us about our instructors?" Slick asked.

"They're two of the best and probably the most liked," he said. Then, abruptly changing the subject, he asked, "Say, do you guys play sports?"

"We sure do," replied Slick.

"Well, you're in like Flynn with these two instructors."

"Why's that?" I asked.

"They just happen to run the sports program in our flight and they like good athletes. If you can help the flight win the Captain's Cup, they'll keep an eye on you like a sea daddy, if you know what I mean."

We both nodded our heads like we knew what the hell he was talking about. Neither of us had a clue.

Knowing that Miller and Warrington were good guys eased the shock of learning our first flight had already been scheduled—a little. But we both had some power studying to do before morning. On our way out we ran into Bennie and he was amazed when we told him we had our first flight in the morning. Evidently our flight had the fewest students, so we got thrown into the fire first.

When we got back to the BOQ, Slick and I decided to study independently for the first several hours, then get together and quiz each other on our procedures. A flight syllabus had been issued at our welcome-aboard brief and it spelled out the requirements for each flight. There was no excuse for not being prepared.

Based on the syllabus guide, the first hop looked pretty much like a gimme. The instructor demonstrated everything. But we had to learn the emergencies for the day, complete a preflight inspection on the aircraft, and start it up. The emergencies and preflight were pretty straightforward, but learning the start sequence would take some studying.

After two hours of reviewing the required material, I went over to Slick's room and knocked on his door.

"It's open," he called, and I entered.

"Well, Slick," I said, "have you got this wired yet?"

He gave me a big laugh. "There's a lot of material to cover. Let's get a Coke and go over what we've learned so far."

Slick unfolded a large schematic diagram of the aircraft and laid it out on the floor. We practiced walking through a preflight and pointed out the major components we would be asked about and explained their function to each other. Then we reviewed the emergencies for our first hop. They included fire during start, brake failure, and lost communications. After an hour of studying, we felt we knew the preflight and emergency procedures cold, so we began learning the starting sequence.

I got two chairs and set them up in tandem to simulate the cockpit. Slick and I practiced our starting procedures with one of us playing the student and the other being the instructor in the back cockpit. After an hour and a half of practice, we both were confident we could start the aircraft. It was almost 12:30 when we finished studying, so I told Slick I would see him after my flight and retired to my room.

It was a restless night for me. I tossed and turned as my subconscious reviewed the procedures for my upcoming flight. I watched the hours pass until four and then I must have dozed off, only to be awakened as my alarm rattled off the dresser at 0530.

When I entered flight 14, there were several other students awaiting their instructor's arrival. I took a seat up front and broke out the books.

At 0700 an authoritative figure entered the room

and barked out my name. "Ensign Matt Sullivan . . . do we have a Mr. Sullivan present?"

I stood up, looked him straight in the eye, and extended my hand. "I'm Matt Sullivan."

"Good morning. I'm Jim Miller, better known as 'Jungle,' and I'm going to be your primary flight instructor while you're at VT-1."

Miller was medium-sized, with blond hair, and had the build of an athlete. He picked up his knee board and said, "Let's brief."

All of the initial briefings were conducted in cubicles near the cockpit trainers, which were adjacent to all the flights. As we entered the briefing area only a few of the cubicles were being used, so I picked one close to our flight. Each compartment had a table, two chairs, a blackboard, a model of the T-34/B, and an area map on the wall.

"Matt, where are you from?" Miller asked as we sat down.

"I'm from Dexter, Maine, home of the Dexter shoe. Have you ever heard of them?" I asked.

"Sure have," he replied, "Got a pair of Dexter golf shoes in my car. Most comfortable set of nails I've ever owned. Do you play, Matt?"

I'd never even thought about golf, but remembered what Big Hands had said, so I bit the bullet. "Not really," I said. "I haven't had the time to learn the proper techniques of the game. But I'm going to buy some clubs and learn this fall."

"Good, maybe we can get out and hit that white one around someday. Do you have any questions about today's flight?"

"No, sir."

"Good. Before we get started, Matt, you don't have to be so formal when we're alone," Jim said, trying to put me at ease. "Do you go by Matt or do you have a nickname?"

"Some call me Matt and the rest call me Sweetwater."

"Sweetwater, where in the hell did you get tagged with that moniker?" asked Miller.

After I told him my story, he said, "So you're the one all the flights have been trying to recruit."

"What do you mean?" I asked.

"Well, when a new class checks aboard, the instructors who run the athletic programs for their respective flights check the records of the incoming students. If you're a good athlete, everyone tries to get you assigned to his flight. As you may or may not know, I run the athletic program for flight 14, and yes, I picked you to be in this flight and as my student."

"I won't let you down, I promise."

"I'm sure you won't. Well, let's get down to business. Today, Sweetwater," he began, wasting no time in using my nickname, "I'm going to demo everything, so basically this hop is a freebie. We'll fly around the entire training area and I'll point out some landmarks which'll help you find certain landing fields and entry points back to Saufley.

"Prior to each flight, I'll go over all the maneuvers you'll be performing, ask some procedural questions about the maneuvers, and quiz you on the emergencies of the day. You'll be expected to know your procedures and your emergencies inside out. I can't

teach you to fly if you're trying to remember procedures while we're in the air."

I acknowledged that I understood how the briefs
and flights would be conducted.

After a nervous trip at the bathroom, I gathered
my flight gear, checked out on the board, and met
Jungle outside the building. As we walked toward the
hangar he explained the particulars of reviewing the
maintenance log for the aircraft we'd be flying and
how to spot repeat gripes.

As we entered the south corner of the hangar, we
walked into maintenance control, a large room where
all the flight logs were kept. Miller went up to the
counter, threw his helmet bag on top, and asked for
an aircraft. A loud voice from a small man almost hid-
den behind a large cloud of cigar smoke, said, "Good
morning, Jungle, your chariot is waiting. All you got
to do is kick the tires, light the fires, and she'll purr
like a new '47 Chevy."

"Okay, Cliff, which plane do you have for me
today?"

"One-oh-five. She's just come back from rework
and is ready to go." Lieutenant Commander Cliff
Cortel was a crusty old maintenance officer who had
come up through the enlisted ranks and been on
active duty for thirty years. He was so well-known in
the aviation community that he was almost a living
legend. He handed the aircraft log to Jungle, who
asked, "How many flyers do you have today, Cliff?"

"Sixty-eight up, and six are comers."

As I looked across the counter at the maintenance
officer and panned back at Jim, I got this insecure feel-

ing in my gut, knowing that today was the beginning of my flight training and that what I learned from now on would become habits for a lifetime.

At that moment Jim opened the metal jacket that housed the yellow sheet and maintenance record for aircraft 105. He explained how to fill in the yellow sheet, which kept track of our flight time and showed me what to look for in the discrepancies section. "Remember, Sweetwater," he said, "you're required by Instruction 3710 to review the last ten discrepancies. But it behooves you to review all the write-ups before signing your bird out. Once satisfied it's airworthy, the pilot-in-command signs the white sheet and this acknowledges that he has accepted responsibility for that plane. Is that clear?"

After the log was reviewed and signed, Jim told me to get my helmet and we headed to parachute issue. The paraloft was on the way to the flight line. The first crews of the day checked their chutes at the paraloft window and took them to the aircraft. All subsequent crews checked the chutes at the aircraft. The last crew of the day brought the chutes back to the paraloft, where they were inspected and stored for the night.

Lieutenant Miller got his chute and laid it up on a table that was used to preflight the gear. "Okay, Sweetwater, here are some major areas which need to be inspected before you accept the chute. You want to be sure that there are no stains or water spots on the outside of your parachute, then unbutton the three small snaps at the neck of the chute and make sure the cable leading down to the pins is not bent or damaged.

Now open the back of the chute and check to see that all the pins are straight and the safety string at the bottom of the last pin is not broken. Your final check is to make sure the d-ring fits into its receptacle. If there are no questions, get a chute and I'll observe while you do a preflight on it."

"Okay," I replied, swallowing the lump in my throat as the rigger handed me my chute.

I had no problems with the preflight of the chute until I had to button up the son of a bitch. The outer flap, which covered the pins, had five buttons to snap. They were not your normal snap-on buttons. There were male and female ends that you had to mate by rolling your finger left or right and it took me some time to master those little bastards.

Jungle chuckled and said, "Don't worry, Sweetwater, you're not the first to have that problem."

As I finished the back side of the chute, I hurriedly flipped it over to cover my embarrassment and caught the d-ring on the corner of the table and popped the chute open. Now I felt like a complete asshole.

Lieutenant Miller stood there shaking his head. "There are those who have and those who will. Go ahead and preflight another chute, Matt, and I'll meet you at the plane."

The sweat began to bead up on my forehead and I started to get a little rattled. I thought, *What* a way to start off. I quickly preflighted another chute and damn near ran out to the aircraft.

Miller had the back cockpit preflighted, his helmet plugged in and resting on the outside canopy rail when I arrived at the airplane. "Okay, Sweetwater, I want you to forget what happened back there. Relax and we'll press on with the flight."

I knew he was trying to put me at ease, but I was still tense.

"Sweetwater, the first thing you want to do is put your chute in the seat. It will act as a backrest for you. Then plug in your helmet and set it on the outside canopy rail. Now let me show you what switches to examine in both cockpits before you do your walk-around."

After the cockpits were checked, Miller walked me through the external preflight, asking questions as we inspected. Luckily I knew the answers and regained some of my credibility. As we finished up the preflight Jungle told me that I was fair game from then on.

I said, "What do you mean?"

"Instructors have a bad habit of leaving flight gloves and other objects in and around the engine," he said, "to see if the students are paying attention to detail during their walk-arounds. If you should miss a glove or pen that was purposely placed in or around the engine, then you're not preflighting correctly. Pride yourself in a thorough preflight and remember—the ass you save may be your own."

By this time the morning sun had warmed western Florida to the point where it was uncomfortable. The survival gear harnessed around my midsection and over my shoulders began to ride tightly, with all the bending and climbing I did during my walk-around. We climbed into our cockpits and the sweat was dripping off my brow as I tried to remember the procedures for starting the machine.

I now began to feel the pressure of responsibility. The instructor couldn't start the aircraft from the aft cockpit, so it was my chance to shine and get back to ground level after that chute incident. There were always little victories to be won and I felt I was one down, even though I answered a few questions right during the walk-around.

After I completed the prestart checklist, I checked to see if the fireguard was posted, the prop was clear, the parking brake set, that my canopy was open, and then I made the call to my instructor. "Ready to start, sir."

Jungle came back with, "Let her rip, Sweetwater."

I made sure the mixture was at idle cutoff, turned on the fuel control valve and boost pump, cracked my throttle a bit, made sure the prop was at full increase. Then I turned the battery on, checked my fuel pressure, and engaged the starter. Once the prop started to turn over, I put the ignition switch to both, slowly moved the mixture to rich, and released the starter when the engine fired. The plane started to vibrate and I moved the throttles up to 1,200–1,400 rpm, then turned on the radio.

Once the equipment had a chance to warm up, I checked the radio by talking into the boom mike attached to the left side of my helmet.

Jungle acknowledged the call. "Nice job, Sweetwater. You handled your first start like a real pro. I've got the aircraft now, so follow me through the pretaxi checklist."

These were my first positive strokes of the day and they felt good.

The pretaxi checklist was pretty simple, but the plane-captain checks were a little more involved. As Jim talked me through the checks he pointed out that each plane captain has his own technique. "Although the procedures are standardized, they may appear different due to variations in the captains' styles. Just don't get frustrated if you see a few different methods."

"Roger that," I replied. The communications in the cockpit were set up for hot mike and a button on the throttle was used when you communicated outside the aircraft, like talking to the tower or center.

After all checks were completed, I signaled to the plane captain to remove the chocks and we taxied out of the line and proceeded to the active runway. As we taxied by the tower we had to report to the instructor which panel was up and what runway was in use. The panel was either green, red, or yellow, and the active runway was posted under the panel.

The panels designated who could go flying. For example, if the green panel was up, all types of syllabus hops could fly; if the yellow panel was up, the weather was not good for solos and only certain instructional flights could launch; and if the red panel was up, nobody flew. The posting of the active runway not only gave the pilot the runway in use, but instructed him where to do his engine run-up.

The engine run-up had about twenty steps to it and it had to be committed to memory. Thank God, Lieutenant Miller demonstrated the first one. We got some backfiring when we advanced the throttle, so we had to do a high-power burnout to ensure that the engine was acceptable for flight. Jungle set the prop for 2,400 rpm's and advanced the throttle to 80 percent for one minute. When he was satisfied the engine was all right, Jim called the tower and requested permission to take off. The tower cleared us for takeoff on runway 36. The wind was calm.

Jim told me to ride the rudders with him to feel what control inputs were required during the takeoff roll and to hold the stick loosely to monitor the back pressure required during the lift-off and climb-out. Once we were airborne and the gear was up, I closed my canopy and went through the after-takeoff checklist. We climbed up to five thousand feet and leveled off.

Jim told me to take control of the aircraft and to fly a heading of 270. The morning sky was clear and the visibility was unlimited. As I flew along he pointed out the different fields we'd be landing at and the boundaries for the training area. With all the excitement of my first flight and all those complex procedures to remember, I began to get a little nauseous.

Into the mike I said, "I'm not feeling 100 percent, Jungle."

"Crack the canopy and get some fresh air, I've got the aircraft."

I said. "You've got it," and cracked the canopy. Within a few minutes I felt much better and I took back the controls.

Forty minutes into the flight I started to smell an odor that had an electrical tang. I didn't want to say

anything because I wasn't sure if it had any signifi-
cance. As we continued the odor became more prominent and I knew something wasn't right. I asked Jim
if he smelled anything unusual.

"Yeah, I do, Sweetwater. Why don't you give me
control of the aircraft and you pull out your emergency pocket checklist?"

As I reached down to pull my checklist out of my
flight suit's leg pocket, the cockpit began to fill with
smoke.

The smoke made me cough to the point where I
was having a problem breathing. Just then Jim
brought the throttle to idle and raised the nose to
reduce our airspeed. He then called me over the
intercom in a rather brisk tone. "Sweetwater, push
the cockpit cold air handle in and pull the hot-air
handle out, then open your canopy."

After I performed these emergency procedures,
the smoke and fumes were still not eliminated. Jungle
immediately made a Mayday call over the airwaves,
telling the world what our problem was, where we
were located, and what our intentions were.

Then he said, "Shut the battery and generator off
and pull all circuit breakers."

The radio and electrical equipment went dead
and we were unable to communicate with each other.
By now I was being overcome by the smoke, so I
leaned over the left canopy rail to get air and started
reviewing my bailout procedures. Everything got real
quiet. Jungle had shut the engine down and we were
falling out of the sky. Within a minute or so the
smoke started to clear and I could see what was going

on. Jim had the aircraft in a controlled descent and was setting up for a high-altitude emergency. There was no airfield below us and we were too far north to glide back to Summerdale, the nearest training strip. Instead we were headed for a stretch of farmland.

Jim was yelling at the top of his lungs to overcome the windstream. He was trying to explain what he was attempting to do, hoping to calm me down. I could barely understand him. He seemed to be in control, but I was scared shitless. He had the aircraft headed for what appeared to be a good-sized field, and when I really looked around, I realized it was the only field in the area large enough to set a plane into.

I prayed that Jim had practiced this procedure while demonstrating it to students over the years. He maneuvered the gliding aircraft to a position 1,500 feet above the field he planned to land in. Our gear and flaps were up and the prop was at full increase. As we descended to low key, abeam the intended point of landing, I started to become concerned. Our emergency landing field had cattle in it and there wasn't room for both of us.

As we rolled out on final Jungle yelled over the windstream, "Turn on the battery and lower the flaps to full."

As the flaps came down it increased our drag and helped slow us to a satisfactory landing speed. I peered out over the motionless prop and noticed the field had a ditch halfway down the middle with a small stone wall dividing it in half. Cattle were spread out all over the field and they were going to be hard to avoid.

Jungle yelled, "Tighten your seat belt as tight as you can stand it and lower your seat. Once all motion stops, get out and away from the aircraft."

At a hundred feet or so I dropped my seat to the floorboards and the last thing I saw was cattle scattering to get out of the way. It looked like Moses parting the waters.

As the aircraft started to settle to land I felt a thump and the plane pitched its nose down. Jungle tried to level the wings and yanked the stick back into his lap. We hit the ground hard, skidded a ways, did a ground loop, and came to rest beside the stone wall.

The next thing I knew, Jungle was trying to get me out of the aircraft. I must have been knocked unconscious for a few seconds. Once I had all my faculties I was up and out of that bird in a flash. Luckily there was no fire.

Jim had gotten a Mayday call out before I secured the battery and radios. There were two planes circling overhead and a farmer racing toward us on a tractor. As we stood on the stone wall Jungle asked, "Are you okay, Matt?"

When I nodded, he asked, "Did you see that goddamn steer I hit?"

"No," I replied, but then realized that the thump prior to hitting the ground must have been the steer. And the steer wasn't dead, just stunned and pissed off. And now he was headed straight for us like a runaway locomotive.

The farmer had to divert his tractor to keep from hitting the raging steer. As the animal raced toward us Jim yelled, "The son of a bitch isn't stopping."

The horrendous screech of tearing metal drowned out the rest of his words as the steer drove his horns straight through the skin of the plane. Jim and I kept the plane between us and the bull. We couldn't believe what we were witnessing. Here we had survived a major plane crash, but were in danger of being gored by a raging bull. Nobody would believe this story unless it was on film.

The animal backed off several times and nailed the side of the plane again and again—*bam! bam! bam!*—ripping gaping holes in the fuselage skin. The farmer was yelling and jumping up and down in his tractor seat, trying to discourage the bull, but to no avail.

The bull turned his attention to the new menace and started to attack the tractor. I don't know whether he was afraid for the bull or for his tractor, but whatever it was, the farmer decided to back off. By this time the crash truck from Summerdale was at the end of the field, barreling down on us. As he got closer he could see the predicament we were in and the crash crewman working the light water turret lit the foam off and started fire-hosing the bull.

The foam was swirling through the air and the bull started to disappear under waves of thick white. Within a few seconds the bull realized the match was over and headed to the center of the field with the rest of the cattle.

After the smoke—or foam—settled, the crash crew and farmer came over to see if we were all right. Jim had a pretty good cut over his left eye and appeared to have sprained his ankle. The crash crew administered first aid to him and looked me over for a concussion. A search-and-rescue helicopter was vectored in to take us to the hospital for further observation. As the helo approached the field I begin to feel a little queasy, and realized that I might be in a mild state of shock.

The crewman from the helo wrapped us in blankets and strapped us to our seats. As we lifted off I began to feel airsick and scared, wondering if I really wanted those wings of gold.

6

UNDER
THE BAG

Since the Navy doesn't take chances, after the accident I was grounded while an assortment of tests were done to determine whether I was physically fit to return to the flight program. The enforced leisure was getting me down, and the rigorous medical tests weren't helping my mood any. I felt like everyone was leaving me behind. Slick tried to help, but the problem was mine and I wasn't going to feel better until I was cleared to fly again.

It took a week. When I finally got clearance, and the chit for my next flight, which would be with another instructor since Jungle was still recovering from a nasty gash he'd received in the crash, it was like the governor had called while the executioner stood there with his hand on the switch. It wasn't that close, of course, but it might just as well have been.

I handled some paperwork, the chit burning a hole in my pocket the way a winning lottery ticket might have, if I'd ever had one, and when I got back to my BOQ room, there was a note on the door from Slick. He wanted me to give him a call before I went to dinner.

As soon as he realized it was me on the line, he said, "Want to go out to eat?"

"Sure, what have you got in mind?"

"Remember that girl I met at Joe's the other night?"

"Which one? There were about fifty or so, as I recall."

"The blonde? Big headlights?"

"Vaguely, I think. Why?"

"She works at the King's Inn, so I thought we might stop by for dinner and I can maybe set something up for us this weekend."

"Us?"

"She must have girlfriends. How about it? Maybe we can take them to the beach."

"Sounds good to me, I guess."

We got to the restaurant about 6:30, and the place was packed. There was a twenty-minute wait for a table, so we sat at the bar for a beer. Slick spotted the girl, but the crowd made it impossible for them to exchange more than a wave. It wasn't until we were seated for dinner that she was able to stop by our table.

Slick wasn't sure of her name, but luckily she wore a name tag, and he pulled the intro off without a hitch. Mary was gorgeous, even more gorgeous than Slick remembered—tall, with her long blond hair done in a French braid and, of course, the assets that had captured Slick's fancy in the first place.

"She's a premed student," Slick said, after the introduction was made. "She works here to pay for school."

Mary smiled. "I really have to get back to work," she said. "But I'll see you before you leave."

We chowed down, sparing no expense in our celebration, and by the time dessert was on the table, the crowd had thinned out a bit, and Mary was free to talk. I had a piece of Key lime pie while Slick tucked Mary away in a corner to unveil his plan for the weekend.

When he came back, I asked, "Well, what did she say?"

"She has a big test tomorrow, but once it's over, she'll be ready for a relaxing weekend. She wants to party."

"What about me?"

"Got it covered. She'll bring somebody along. She's got a friend in mind. We'll meet them tomorrow for a drink. If you like what you see, we'll set it up for Saturday at the beach."

But first there was the business of flying to attend to. I was scheduled for my first flight since the accident the next morning and decided to brush up a little before hitting the rack.

Feeling excited about the promising weekend, Slick and I studied a bit and planned our strategy before going to bed. At 0900 the next morning,

Lieutenant Charles "Warbucks" Warrington called out my name. I stood up and walked toward him. "Good morning, sir," I said, extending a hand. I knew him by reputation, because he happened to be Slick's instructor. Jungle had promised to get me a decent replacement until he was up and running again, and he'd come through.

"Hey, Sweetwater, how's it going?"

"Great, sir. Thanks."

"Jungle called and asked if I would take you on until he can get back in the air."

"I appreciate it, and I won't let you down."

"That's the spirit. Let's go brief." We sat in one of the cubicles, and Warrington started right in. "Matt, since you've already had the long-drawn-out brief and walk-around, I'll just touch on some major points and we'll go do it. I plan on letting you do everything today. I'll help you along if you need it, but this will better prepare you for your upcoming flights."

"That'll be great, sir."

As we walked toward the hangar he quizzed me on some emergencies. "Matt, what would you do if you had an engine fire after start-up?"

"I'd shut the mixture off, push the throttle to full open, shut the fuel control off, shut the battery and ignition off, and abandon the aircraft."

"Very good, Sweetwater. What if you suspected carbon-monoxide contamination?"

"Open the canopy, pull out the cockpit cold- and hot-air handles and land as soon as practicable."

"Looks like you've been hitting the books and not resting on your laurels."

After entering the hangar, we signed the log-book, got our chutes, and made it to the plane. He watched me preflight both cockpits and inspect the outside of the plane. Before we strapped in, he pointed out a systematic way of setting up the front and back cockpit switches before start. The system would save a lot of time and was easy to remember. I thanked him for the tip and strapped in. To my surprise, the prestart and starting sequence both went as they were supposed to. The studying had paid off.

My taxiing wasn't the best, but wasn't bad for the first time. Warbucks talked me through the engine run-up and rode the controls with me at takeoff. Not used to retractable landing gear, I forgot to raise it until he reminded me. All in all, though, I was pretty proud of my efforts. The important thing was to remember the mistakes and not make them again.

The flight itself was flawless. I did the required maneuvers without a hitch and got a thorough area checkout. Then we revisited the field where Jungle and I had gotten our matador quals. The flight lasted almost two and a half hours, and I felt confident when we landed.

Warrington congratulated me. "I'm going to recommend that you push on with the scheduled syllabus. I don't think you need another warm-up flight, Matt."

It felt good going into the weekend a winner. It was time to light my hair on fire and have a little fun, if the girls would cooperate. I was walking a tightrope, and even though I still had a long way to go, I figured I was due a little R&R. Especially when I realized that more than half of the men who'd started with me at Pensacola were already civilians again.

As I approached my BOQ room I could tell that it was almost the weekend. Radios and stereos were blasting everything from blues to opera. Some of the aviators were standing in the halls drinking beer and telling sea stories. We'd all survived another week in the Pensacola pressure cooker.

At 1600 the famous Tailhook Bar in the BOQ lounge opened, and that was the official beginning of the weekend. Instructors and students gathered without regard to rank or experience to unwind and indulge in that camaraderie that makes the Navy unique.

I gave Slick a call before I headed to the bar and told him I'd meet him there. He already had a snoot full of beer when he joined me. It was almost time to meet the girls, so we ate quickly and went to freshen up.

At 8:30, I rejoined him at the Blue Goose and we headed for town. The drive to the Sheraton took twenty minutes, and when we got to the parking lot it was already full. That could only mean one thing—a great band was on tap.

By the time we found a place to park and reached the bar, we were fashionably late. Slick made a combat sweep of the bar to see if he could find them. He was back in a few minutes, and he was in a huff.

"Did you find Mary?"

"You bet I did. She's dancing with some jarhead."

"How do you know he's a marine?"

"His haircut gave him away."

"Let's play it cool and stand by the bar until she spots us. We were the ones who were late, after all. She has to go by the bar sometime. And I want you to remember one thing—if her friend looks like her mother fed her with a slingshot, I'm outta here."

"Okay. Just let me know if you need a ride home."

"Roger."

At the end of the dance, Mary came straight over to us. "Hi, guys," she said. "Where've you been? We waited, but when you didn't show, we came in for a drink."

"The parking lot was full," Slick said. "We had a bit of a hike."

Slick was about to raise the issue of the jarhead when another woman, whom I took to be Mary's friend, showed up. Mary introduced her as Amy and said they were roommates.

I was speechless. Amy was, if possible, even more spectacular than Mary. She wasn't quite as well endowed, but her face was marvelous and her figure nonpareil.

After the pleasantries were finished, Mary said that Larry, the jarhead, was leaving, and we could have his table. It was a great beginning to what I hoped would be an even better weekend. To make sure, I immediately invited the girls to the beach and could barely conceal my eagerness when they accepted. Everybody was tired, and the booze had made us all a little sleepy, so after a nightcap, we walked the girls to their car and got directions to their place for the morning.

When they drove off, I looked at Slick. "Can you believe it?" I asked. "How often do you find room-mates who are both knockouts?"

We were up bright and early, getting our beach and barbecue gear shipshape. The girls were supply-ing the food. We packed the trunk with chairs, towels, a grill, and enough charcoal for a whole day. The ice chest was too large to fit, so we put it in the backseat. It was a beautiful day for the beach. The sun was out, the sky was bright blue, and there was a slight breeze, perfect for an outing.

We arrived at ten on the button, and they were already outside, waiting under the carport. The house was a small single-story affair on Scenic Highway twenty minutes from the base. Amy was leaning against a red TR-7, wearing one of the skimpiest two-piece bathing suits I'd ever seen. Mary was some-where under a white cotton beach top, but it was easy to see exactly what it was she was hiding.

Trying not to stare at Amy, I said, "Nice suit."

"Do you like it?"

"It's very becoming."

"Thanks, Matt. I made it myself."

"Everybody ready?" Slick asked, before I could make an ass of myself by responding.

Within an hour we were basking in the sun on the prettiest beach in the world. The sand was like pure white sugar and the water was a warm eighty degrees. By two o'clock everyone was getting hun-gry, so I started the charcoal. While we waited for the grill to heat up, Amy and I went for a walk on the beach and Slick and Mary went for a swim. Amy and I talked about our families and what we wanted to achieve as we strolled down the beach. By the time we returned, the grill was ready, so I threw on some hot dogs and hamburgers.

Slick and Mary came out of the water just as we started to dish up the food.

"All right, Sweetwater!" Slick said, "It looks like you've got everything under control."

When the day came to an end and the sun started to set, we waited until the beach traffic subsided before we drove the girls home. At their house, they invited us in for some dessert and showed us around. After a piece of homemade apple pie I said good night to Mary and Amy walked me out to the car. Leaning up against the Blue Goose, we lip-wrestled until the lust got too heated and Amy called it quits.

I asked, "Would it be all right if I called you? I'd really like to see you again."

She didn't hesitate. "Sure. In fact, I'd be mad if you didn't."

As she walked into the house Slick came bouncing out and hopped into the Blue Goose.

"What a weekend! Goddamn it, Water, what a weekend," he said. We talked about our luck as we drove back to the base. It appeared we had a couple of hot ones on the line for the rest of the school year, and if we were lucky, as long as we were in the Pensacola area.

We spent most of Sunday relaxing and hit the hay early. As I lay in bed I thought it was about time I got myself a car. I had never owned one, and if I wanted to date on my own, I had better have a set of wheels.

My next three flights went well. I was prepared for all of them and my grades reflected my performance. I didn't fly on Thursday and I was scheduled for my fifth hop on Friday. Number five was an important flight, since you had to perform all the maneuvers to date and be prepared for any emergency. There was a lot of reviewing necessary prior to this hop and I was thankful I had Thursday off.

Friday's flight would include entry into the outer fields' landing pattern and home-base pattern without coaching. I would be fair game for any emergency learned to date and all procedures had to be executed correctly. Our instructors had been helping us along up to this point, but now we had to show them we could think for ourselves.

Slick, who'd already done the flight, said, "There's so damn much to remember and so many ways to foul up. You've got to know everything cold. When your instructor tells you to do a certain maneuver, you've got to know the procedure so well that it's second nature. I'm telling you, Sweetwater, when you think you've got your shit in one bag, stand by for an emergency. Your instructor will set you up, just to see how well you react."

The flight prepares you for your solo hop and the instructor tries to overload you to see how you handle the pressure. He can tell within the first fifteen minutes how well you're prepared.

Slick laid out the runways for the outlying fields, using tape on the floor of my room. I practiced entering the patterns by walking them through while Slick acted as my instructor. After several practice runs Slick started to throw some problems into the kettle. After three hours of studying, I had had it and we turned in.

My flight was scheduled for an 0730 go. I got up around five, reviewed my procedures again, had breakfast, and headed over to the flight. Lieutenant Warrington was waiting for me and we went right into the brief. One thing about Warbucks, he didn't play the "I got ya" game. Everything was up-front—you knew it or you didn't.

The brief, the aircraft checkout, run-up, and take-off went smoothly. Then the wheels started to come off the wagon. The first maneuver he wanted me to perform was slow flight. I had done it many times, but for some reason I drew a blank. My entry was sloppy and I couldn't maintain altitude. Naturally Warbucks decided to capitalize on the moment.

He knew I was frustrated, so he threw a high-altitude emergency at me, telling me that I had lost oil pressure and the engine was running rough. Luckily I remembered what Jungle had taught me from day one. Fly the airplane and react to the situation at hand. Well, I knew I had gooned the slow-flight maneuver and this was a different ball game.

I immediately looked outside the cockpit for a place to set the plane down, having flashbacks of what had happened to Jungle and me on my first flight. I saw Summerdale within gliding distance.

Getting Warbucks on the horn, I said, "I'm going to use Summerdale as my emergency field."

He said, "Great choice, but I want you to pick another field."

I wanted to chew him out, but knew that would be a big mistake. I looked to the left and right and spotted a long green field about four miles east of Summerdale.

The T-34/B had a thirteen-to-one glide ratio. This meant for every mile up in the air, you could glide thirteen miles over the ground. I had enough altitude to glide to the field selected. Now the trick was to maneuver the aircraft so I would be at 1500 feet over the field in which I intended to land while headed into the wind. This position was called "high key."

Once I hit high key, I would spiral down to hit the other checkpoints described in the procedure. As I glided to the field I slowed to ninety knots, keeping my gear and flaps up and canopy closed to reduce drag. Once over the field, I saw I was two hundred feet high, so I immediately lowered my gear and flaps to approach and transitioned to eighty-five knots. As I completed my spiral down to one thousand feet, which was called "low key," I was still high, so I extended my circle a little to lose the extra altitude.

When I passed through the ninety-degree position of my intended point of landing, I lowered my flaps to full, completed the landing checklist, and slowed to seventy-five knots. I rolled on final with eight-hundred feet of straightaway and was about two-hundred feet above the ground. At that point Warbucks said, "I have the aircraft."

He added full power, raised the gear and flaps, and flew it back up to three thousand feet. Once we had leveled out, he told me to take control of the aircraft again. Warbucks praised my performance, which boosted my confidence a bit.

As I flew toward the ocean Warbucks asked me about the fuel and electrical systems. We were headed for Wolfe Field, a practice site for crosswind landings. It was close to the ocean and there always seemed to be a nice crosswind to practice with.

My entry into the pattern was nothing to be proud of. Warbucks made me redo it. By the time I got back into the pattern, it was full and I really had to keep an eye out. My pattern work and landings were very rough and I had a lot of trouble with my crosswind landing technique. After seven landings and two wave-offs, he told me to head for home. After exiting the area, he took the aircraft and told me to relax.

As we approached Grassy Point, the southern entry for Saufley Field, Warbucks gave me back the controls. "Let's see if you can get us home," he said.

This would be my final test of the day. The home-field entry at Saufley was set up so you didn't have to talk to the tower. There were a lot of checkpoints that had to be met as you circled down to land.

The procedures required you to enter overhead at 1,200 feet. While circling, you had to establish which runway was active. Once this was confirmed, you would then descend downwind to eight hundred feet and continue around the circle. When you returned over the active runway at eight hundred feet, you performed your landing checks and descended. There could be ten planes in this circling pattern at different stages in their descent and not one word had to be said, unless someone was unsafe or cutting another plane out.

My entry was safe, my procedures were solid, and I got us on deck without Warbucks having to touch the controls. My airmanship wasn't as smooth as I would have liked it to be, but I had completed the procedure without help.

As I walked from the plane I felt pretty humble and my head hung low. Warbucks tried to make some small talk to pick my spirits up a little, but I was not buying it. The debrief took almost an hour. All in all I really hadn't done that poorly, but my pride was bruised.

Warbucks told me that Jim had received his up-chit and would be flying me for the rest of my presolo hops. I thanked him for his instruction and left for my room.

Talking to myself as I walked back to the BOQ didn't make things better. Slick was on his way back from the gym when he spotted me. He quietly came up behind me and said, "Hey, Water, who in the hell are you talking to anyway, Topper?"

"You son of a bitch, Slick, you scared the shit out of me."

"How'd your flight go?"

"Not so hot. I flew like a plumber."

"I told you the instructors work you over on this flight. Don't sweat it. Learn from what you did wrong and press on."

"You're right, Slick. Let's get cleaned up and take a look at some new cars."

"Why, are you planning on getting one?"

"I've been thinking about it. I really do need a set of wheels."

"What have you got in mind? An ensign mobile, a Corvette?"

"Yep, I've always wanted one and I won't be happy until I own one. So I might as well get it out of my system."

By Saturday afternoon I was the proud owner of a steel-city-gray, white-convertible-top, saddle-brown-interior Corvette. It was an eye-catcher and Slick and I spent most of Sunday cruising around town. By that evening I had washed and waxed the car and put a hundred miles on her. Since Slick had a name for his car, I had to come up with one for mine. I named it the Silver Fox.

My sixth hop went pretty well and Jungle was pleased with my progress. I made some minor mistakes, but for the most part I performed above average. The seventh hop, which was scheduled for the next day, would be another eye-opener. This was the spin flight, and the stories about how dangerous it was got students uptight before they flew, almost to the point of getting sick.

Slick had already flown the spin hop. "It's more fun than a C-ride at Disneyland," he said. "I can't understand why so many guys get nervous." But I *was* uptight, and he knew it. To try to put some of my fears to rest, he briefed me on what to expect. By the time he was finished with me, I was confident I could handle the maneuver without any problem.

The brief the next day was a bit longer than normal. Jungle wanted to make sure I understood why the spin was taught and that I knew the proper procedures for getting into and out of the maneuver. I could tell that I was still a little stressed because my palms were sweating and I had a nervous cough as we walked down to maintenance control.

We checked out the aircraft and were airborne in twenty minutes. We climbed quickly up to seven thousand feet, where I practiced my steep turns, slow flight, stalls, and unusual attitudes. Then Jungle said, "I have the aircraft."

It was time for the big C-ride. "Okay, Sweetwater, what we are going to do now is review the spin checklist. Check to see that the fuel boost pump's on, and your harness is tight and locked. Then push the prop up to 2,400 rpm, check and make sure the canopy is closed and locked, cage the directional gyro, and ensure all loose gear is stowed."

Once all the checks had been done, Jungle picked a heading of north.

"Now, before you enter into a spin, make sure you do a clearing turn to be sure there are no other aircraft in your airspace." He rolled ninety degrees to the left and right, checking for other machines in the area. Once satisfied the area was clear, he rolled back on a heading of north, raised the nose ten degrees above the horizon, and brought the power back to idle.

"Okay, Sweetwater, continue to hold the back pressure in until you start to get a strong stall buffet. Just prior to the aircraft stalling, put in full left rudder and pull the stick straight back into your lap."

I whispered to myself, "Oh . . . oh . . . oh shit! Here we go."

"Okay, Water, there's one turn, and . . .here comes two. You can see that the more turns we make, the faster and tighter the revolution becomes. After the completion of your third turn, recover by positioning the rudders to the neutral position like this, release the back pressure on the stick, and move it forward to the neutral position. When the rotation stops, level your wings, the aircraft will be in a sixty-to-seventy-degree dive. Start a pullout immediately to keep your altitude loss to a minimum. Be careful not to pull up too fast or you'll enter an accelerated stall."

As we started to gain altitude Jungle added power and gave the controls over to me. "Okay, Sweetwater, let's climb back up to seven thousand feet, pick up a heading of north, and you try a couple."

"Roger!"

I started reviewing my procedures mentally as I took over the controls. After the completion of my third spin, I felt comfortable with the maneuver and enjoyed the rest of the ride.

After the spins, we went down to Wolfe Field and I practiced some more crosswind landings, then we headed home. I was beat by the time we landed back at Saufley and I knew what the term "wrung out" meant—I felt like a wet noodle. Jim gave me a good debrief and told me what to expect on my next two flights.

"Sweetwater, your next two flights will be basic radio navigation. It's just been added to the syllabus, so you and your classmates will be the first students to fly these hops. The flights are instrument trainers and you'll be flying the aircraft from the backseat. There's a special bag that you'll pull over your head. It blocks your outside view, simulating instrument conditions. The training is designed for the student who may get disoriented or lost on his solo flight. Some knowledge of radio navigation could help you navigate back to Saufley should you find yourself in this predicament. I must caution you, though, that you are not instrument-qualified after these flights. This is an introduction only and a tool to assist you if you get in trouble. You'll get your formal training at your next squadron."

After the brief on the instrument flights, Jungle gave me a handout on the procedures I needed to know for the hop. The flights were so new that the procedures weren't even incorporated into our syllabus books. I left the debriefing room and checked the scheduling board to see when I flew next. My first "under the bag" flight was scheduled for Friday morning. This would allow me an extra day to study.

The phone woke me up and it was Slick. He was ready to party. "Come on, Sweetwater, it's Wednesday night. Time to get ready for Dirty Joe's."

I had forgotten it was Dirty Joe's night, but it didn't take me long to get fired up. The timing was perfect—I didn't have to fly Thursday and I was ahead of the power curve study-wise. "Do you have to fly tomorrow?" I asked.

"No way, José! I'm like you, under the bag on Friday."

"How did I catch up with you?"

"Warbucks had some meetings over at Sherman Field all week and I've been canceled twice. Come on down to the room and have a beer before we go."

After a couple of beers we decided to practice our instrument training while driving the Silver Fox. I drove to the back parking lot behind the BOQ where there were hardly any cars and I put a paper bag over my head, simulating the flight training. Slick gave me directions as I drove to the opposite end by telling me when to turn and how much. Once I got to the other end of the lot, we traded places and Slick tried his skill at it. After a couple of trips we had it mastered. Then we headed for Joe's.

I spent Thursday reviewing procedures and learning some instrument maneuvers that were on the handouts given to us. When Friday rolled around, I felt prepared for my flight. I spent an hour under the bag learning how to find my way back to Saufley and to other surrounding bases. Once Jungle felt I had the picture, he landed the plane at an outlying field and we switched seats. I did some landings and then we climbed up and did a couple of spins before heading home. Flying from the backseat under the bag took some getting used to. It took me a while to believe my instruments and not my instincts.

I landed before Slick, so I hung around the ready room until he finished debriefing. We compared notes about our flights as we walked back to our rooms and it was amazing how similarly we had reacted to the various maneuvers. We had both experienced vertigo and the leans.

Just before we split to go to our rooms, Slick said, "Let's call Mary and Amy and see if they want to go to the beach tomorrow."

They accepted our invitation, but were hoping we would wine and dine them that night. We had some tickets to Gulf Coast Wrestling but they weren't into Gorgeous George and the tomfoolery of professional wrestling, so we had to go alone. We got home about eleven and hit the hay.

We had told the girls we would pick them up between nine and ten. It was a little after nine before we had all our beach gear collected and packed into the Blue Goose. The girls didn't know that I had bought a new car, and I planned on surprising them that evening when I picked Amy up for a date that she didn't know about yet.

On the drive over to the girls' house, I asked Slick, "How are your instrument reflexes?"

He said, "Let's find out."

I took some beer out of a bag and said, "Whenever you're ready, Slick, put it over your head and I'll guide you down the highway."

When we hit a straightaway, Slick slipped the bag over his head. We were traveling about fifty miles an hour. I said, "Hold the Goose steady. You're looking good." As he started to drift toward the center-line dividers, I said, as calmly as I could, "A little right," which he did, then "Straighten her out," which he also did, and very nicely. But the real test was coming up—we had some oncoming traffic. Trying not to spook him, I told him. "Traffic's coming, hold what you've got."

He didn't flinch and we passed the oncoming vehicle with plenty to spare. I said, "Okay, Slick, take off the bag. You've made the grade."

"Not yet, Water. I'm having too much fun."

He goosed the accelerator, and we started to pick up a little more speed. The Goose was not the swiftest thing on four wheels, so I wasn't too worried.

"How'm I doin?" he asked.

"Steady as she goes, I . . . uh-oh!"

"What? What's uh-oh? What does that mean?"

"Don't panic. It's just a truck."

"What kind of truck?"

"I don't know, it doesn't matter. He's going to turn off." I saw him reaching for the bag, but then the truck changed course. "Look out!" I shouted.

He let go of the edge of the bag, his knuckles whitening on the wheel. "What shall I do?" He slammed on the brakes, and the truck cut back the other way. The Goose fishtailed a little, and the truck veered sharply to avoid us. The truck driver was hanging out his window, staring at Slick, his jaw slack with amazement as he roared by out of control. By now I could see that the truck was loaded with wooden crates. And the crates were loaded with white chickens.

We drifted on by kind of close, and the truck's cargo was wobbling. The rope holding some extra crates on the tailgate snapped as we went past, and I heard a crash, followed by a firestorm of clucking.

"What was that?" Slick shouted.

"Nothing. Keep driving."

"Don't tell me nothing. I heard a crash. What was it?" Once more he slammed on the brakes, reaching for the bag even before the car stopped.

I looked over my shoulder and saw that a half dozen of the crates had fallen off the tailgate. The impact had sprung them open and the chickens were flapping as they climbed out of the wreckage and running in circles on the highway. The commotion kicked up a blizzard of white feathers that kept swirling like snow, propelled by the flapping wings.

Slick ripped the bag all the way off and jerked his head around. "What the hell . . ." he shouted. "Did we do that?"

Before I could answer him, I heard the heart-stopping *whooop, whooop, whooop* of one of those newfangled sirens and swiveled my head toward the front so fast I thought I might have whiplash.

Red and blue gumballs flashing, a police car was speeding toward us, two plumes of black smoke fanning out from its tires as its big engine spun the wheels in place for a moment before they got traction.

"Quick," Slick shouted. "Hide the bag!"

"Where? Why?" I didn't know what he was worried about, but his panic must have been contagious. I rolled the bag into a big ball, crushed it in my lap, then sat on it, just as the cop car screamed past. I glanced at it and waved at the driver, or what I could see of him under his smoky hat and behind his mirrored shades.

"Let's get the flock out of here," Slick snapped, stomping on the gas. "That truck driver will try to have our asses hauled into court." Without waiting for an answer, he floored it. I could hear the Goose straining, but zero to sixty took a while in the battered old hulk.

It was several miles before we would get to the girls' house. "I'll never do that again, never again," Slick kept repeating. "I must be crazy. I'll never do that again."

At the end of their block, he stopped, and I looked at him. "What's wrong?"

He had this big, shit-eating grin. "Are you thinking what I think you're thinking?" I asked.

"Where's the bag?"

I was still sitting on it, and he knew it. He held his hand out, palm up, and wiggled his fingers. "Gimme, gimme."

"No way, Slick. You said you must have been crazy to do it once, remember?"

"Remember what? Come on, Water, gimme that bag."

I gave it to him against my better judgment, watched him smooth out the wrinkles before slipping it over his head. "God," he said, "it stinks in here. Did you cut the cheese, or what?"

Then, gripping the wheel firmly, he said, "Cleared for takeoff, Water," and stepped on the gas.

The street was deserted, and there was only a handful of parked cars to avoid, so the approach went smoothly.

"Coming up on the driveway," I said.

"Are they watching?" he asked.

"Nope, they're not outside."

He laid on the horn as he rolled. The door opened and out they came, along with their cat.

"There they are," I said.

"Let me know when to turn."

"Roger. Three . . . two . . . one . . . turn!"

Slick made the turn beautifully and started to brake. That was when the cat made his move, darting straight toward the car. "Look out for the cat," I yelled, "Right! Stop! Stop!"

But before Slick could react, the car hit the right support leg of the carport and collapsed the whole damn thing onto the Goose and broke the windshield.

Slowly Slick removed the bag. Mary and Amy looked like disapproving bookends as they stood there, hands on hips, scowling through the wreckage. Slick grinned and said, "Hi! What's for dinner?"

RUGDANCE

My next flight would be the second instrument hop and pretty much the same as the first. Jungle was a good instructor, and I was looking forward to getting back in the air with him.

When he met me in the flight, the brief had no surprises. We walked after I checked out on the board. The weather wasn't good and we probably wouldn't get off on time. The ceilings were only eight hundred feet and we needed a thousand to launch.

Since we had some extra time while we waited for the weather to clear, Jungle gave me a good workout on my preflight. When I was setting up the switches in the front and back cockpit, he dropped a few Easter eggs for me to find.

By the time I finished inspecting the cockpits he

was standing by the starboard wing. He told me to go ahead and complete the exterior preflight and we'd fly a weather-check flight once I was finished. As I started my checks our plane captain came over and started talking to Jungle.

The inspection was routine until I got to the underside of the nose section. I looked up the port augmenter tube and it was clear, but when I inspected the starboard one, I spotted an old leather glove. I pulled it out and rushed over to Jungle to show it to him.

"Hey, Jim, look what I found."

"Son of a bitch! One of those maintenance men was pretty sloppy in picking up after himself. I'll have to speak to Cliff about this," he said as I went back to my business.

I opened the engine cowlings and started to look the engine over. Within seconds I spotted a greasy rag and I now realized I was being tested on my pre-flight performance. At this point I called Jungle over to where I was standing.

"What's up?" he asked. I figured he knew very well what I was referring to.

"Seems that the crew that worked on this plane had their heads up their asses. Look at this shit, will you?"

"Well, I'll be damned! We better go over this bird with a fine-tooth comb. Who knows what else is wrong with it."

"Yeah, I bet!" I said, looking him straight in the eye.

Not able to keep a straight face any longer,

Jungle told me to continue and keep up the good work. By the time I got around to the static air vent, I was pretty paranoid. It was actually a relief to find one more aberration. When I finished removing the duct tape he'd placed over the vent, Jungle gave me a pat on the back.

"You never know, Sweetwater. Weird things can happen, so you should never take a preflight lightly."

Thanks to Jungle's sadistic instruction methods, I had learned a valuable lesson in a very short time.

At 10:30 the weather was still marginal and the red board located on the tower was still visible. This meant that all flights were suspended until further notice. But I didn't get off the hook that easily. Jungle was a weather-check pilot, so we still got a go on our launch to report weather conditions back to the tower. We went over to operations and filed an instrument-flight plan so that we would be under positive control while we checked the area out.

I couldn't buy any better training than this. Most students wouldn't get this experience until they were in basic instruments in their next squadron.

Most of the flight was in and out of clouds and it didn't look like the weather was going to get much better. We flew around the whole training area and the ceilings were below visual flight rules in all quadrants. The hop was longer than normal due to the reporting required.

Throughout the flight, Jungle gave me a lesson on the weather patterns for the Gulf Coast and explained how quickly the ceilings could drop. He briefed me on the reentry procedures in the event there was a recall of planes already in the air due to decaying weather, which sometimes happened.

On our return to base, he called the tower and recommended that flight operations be canceled for the day. By the time we landed, all aircraft were shut down and the place looked like a ghost town.

We turned in our chutes, filled out the yellow sheet, and headed up to the flight to debrief. The squadron was empty except for the scheduling officer, who was finishing up the flight schedule. I was due for an off-wing flight with another instructor from flight eighteen, but wasn't on the schedule for the next day. This flight was incorporated in the syllabus to see if a student had picked up any bad habits and to maintain standardization among the instructors.

Jungle gave me a thorough debrief on my instrument flight and briefed me on what to expect during my off-wing hop, including a rundown on the instructor. When he was finished, he said, "You're ready to solo now. You already have the reputation of a good stick throughout the squadron, Sweetwater."

I thanked him for the kind words and he said, "Don't thank me, Sweetwater, you earned it."

I put my helmet and survival vest in my locker and headed over to my room. When I got there, I slipped the key in the lock, turned the knob, and the whole door fell into my bedroom. My clothes and uniforms were all over the place and the room was turned upside down.

I had a flashback to Splinterville, when the DIs had ransacked my room. I said to no one in particular,

"What the hell is going on?" Then I heard some snickering coming from the bathroom.

"All right, you bastards, get out here." At that moment the door flew open and I was charged by several men. Slick was leading the pack when he grabbed me and threw me on the bed. Two apes were already trying to get my flight suit off before I realized what they were up to. They had plans to shave me where only your doctor goes. I put up a valiant fight, but to no avail.

When they were finished, my genital area looked like a bald-headed mouse and I was hot enough to blow up when they finally let me loose.

"All right, you sons of bitches, what's this all about?"

"Haven't you heard?" Slick asked.

"Heard what?"

"You were selected student of the month." He slapped me on the back, and then they started to sing "For He's a Jolly Good Fellow." I threw my hands over my head and fell back on the bed in disbelief.

After I took a shower and got cleaned up, Slick and the rest of the guys helped me straighten the room and hang the door back on its hinges. No sooner was the door up than someone knocked on the outside. I opened it, ready for just about anything from a pie in the face to a topless singing telegram, and there stood Jungle with an outstretched hand. "Congratulations on your selection as student of the month," he said.

"Thank you, sir," I replied. "By the way, you didn't have any input as to what the initiation would be, did you?"

"Who me? Certainly not."

But he was laughing, and I knew he'd been behind it. As he started to do a 180 and head out the door, I said, "I'll get even with you before I leave this base."

"Yeah, yeah, yeah, Sweetwater, I've heard that one before."

"Don't laugh, Jungle. I don't get mad, I get even."

At that point I wasn't sure if they were joking or if I had really been selected student of the month.

It was officially confirmed at quarters the following afternoon that I had been selected for the honor. I received a nice plaque and letter of commendation from the commanding officer. This recognition was good both professionally and psychologically. With my solo flight coming up in a few days and my precision flights to follow, I was pumped up for anything that might come my way.

The next morning I was scheduled for my off-wing-check ride. These rides covered everything taught to date and you were expected to have command of the material. When I got up, I went over my maneuvers one last time before my brief at ten o'clock. I felt good. I knew the systems and aircraft. I knew my procedures and was prepared for my flight. I wasn't cocky, but I was ready for whatever the instructor had to dish out.

My check ride was with Lieutenant T. J. Bean, a flight-eighteen instructor and standardization pilot for new instructors. He had the reputation of being a hard-ass but a fair one. Jungle had briefed me on his demeanor and idiosyncrasies.

At 1000 Lieutenant Bean walked into the flight and shouted, "Sullivan, has Sullivan shown up yet?"

I raised my hand. "I'm Sullivan."

Bean said, "Let's brief." As I approached him I extended my hand to shake his. "Don't try to butter me up, Ensign," he said. "You just better have your shit in one bag today."

I thought, What a horse's ass this jerk is, and hoped my opinion didn't show on my face.

"Why aren't your flight boots shined, Ensign?" he asked.

"I didn't realize it was required, sir."

"They look sloppy and it gives the impression that you're sloppy."

"I can assure you that I'm not sloppy, sir, and—"

"I don't want to hear your candy-ass excuses."

"It's no excuse. I just—"

"Enough bellyaching! Let's brief." The prick wouldn't even let me defend myself. The harassment lasted almost an hour and a half. He asked me every question in the book and drilled me on the emergencies until I was blue in the face. Throughout the brief, he didn't have one nice comment to make and he hardly cracked a smile. After the brief, he told me to get my gear and meet him down at maintenance control.

As I walked to the hangar by myself I wondered if it would be wise to go flying with this wild man. He had me so pissed off at this point that I didn't know whether I was coming or going. The morning was seasonably hot and I was soaked with perspiration before I got to the hangar.

When I got to maintenance control, Bean was waiting for me. He threw the maintenance log at me as I walked up to the counter and told me to fill it out. At that point I almost threw it back at him and told him to shove it up his ass, but my better judgment told me not to. I filled out the log and checked out my parachute.

This was the first flight of the day for this aircraft, so there were no chutes in it. Bean walked behind me like my shadow and watched me preflight my chute. The chute had stains on it and the release pins were slightly bent. I told the man at parachute issue that this chute was down and I needed another. Bean jumped in, saying, "What's wrong with this chute? It looked okay to me."

When I told him about the water and bent pins, and he said, "Oh, I must have missed them," I knew something was up.

I got a new chute and headed to the aircraft. Bean's chute and helmet were already set up in the backseat, so I knew he had time to screw with the aircraft before I arrived. As I started my preflight I found one thing wrong after another. The backseat wasn't set up correctly, the tires needed air, gloves and rags were lying in different parts of the engine, and the straw that broke the camel's back was when I found a chunk of metal missing from the prop.

I called Bean over and told him. "This plane is down for an unsatisfactory prop," I said.

He looked at it and said, "Good show, Matt. Get

your gear out of the plane and let's get another bird."
I thought, He *is* human, he finally had something nice
to say.

As we walked to maintenance control Bean let
the cat out of the bag. "Sweetwater, I've been riding
you hard all morning and it was done for a purpose.
This is the first of many check rides you'll have to
perform while in the flight program and I wanted you
to experience the drill. You did remarkably well. I
knew what kind of student you were before the brief.
I reviewed your training record prior to the flight and
checked out your reputation in the squadron."

He actually smiled before continuing. "The chute
problem and the plane were all plants and I wanted to
make sure you weren't a yes-man. Too many times
I've seen student pilots let items go that they knew
were wrong because they were afraid to speak up.
Don't ever let anyone talk you into something that's
going to get you killed. Now let's get an aircraft and
go have some fun."

Now that things were out in the open and I knew
where I stood with this man, I relaxed a bit and
started to run cool again. The flight went well and I
performed all maneuvers without a problem. After we
finished all the required items, Bean showed me
some acrobatic maneuvers that I would perform after
my solo flight.

Bean's debrief was short and sweet. "Matt," he
said, "I want you to continue the same study habits.
You've got a good system going and you'll do well if
you follow it."

"Thank you, sir, I appreciate that. But I have to

tell you, I almost lost it when you threw the maintenance log at me."

Bean grinned. "It's all a test, Matt. We try to get under your skin to see how much pressure you can take. Remember, getting aboard a pitching deck at night with no other place to land might be to a life-or-death situation. If you can't hack the heat here, we don't want you in the fleet. That's why we try to weed out the weak sisters early on. Have fun on your solo and I'll see you around the squadron."

The lieutenant had another flight after mine, so he waited in maintenance control for his next student. I walked back to flight fourteen still a little hot under the collar, thinking about the way he'd treated me prior to takeoff. When I walked into the flight to check in, Jungle was getting ready to go fly.

"How'd it go?" he asked.

I rolled my eyes and said, "It wasn't fun when we started, but I managed to survive the humiliation."

"It's a psych game, Water. The better student you are, the harder you get pushed. Smile, shipmate. I'll see you bright and early tomorrow morning. The nest may get emptied out if you've got your shit together."

I knew what he meant—I'd probably solo, if the weather held up.

Slick wasn't back from his flight, so I headed back to the room to wait for him. Not knowing how long he'd be, I decided to wash and wax the Silver Fox. About the time I finished washing, I spotted Slick walking across the lawn heading for his room.

"Hey, Slick," I yelled.

He didn't acknowledge my call and kept on walking.

Oh boy, I thought, someone's got a hair up his ass and I better find out what's going on.

When I got up to the room his door was half-open, so I knocked and let myself in. I could hear him in the bathroom coughing and gagging. I went in to see if he was all right and found him on his knees talking to the toilet. He was straining so hard to vomit that I put my hand on his forehead to help him get it up. Once his convulsions subsided, he lay down on the bed.

"Slick," I said, "are you all right?"

"Yeah, I just need to catch my breath."

"What happened?"

"After my check ride we did some acrobatics and I got real sick. I filled my puke bag and then my helmet. I've never been so embarrassed in my life."

"Don't worry about it, you're not the first one to puke on an acro flight. Lie still and let your semicircular canals and vestibular apparatus quiet down and you'll feel better."

"What the hell are you talking about, Sweetwater?"

"Trust me, Slick, I got my medical degree at home."

Once I knew he was resting, I went out and waxed my car. After an hour or so, Slick wandered out to see how I was doing and thanked me. I could tell he was feeling better by looking at him. Another tip-off was that the smell of puke of was gone.

"You know, Sweetwater," he said, "after you left I began to feel better by the minute."

"Those things I mentioned are in your inner ear. If they get out of whack, you tend to get sick. Once your semicircular canals stop spinning, you get back to normal."

"How did you know about that, anyway?"

"My dad explained it to me one time when my sister got sick flying."

"I hope this isn't an ongoing thing for me."

"Nah, your system will adjust easily. Some people are just more sensitive than others. I got a taste of acro today myself, and I started to get dizzy, too, so don't worry about it."

He looked doubtful, so I thought I'd cheer him up. "After I finish waxing the car, do you want to get something to eat?"

"Yeah, but I think I'll go light tonight."

"Okay, let's go to the soup exchange and get some homemade vegetable soup and a chicken sandwich."

"Sounds good. Come get me when you're ready to go."

"See you in ten minutes."

We had a nice light meal and were back at the BOQ by seven. After an hour of discussing our check flights and reviewing our solo procedures, we called it a night. We both had check rides in the morning, and if everything went well we would solo. The flight would be conducted like the last three. High work first, a couple of emergencies, and then to the landing pattern. Once your instructor felt confident that you could land and take off safely, he would kick you out of the nest and you would solo.

After two touch-and-go's and a full stop to pick up your instructor, you returned to Saufley and were debriefed. Once you were debriefed and cleared safe for solo, you got to take the plane out for an hour-and-a-half flight and practice on your own.

For some reason, I didn't sleep very well during the night and I was a little slow getting a move on in the morning. I ate breakfast on the run and was almost late for my brief. Lieutenant Miller went over the flight thoroughly and confirmed that if things went well, I'd solo. Normally the instructor doesn't tell you when he plans to boot you, but in my case he did because he felt I wouldn't choke. But if the way I had slept was an indicator of what was to come, I knew I'd better regroup.

The preflight, start-up and takeoff went very smoothly. We climbed up to seven thousand feet, did all our high work, then headed for Summerdale, the practice landing field. En route Jungle gave me my high-altitude emergency, and after my second touch-and-go he simulated an engine loss for my low-altitude emergency.

On my third approach he said, "Make this a full stop. I've got to make a head call."

As soon as he said it, I knew it was time for me to go flying on my own. Although I was well prepared, my adrenaline started to pump.

I pulled off the runway and back-taxied to the approach end of runway 32. With the engine still turning, Jungle got out of the back and strapped his chute to the seat with the safety harness and closed his canopy. He leaned into my cockpit, slapped me on the shoulder, and said, "Have fun and don't leave me here." Then he walked over to the duty truck.

The outlying fields did not have a control tower, but they had a runway duty truck equipped with radios so that the planes in the pattern could be monitored and given instructions in case of an emergency. As I looked over my shoulder, I saw Jungle get into the duty truck and then I received my call. "Sioux Falls 201, how do you read this transmission?"

"Loud and clear, sir, how about me?"

"Loud and clear. You're clear to the hold short line."

"Roger," I said, and cleared to the line.

"Two-oh-one cleared for takeoff."

"Roger, cleared for takeoff," I repeated.

All my checklists were completed and rechecked by the time he cleared me. I lined up on the center line of runway 32, ran my engine up to two thousand rpm, sat there for a few seconds, then pulled my power back to idle, leaned over the right canopy rail, and threw up.

After a good projectile vomit, I wiped my face with my left arm sleeve, went to full power, and took off.

My first approach was a little tight, which caused me to overshoot the runway. I didn't like my setup, so I waved it off. My next approach was right on and I greased it to the blacktop and then roared back into the sky for my second landing. My approach and landing were picture perfect and my confidence was building. As I reached the upwind end of the runway, climbing to five hundred feet, I heard Jungle call my side number.

I keyed the mike and said, "This is Sioux Falls 201, go ahead."

"Two-oh-one, I want you to clean up the aircraft then climb to two thousand feet and circle overhead until I call you back down. We have an emergency in progress and he's landing at Summerdale. Do you read me?"

I rogered, raised my gear and flaps, and started my climb to two thousand feet.

Once anchored overhead, I listened in on the emergency frequency until I could see the plane in distress, then I switched back to the runway duty truck. The plane had a rough running engine and the pilot planned to fly to a high key position over Summerdale and execute his high-altitude emergency procedures. He landed at Summerdale without mishap.

By the time Jungle called me down for my final landing, there were several other planes doing touch-and-go's in the landing pattern. Now my training had to be put to use. I descended away from the field and got down to the pattern altitude before I turned inbound.

Jungle must have had confidence in me, because he didn't panic and call. I entered the pattern as we were instructed, lowered my gear and flaps, and landed like a pro. As I back-taxied to pick Jungle up I could see that Slick was in the pattern by the markings on his helmet.

I couldn't wait to tell him all about my experience. But I figured it best to leave out the pretakeoff puke episode. As Jungle approached the right side of the aircraft, he just shook his head when he climbed in the backseat. I knew I wouldn't hear the end of this one.

Once Jungle got strapped into his seat and hooked up his helmet to the mike jack, he asked, "So how'd you like it?"

"It was everything I expected and more. Sorry about that first approach. I got too tight and gooned it."

"Hey, you did it right. You didn't like the setup and you took it around again. That's what you're supposed to do. And you did a good job during that emergency; you handled it like a seasoned veteran."

"Thanks," I said, still waiting for him to say something about the puke along the starboard side of the aircraft.

Not much was said the rest of the flight home. I made the home-field entry like I had been doing it for years, landed, then taxied up to the front line where the plane captain parked me. I could see that he'd spotted the vomit on the side of the plane and couldn't wait to chock the aircraft and get upwind.

Jungle and I unstrapped and got out of the aircraft to do our postflight walk-around. As we were finishing up he said, "Sweetwater, you've got some cleaning to do before you go out on your solo flight."

"Yes, sir," I replied, and walked in to maintenance control to get a bucket and some cleaning gear. The squadron had a policy that if you puked in or on an aircraft, it was your responsibility to clean the mess up and not the plane captain's.

Before I got the cleaning equipment, Jungle debriefed me on my performance. He said, "You did a great job and don't do anything stupid while out on my solo flight." Then he broke out laughing.

"What's the matter?" I asked.

"Sweetwater, I've been here almost two years and seen just about everything; when you puked out the side of that aircraft and took off without missing a beat, that took the cake. That stunt will go down in the history books, I guarantee you. And you haven't heard the end of this."

"Yeah, I bet I haven't! Can't you keep it to yourself?" I asked, heading for the cleaning locker.

"Nope!"

I filled a bucket with hot water, got some cleaning soap, and headed out to the aircraft. As I passed through maintenance control it was full of instructors giving debriefs and students waiting to go out on their solo flights. They all knew what had happened and I felt like a horse's ass as I left the hangar.

It took me about twenty minutes to clean up the mess. It had baked on pretty good, so it took a little extra elbow grease to remove. As the maintenance personnel stood by I said, "Sorry about this, I guess I'm not as tough as I thought I was."

"It's all right, sir, we see this all the time. Hang in there, you'll get over it."

"Thanks, gents, I think she's clean now."

"Good, why don't you take a break? We'll gas it up and check her safe for flight."

"Roger that," I replied as I picked up the cleaning gear and headed back to the hangar. While I was waiting for maintenance control to release the plane to me, Slick walked in.

"Hey, Slick, how'd it go?"

"Okay, I think." He looked at his instructor, who gave him a thumbs-up.

"All right!" I said. "I'll see you in the landing pattern at Summerdale."

"You've got it," he replied as they went to debrief.

Once the aircraft was released to me, I signed the white sheet, taking responsibility for the airplane, and walked out to the flight line. Boy, did I feel like I was somebody now. I could remember how I felt when I was on my second or third hop and saw students heading out on their own. I couldn't wait for my turn.

I did a thorough preflight and reviewed procedures before starting the aircraft. I felt confident in my ability to take off, do the required landings, and return to home field safely. Once comfortable, I started the aircraft, taxied to the engine run-up area, did my checks, and took off when cleared.

As soon as I was off the runway with a positive rate of climb, I raised my gear and checked my instruments. I made a climbing left turn to three thousand feet, leveled off, and started heading toward the town of Fairhope, Alabama. Then I rotated my head to the right and looked over my shoulder and saw that I truly was alone. What a thrill it was knowing that I was controlling an airplane all by myself. I had been doing it for many hops, but the fact that there was no one back there to help if I got into trouble made it exciting.

Flying along the coastline and near the southwestern border of the training area, I turned to the right, descended to 1,500 feet, and headed up toward Point Clear. There was a big resort close by, and rumor had it that women liked to sunbathe topless on a dock offshore. Although over the water was slightly out of our training area, I figured I could pull it off without getting caught.

As I approached the area from the south I could see several women on the dock, and yes, they were unclothed. After a couple of circling passes and some good eyeball liberty, I proceeded toward Summerdale, where I was to meet Slick.

After two touch-and-go's Slick entered the landing pattern and we bounced together. Once we'd completed the required number of landings, we left the pattern and I headed for home. My time was almost up, but Slick still had forty minutes or so left. Prior to the flight he and I had come up with a personal frequency to switch up on so we could talk while we were soloing. After I cleared the landing pattern and was on my way home, I told Slick to "come up tactical," the key word we used to switch to our private frequency. We both switched and I briefed him on the eyeball liberty.

He rogered my scouting report, and just as I started to switch back to the base frequency, I heard over the radio, "This is the flying Hershey bar, eat me, eat me, eat me." I laughed and wondered who else knew about this frequency.

After I landed and parked the aircraft, I went to maintenance control to check in. As I was filling out the yellow sheet the maintenance officer came out of his office smoking one of his nasty cigars and said, "Ensign, the ops boss wants to see you in his office and he didn't sound like a happy camper."

"Yes, sir," I replied. Quickly I finished up my paperwork. A sickening feeling came over me as I hurried to his office. The operations officer was Lieutenant Commander Tim "Dirt" Oliver. He was a slender man who stood about six feet tall and got the nickname Dirt from knowing all the untold stories about most of the students who were under his safeguard.

As I walked into the office area a yeoman was sitting behind a desk outside Oliver's office. "Good afternoon, sir," she said. "May I help you?"

"Yes, I'm Ensign Sullivan and I was told that Lieutenant Commander Oliver wanted to see me."

She got up, knocked on his door, and announced my arrival, then asked me to step into his office.

When I walked in, Oliver was standing near the window. He said, "Close the door," and it wasn't in a friendly tone, then he went behind his desk and sat down.

After I closed the door, I came to attention and said, "Reporting as ordered, sir."

He told me to come over by his desk. I followed orders and squared off in front of his desk and went to parade rest.

He barked, "Who told you to go to parade rest? Lock it up, Ensign."

I now knew I was in a world of brown, but I couldn't figure out why. My throat felt like cotton and I could feel the sweat dripping under my armpits.

"Ensign, do you know your course rules?" he asked.

I said, "Yes, sir," in a confident manner.

"Then what were you doing out over the water near Point Clear resort? You know that's out of our training area, don't you?"

How in the world did he know I was out there? I wondered. I knew I'd better not bullshit him, because it looked like he had some good info.

"Well, what do you have to say for yourself?"

"I flew out there for some eyeball liberty."

"What in the hell is eyeball liberty, Ensign?"

I knew darn well he knew what I was talking about. He just wanted to watch me squirm and do a little rugdance before he lit into me.

"The word was out that women liked to sunbathe nude on this dock near the shoreline, so I took a closer look."

"Do you not adhere to rules and regulations?"

"Yes, sir," I said.

"Then why did you violate the course rules?"

"No excuse, sir." I thought the rugdance was about over. But I was wrong.

"What do you know about a 'flying Hershey bar,' Ensign?"

"Nothing, sir. That wasn't me, honest to God. I just heard it over tactical, I mean over the air."

"What do you mean when you say 'tactical,' Ensign?"

"Well, sir, that's the special frequency that a friend and I decided to use to talk on when we were out in the training area."

"Where did you get that tactical frequency?"

"One of the guys that lived near us told us about it before he headed out to Ellyson Field."

"Stand at ease, Sullivan," Oliver barked. "Have you ever heard of the guard frequency?"

"No, sir," I replied.

"I bet your special tactical frequency was 121.5."

"How did you know that, sir?"

"How do you think I knew what you did? That frequency overrides all other frequencies when you transmit on it. It is the emergency frequency and you told the world what you did when you briefed your friend Morely. My tower people and everyone in the area heard about your little excursion. My friend, you've been suckered into one of the oldest aviation tricks in the book."

"Oh shit," I said, under my breath.

"You've got a pretty impressive record going, Sullivan. Don't fuck it up by breaking the rules. That's how people get killed. Now get out of my office. I hope you've learned a valuable lesson and you had better not have been the one who made that flying-Hershey-bar call."

"No, sir, it wasn't me."

"You're excused."

I left his office in a flash and I didn't wait for the door to hit me in the ass. I hadn't done a softshoe like that since I'd hopped a freight train and gotten caught by my dad. That little stunt cost me three months of grounding. By the time I got to my room and changed, Slick was pounding on my door.

"Hey, Water, what did the dirt man want?"

"I can tell you one thing, Slick. It wasn't a social call and I'm going to kick Bennie Nunn's ass if I can find the son of a bitch."

"What the fuck did Bennie do?"

"You know that great frequency he gave us to talk on?"

"Yeah, what about it?"

"Well, that frequency overrides everything, and when you transmit on it, you talk to the world."

"Holy shit!"

"That's right, everyone in the area got the same brief I gave you about the sunbathers."

MARDI GRAS
LIBERTY

After the rugdance in Dirt Oliver's office, I was ready to relax and have some fun. The weekend was upon us, and Slick and I decided to spend two days at the beach. Rentals were fairly inexpensive, so we booked ourselves in a condo a thousand feet from the ocean.

Our main objective was to meet some new talent and have a fun weekend. Amy and Mary were off to Boston to look at medical schools, so we had the opportunity to expand our star search. Neither Slick nor I were going steady with the girls, but it would be uncomfortable if we were to run into them with two other girls.

We checked in at the rental office by seven, got unpacked, and relaxed on the balcony with a couple of beers while we watched the ocean devour the sun. By nine we were ready to shake the trees and rake the leaves.

By the time we got to Dirty Joe's, a large crowd was gathering outside. Joe's was funny on weekends—sometimes the place was like a morgue, and other times you couldn't find a place to stand. I always liked standing near the jukebox, because I got to screen everyone who came into the place. Slick liked standing at the end of the bar near the pool table.

At ten o'clock the place was a mob scene. There were a lot of new faces and some foxy talent pawing around. Just as I was about to roll in on a girl, Slick came up to me and said he had a couple of hot ones lined up. He yelled into my ear over the noise, "Water, just go along with my scam and let's see what develops." I started to ask him what role we were playing, but got drowned out by the overwhelming noise.

As we approached the women I liked what I saw. They were both good-looking, and classy to boot. Slick gave a head nod toward the door and we all headed in that direction. Once outside where we could talk, he made the formal introductions.

"Sweetwater, this is Jill and Susan. They're schoolteachers from Mobile, Alabama." I extended my hand and received a firm handshake from both women.

Jill said, "I understand that you fly with the Blue Angels."

"That's right. I've just joined the team and that's where I met Slick."

"What's with these nicknames anyway?" Sue asked.

"Your squadron mates usually tag you with a name that you've earned through brilliance or stupidity, and if it sticks, you'll probably have it as your call sign for the rest of your naval career."

"Well, how did you two get your names?" Jill asked.

Slick jumped in and said, "We'll divulge those secrets at a later date. Right now let's party."

As the night progressed we learned more about the girls and dug a deeper hole for ourselves. By the time 1:00 A.M. arrived, we had decided to meet in the early afternoon and go sailing on the bay. The girls were staying in the high rise hotel across the street from our condo, so it made things easy.

When we got home, I asked Slick, "Do you think they bought that Blue Angel bullshit?"

"They seemed impressed."

"Yeah, but they asked too many of the right questions. I think they've been on the Pensacola naval-aviator circuit before and know we are probably only students."

"You're probably right, Sweetwater. We'd better come clean tomorrow before we embarrass ourselves. Let's get to bed. We have a big day."

Bobby Melon is a retired navy dentist. He lives six months in Minnesota, where his private practice is located, and the other six months he runs Molar Man's right down on Pensacola Beach. He's a legend in his own right and his bar has a fantastic collection of aviation and dental memorabilia. Pilots and aircrews loved to drop items off for him to hang on his walls, and he'd converted one room into a small museum where he displayed antique dental equipment.

Several weeks before, Slick and I got to know Bobby when he returned to open Molar Man's for the spring and summer months. We had helped him move some gear around and he took care of us when we visited the bar.

It was late afternoon when Slick and I arrived with Jill and Sue, and the place was packed. All the outdoor tables were full and there was no room at the open-air bar. As we walked in, Molar Man spotted us and gave us a gracious welcome. He could see that we wanted to sit outside and without hesitation had a couple of his waiters bring a table out from the back to accommodate us.

"Hold on, Bobby," I told him. "It isn't necessary to go to all that trouble. We can wait until a table's available."

"Nope," he said, "when you to come in to Molar Man's, the place is yours. Without your help that Sunday, I'd have been three days behind schedule. Besides, when you're in my bar, I'm the boss, when I'm flying with you, you're the boss, got it?"

"Roger that," I replied. There was nothing to do but wait for the table to be set up.

Once it was ready, we all sat down and Bobby took our orders personally. After a few drinks Slick said, "I have a confession to make."

Sue grinned at him. "I bet you're going to tell us that you're really not Blue Angels."

"How did you know?" Slick asked.

"Jill and I have dated most of the Blues and you two are a bit young to be on the team. You both have the personality and looks to make it one day, but you have to survive Vietnam first."

"Now that you've broken our cover, will you still go out with us tonight?"

"Only if you and Sweetwater will go to the Mardi Gras with us next week."

Slick looked at me, I looked at him; we gave each other the thumbs-up and Slick said, "We're players."

"That's great," Sue said. "We go every year and it'll be fun to have an escort for a change. Don't get me wrong, we'll pay our share of the trip and we can take my car—it's bigger. Do you think you can get next Friday off?"

"Not really sure," Slick said. "We'll have to check on Monday and get back to you."

"If things work out, you can stay on my daddy's boat Thursday night and we can leave for New Orleans early Friday morning."

"Sounds good. We'll see what we can do," I said.

After another round of drinks, we thanked Molar Man for his hospitality and hit the bricks.

We drove the girls back to their hotel and told them we would pick them up at eight for dinner. Slick and I left the Blue Goose in the parking lot and walked across the street to our condo. We couldn't wait to get back to our place and figure the girls out.

Monday Slick and I talked with our flight leader and asked him if it would be possible to take Friday off.

We were up front with him about our reasons. He had no problem with granting us special liberty as long as we got our check rides completed by Thursday.

Tuesday we were scheduled for our first instructional acrobatic flight with a solo hop to follow. Wednesday was two solo flights, weather permitting, and Thursday was our final check ride. The following Monday we would find out if we got jets, check out on Tuesday, and head for our new duty station on Wednesday. The next week and a half was action-packed and would determine our naval careers.

Slick and I were both scheduled for an 0700 brief with an 0830 launch. We were up early, ate a light breakfast, and were in the ready room by 0655. Lieutenant Miller walked in at 0700 and said, "Let's brief."

Once we were seated, he asked me the acrobatic checklist then got into the technique of each maneuver. "On the wingover, Sweetwater, I want you to enter it at 130 knots of indicated airspeed, and after you have completed ninety degrees of turn, you should be at or approaching 70 knots IAS. Then as you start to recover, relax the back pressure on the stick and roll out 180 degrees from your original heading with 130 knots of airspeed. Any questions?"

"No, sir, it sounds pretty straightforward."

"It'll make more sense once you see one demonstrated. The loop is probably the easiest of all the acrobatic maneuvers. The best way to enter this maneuver, Sweetwater, is to pick up a ground reference line and use it throughout the loop. Your entry speed needs to be 150 knots with a firm three-G pull-up, keeping your wings level as you approach the top of the loop. Once you're inverted, put your head back and pick up your reference line, release the back pressure on the stick, and recover at 150 knots in your original direction."

The barrel roll, half-Cuban eight, and split S were also briefed. They all had pretty much the same entry and airspeed techniques. After the brief Jungle asked if I had any more questions and I shook my head.

"Okay, Water, check out on the board and let's do it."

As I walked out of the briefing room I saw that Slick was just finishing his brief, so I waited for him and we checked out together.

As we walked to maintenance control I could tell Slick was uptight about the flight. I said, "Hey, partner, lighten up. Just go up there and have fun. If you feel sick, tell the instructor. Don't wait until it's too late. It's all mind over matter."

"Yeah, you're right, Sweetwater. I've been worrying about this day since I got sick a few flights ago."

"So what if you get sick again? You'll overcome it."

By the time we entered maintenance control, Jungle had checked the book and signed the white sheet. "Let's go," he said, "we're running late." We checked out our chutes and walked to the aircraft. Jungle preflighted half the airplane and I did the other half. After we strapped in, I did the start checklist, fired the plane up, and taxied to the run-up area. Once all checklists were completed, I called for take-off clearance.

After I was cleared for takeoff, I headed west and climbed to eight thousand feet. We planned to work the upper west corner of the training area and Slick would be down in the southern part. As I leveled off Jungle said, "I've got the aircraft."

I replied, "You've got the aircraft."

"Okay, Water, after you've completed the checklist, do your clearing turns—ninety degrees to the left and right and remember to check above and below you."

"Yes, sir."

"Okay, I'll demonstrate the wingover first. Here we go. Once your turns are done, select a road going east and west or north and south and increase your speed to 130 knots. Now, once you're lined up on a section line and your airspeed is 130 knots, raise the nose smoothly and roll into twenty degrees angle of bank. As your airspeed slows to seventy knots continue to increase the angle of bank to ninety degrees. Once perpendicular to the section line, relax the back pressure on the stick and let the nose fall through. You want to recover 180 degrees from the original heading with 130 knots of indicated airspeed. Okay, any questions?"

"No, sir."

"Go ahead and give me a couple in either direction."

I did two to the left and two to the right. By the time I finished my fourth one, I had it down. We went though each maneuver the same way, and I did pretty well except for the barrel roll. I wasn't getting my nose up high enough before starting to roll inverted, which made me fast on the recovery. Jungle was pleased with my performance and he told me to practice my barrel rolls while I was out on my solos.

When we landed and filled out the yellow sheet Jungle debriefed me and cleared me for solo. Within a half hour I had a plane, and while walking out to preflight, I spotted Slick getting out of his plane. He had puke all over his flight suit and his helmet looked full the way he was holding it. He didn't spot me and I didn't approach him. It seemed likely he wouldn't be going out on his solo, at least in the next few hours.

I went out and had a ball practicing my maneuvers and was back in the chocks by two. As I walked from the flight line to maintenance control, I knew I was somebody now, just by the way the other students looked at me. I knew what was going through their minds, because when I had seen a student returning after his solo, flight I had been pretty envious myself. As I filled out the yellow sheet the old maintenance officer stepped into the room puffing on a cigar.

"Say, Sweetpea—"

"It's Sweetwater, not Sweetpea."

"Whatever. That buddy of yours, Slick, is a pretty tough cookie."

"What do you mean, sir?" I asked.

"He puked the whole flight, wouldn't give up, and he's out on his solo as we speak."

"All right!" I yelled, "I knew that son of a bitch could do it."

"Beer muster and tie-cutting ceremony tomorrow afternoon. Are you going to be there?"

"Yes, sir, you bet I am."

* * *

The next day was picture perfect, not a cloud in the sky. Slick and I both punched out our two solo flights and were on deck by 3:30. The beer muster started at five, so we had time to change into our uniforms before the gala festivities began. The beer muster was a tradition at Saufley Field and over the years had turned into a rather elaborate ceremony.

Each month a different flight sponsored it. A couple of kegs of beer were on tap as well as soft drinks for those who didn't drink. The tie-cutting ceremony and storytelling were handled by the instructors and each student presented a bottle of his instructor's choice for bravery above and beyond the call of duty.

There were fifteen ties to be cut and a lot of embarrassing stories to be told. Some of them were so funny you would cry laughing so hard. Slick and I were the last two to be done. Slick's instructor hadn't shown up yet, so I got the honors. Jungle started off with our crash landing, which got everyone's attention. Then things began to deteriorate real fast. By the time he finished telling about my little sight-seeing venture, the place was in an uproar.

Jungle was known for his close tie cuts and I could sense that I would be no exception. The traditional knife used was a twelve-inch razor-sharp machete. Everyone stood by as Jungle took the bottom of my tie and held it straight out from my windpipe. He told me to turn my head toward my left shoulder as he cocked the knife back and made a couple of practice attempts at the knot. Then with a flick of his wrist, he cut the knot in two and the crowd went wild. I almost shit my pants as the tie separated a fraction of an inch from my Adam's apple.

As Jungle ended his speech he made me very proud. He said, "In all seriousness, Ensign Sullivan is a fine young officer, an outstanding pilot, and I would follow him to hell with two cans of gasoline under each arm. Thank you." The place exploded with applause.

The applause quickly changed to laughter. The place went wild because in came Slick's instructor, his flight suit covered with fake rubber puke. When the crowd finally settled down, Lieutenant Warrington told Slick's tale, but in a way that made everyone proud that he had the fortitude to continue in such adverse conditions. After he cut Slick's tie, we all congratulated one another and partied until the beer was gone.

After we said good-bye to all the heavies, Slick and I headed to our rooms, changed, hopped in the Silver Fox, and were off to Dirty Joe's by eight. We knew we had our final check ride in the morning, but it was Miller time and the party was on. Joe's was hopping when we arrived and we mingled in with the crowd. After several hours of telling sea stories, I stopped drinking and filled up on water, knowing I had to drive home.

I had just gotten a refill of water when Slick came up to me and asked if I had seen Amy and Mary.

"No, where are they?"

"They're outside and they want us to go to Mardi Gras with them."

"Oh shit, what did you tell them?"

"I told them we had to fly over the weekend so that we could finish up by Monday."

"Good call. Do you think they bought it?"

"Hook, line, and sinker."

"Great! Did they find a suitable medical school?"

"Yeah, they did. Harvard."

"Did they get accepted?"

"Not yet, but all indications are that they will."

"Goddamn it, they must be some smart cookies. I better go out and say hi and congratulate them. Slick, give me a few minutes, then come get me so we can head home."

"Will do."

I walked out the door and looked over the crowd and spotted Mary talking to a jarhead. I knew he was a marine by his squirrel haircut. That kind of got my blood boiling a bit, but who was I to be judgmental? When I approached them, Mary introduced Jim Lott, a marine instructor pilot. If I didn't know any better, I would have thought it was myself standing there. We were the same size and looked a lot alike, except for the haircut.

As a matter of fact, Mary said she thought it was me when she went up to him. He was an instructor in A-4s at Sherman Field over at NAS Pensacola.

Mary said, "Sorry you couldn't join us."

I shrugged apologetically. "We have to fly."

Lott piped up. "I didn't think you guys flew out at Saufley on weekends."

I thought for a microsecond before answering, "We usually don't, but the pilot training rate is behind, so we have to make up some time."

Lott said, "I think I heard our ops boss mention something about Saufley being behind in training. Too bad you're going to miss Mardi Gras weekend. It's a real blowout."

"So I've heard. Maybe we'll get to go next year." Just then Slick showed up and we said our good-nights and left.

As we walked away I said, "Good timing, Slick. The heat was on."

"What do you say we get packed and start celebrating? I'll call Sue, tell her we're inbound and reconfirm the directions."

The directions were fairly simple. Her dad's boat was docked at Grand Bay Yacht Club, which was right on our way to New Orleans. I told Sue we'd arrive around five or six and she said she'd have a guest pass waiting for us at the entrance. Slick and I planned to take the Silver Fox and it was comforting to know that it would be in a guarded area while we were at Mardi Gras.

We were packed and on the road by three. We figured it would take us about three hours to get there. We arrived at the main entrance just before six. Upon arrival at the Yacht Club, a guard presented us with a pass and directed us to the girls' boat. When we pulled into the slip's parking area, I couldn't believe my eyes. The boat had to be eighty feet long and twenty feet wide. The girls were sitting on the stern having drinks as we drove up.

Trying not to show how overwhelmed we were,

we took our time getting out of the car before covering it. As we approached the walkway that connected the pier to the boat, the girls were waiting topside for us. As protocol dictates, we requested permission to come aboard.

Sue said, "Permission granted," and we headed up the brow. The girls had on flowery halter tops and skimpy wraparounds. We exchanged hugs and then were directed to our staterooms to drop off our luggage.

After a breathtaking tour of the unbelievable yacht, the girls offered us a drink and some snacks before we went to dinner at the yacht club. While Slick and I relaxed on the stern of the *Cajun Queen*, the girls went to the store.

As we headed down to our staterooms I said, "Slick, is this for real or a goddamn fairy tale?"

"So far, Water, it looks pretty fucking real to me."

"Yeah, but these gals are old pros at this shit. They can get anyone they want."

"Maybe so, but they haven't strapped on a couple of horny student pilots who haven't had their ashes hauled for months, either."

"You've got that right."

I had just stepped out of the shower when the door opened and in walked Sue with champagne, glasses, caviar, and crackers. I had just covered myself with my towel when she said, "Let's have a party, sailor."

"Sounds good to me. Let me get dressed."

"Wrong," she said. "Let's enjoy this feast while taking a warm bubble bath together."

"I like it," I said, and let the towel fall to the floor.

Two hours later we emerged from my stateroom rather tattered. Slick and Jill were gone, so we assumed they were still at the club having dinner.

At eleven they strolled back to the yacht and seemed to have had a grand evening as Slick carried Jill up the brow. Slick said, "You two lovebirds missed a fine meal."

"Maybe so," I said, "but the dessert was better on the boat." Slick got my drift and rolled his eyes.

The girls shared our staterooms with us and we didn't get much sleep, but at least we were warm. After breakfast we loaded up Sue's 500 SEL and headed for New Orleans. I could see why she had wanted to take her car. It had the room and class they were accustomed to. I lost the draw of straws and had to drive while the rest partied.

The traffic started to back up from about Bay St. Louis to the New Orleans Tunnel. As we approached the tunnel to go under the bay, the traffic was stop-and-go and Jill started to get concerned about getting stuck inside the tunnel. Slick made a wisecrack about water trickling down the wall, which set Jill off. She broke out in a cold sweat and wanted to get out of the car.

When Slick realized she was upset, he tried to comfort her, but it was too late. She was distraught to the point of hyperventilating. Luckily we were out of the tunnel before it got too bad. I pulled over to the side of the road as soon as I could and we got Jill out of the car. Once out in the open air, she started to calm down quickly.

"Sorry, gang, but I get claustrophobic when I get stuck in tunnels."

"Why didn't you tell us?" I asked.

"I've never freaked out that badly before."

"If you start to feel uneasy again, let us know and we'll help you through it."

"Okay, thanks. I feel much better now." We were all pretty quiet until we reached our hotel in the French Quarter. We dropped the girls off with our luggage at the entrance and Slick and I parked the car.

"Boy, Water, I thought she might lose it in that tunnel," Slick whispered.

"What do you mean *might* lose it? She flipped out. We need to keep an eye on her with these crowds. She's liable to go wacky on us again."

"Hey, I'm not going to be a baby-sitter for her. I want to raise some hell."

"Don't worry, Slick, we'll get plenty of that, and don't forget how we got down here. Walking isn't too crowded back to Mobile."

"I gotcha."

We had two adjoining rooms that overlooked Bourbon Street. As I looked out the window at the famous street, I could see the crowds building by the minute. Slick and I were ready to party, but Jill was still visibly shaken. Sue told us to go ahead and they would meet us in the lobby at 9:00 P.M. That was the liberty card we were waiting for, and without hesitation we were out the door.

Our first stop was Pat O'Brien's, a famous bar in the French Quarter. When we walked in, we noticed a crowd gathered in one corner near the bar, so we went over to see what all the excitement was about.

We should have guessed. There was a table of five men and three women drinking "Flaming Hookers." One of the guys at the table was my flight instructor, Jungle Jim Miller.

I said, "What are you doing down here?"

"The same thing you're doing, shipmate, getting all fubar."

"Fubar? What's that?"

"Fucked up beyond all recognition." After a good laugh, one of the girls placed a couple of Flaming Hookers on the table in front of Slick and me and said, "If you want to join the party, you've got to shoot a Hooker."

I leaned over to Slick and asked if he had ever drunk one of them and he said no. "Me neither, but we can't let them think we're pussies, so I'm game if you are."

"Let's do it."

Jungle lit the whiskey on fire, then Slick and I each grabbed a shot glass and proposed a toast to naval aviation before downing the drinks. Within seconds I felt like a raging bull with smoke coming out his ears and nose. I thought the top of my head was coming unscrewed.

There was one fellow, called Sundance, who had already had one too many and his steady hand faltered. He set his mustache on fire when he misjudged the angle to his mouth. The guy looked like Robert Redford—at least he did before he lost half his mustache—and that's how he had gotten his nickname. Most of the guys at the table were flight instructors and the girls were navy nurses, so we were in our element.

One of the nurses got a towel with some ice and had Sundance hold it to his scorched facial hair. Jungle said, "I think we've seen enough here. Let's press on down the street to the Fats Domino concert." He asked us to join them.

I looked at my watch, saw that it was almost nine, and told them we had to meet some people, so we passed.

By the time Slick and I left to meet the girls, we had a snoot full of whiskey. When we entered the lobby of our hotel, we looked around, but the girls were nowhere in sight.

I said to Slick, "They must still be in the room. I'll give them a call and see what's shaking."

The phone rang twice and a male voice answered. "Yes, may I help you?"

"Is Sue there?"

"No, there's no one by that name here."

"Is this room 820?"

"Yes, it is."

"Okay, sorry to bother you."

"That's quite all right."

"Good evening," I said as I hung up.

I walked back to Slick and asked him what room I was in.

"Hey, Water, I know those drinks were strong, but I didn't realize they had fried your brain. You're in 820 and I'm in 821. Why, what's the matter?"

"Well, I called our room and someone else is in there."

"Bullshit!"

"No, I'm not shitting you, Slick. Some guy

answered. Let's talk to the desk clerk and find out what's going on."

When we identified ourselves, the desk clerk handed me a sealed white envelope. I opened it and couldn't believe what I was reading.

"Slick, the girls flew the coop. Jill was going nuts with the crowd, so Sue took her home."

"What did they do with our gear?"

"They took it with them."

"Oh, that's just fucking beautiful," Slick replied.

"She said she tried to find us but had no luck and she didn't want to leave our bags, so she took them with her."

"Why didn't they leave a room for us?"

"I don't know. We'll get that answered when we see them."

"This is just fucking beautiful—no room, no clothes, and no fucking wheels."

"Listen, Slick, why don't you say fuck one more time? It may make things better."

"Fuck you, Sweetwater."

"Well, Slick, we might as well make the best of it. Let's hit the concert and see if we can get a ride back with that crew we met in Pat O'Brien's."

"Good idea."

The concert was being held in Jackson Square, and by the time we arrived it looked like Times Square on New Year's Eve. As we got close to the concert we could hear the Fat Man playing "I'm Walking to New Orleans." The closer we got to the show, the more difficult it was to believe my eyes. Jungle Jim was up on the stage with Fats, playing the piano right alongside him.

"All right," I hollered, "Hit it, Jungle." We worked our way around to where we could get to him when he got off the stage.

Once the song ended, Jungle shook Fats's hand and jumped into the crowd close by. After some pushing and shoving we finally caught up to him.

"Hey, Jungle, over here," I hollered. Once he spotted us, he came over to see what was up. "I didn't know you played the piano."

"I don't advertise it, but I've been tickling the ivories for almost twenty years."

"Well, you sounded great, and kept right in time with the Fat Man."

"He's one of my favorite musicians and I've been playing his music for years."

"Any chance you have room in your car to give us a ride back on Sunday? The people who drove us down left us stranded."

"We don't, but I've seen a lot of people down here from Pensacola. I'm sure we can get you a ride back. Where are you guys staying, so I can get in touch with you if something comes up?"

"You're looking at it."

"What do you mean?" asked Jungle.

"The girls checked out of the rooms we had and the hotel rented them to other guests. We have to find another room somewhere or else sleep here."

"I can tell you fellows right now that if you don't have a room, you're not going to find one within a hundred miles of here."

"Well, it looks like you're looking at our sleeping quarters as we speak. We'll be in the area, Jungle, so

I'm sure we'll run into each other before the weekend is over."

"Okay, see you later and be careful."

As the night lingered on we jumped from party to party, not worrying about our dilemma. By three in the morning things started to wind down and we hadn't had any offers to share a room, let alone a bed, so we headed back to Jackson Square.

When we got back to the area where the concert had been held, it looked like a national park campground. There were hundreds of people in sleeping bags and a dozen tents were pitched. We went to the stage area to get under it, but it was already filled up. There wasn't much space to stretch out in the grass, so we walked along the perimeter of the park and found a dry drainage ditch that had some space available. Slick and I huddled up against each other and fell fast asleep within minutes.

What seemed like ten minutes of sleep turned out to be a couple of hours. We were awakened by the noise of a payloader cleaning up the debris in the streets. As we gathered our faculties and realized where we were, it took a few minutes before I could move. When I started to get up, my back went into a muscle spasm, which kept me on my knees for a short period.

Once I got out of the ditch and stood up, my body parts started to function normally. I looked at Slick and said, "You look like shit, Morely."

"You wouldn't win any beauty contest either, shipmate."

Feeling like we'd been hit by a Mack truck, we

decided to hitchhike back to Mobile. At least we had a place to sleep, and if things had deteriorated to the point where the girls didn't want us around, we could hop in the Silver Fox and head back to the base. As we walked toward the freeway I looked at Slick and said, "Some Mardi Gras liberty, huh?"

"Yeah, but you can't buy training like this, Water."

9

PRINCE OF
DARKNESS

At 8:00 A.M. Slick, I, and the rest of the students
who had completed their primary flight training sat
in the base auditorium. While we waited for the
training officer and his staff to arrive I could feel the
tension mount. At 0815 they arrived and posted the
aircraft selections on the front of the podium.
Before we were allowed to look at the results, the
training officer had a few remarks to make and pass
out achievement awards to the outstanding students
in the class. Slick and I were not among the chosen
few.

After all the administrative business was completed, we were called up alphabetically to look at our
class ranking and pipeline selection. What you got to
fly was based on three factors—the needs of the

Navy, flight and academic grades, and finally your individual preference. You got your choice as long as there was a training quota available for the type of aircraft you selected.

The anxiety that built up inside me while I waited my turn was almost overwhelming. When Slick's name was called, I said, "If you see jets next to my name, turn and give me a thumbs-up and I'll meet you in the admin building."

Slick walked to the podium, hesitated for a moment, then walked out of the auditorium with his head hung low. My heart skipped a beat and I became real concerned with my future.

When my name was called, I broke out in a cold sweat as I walked to the podium. This reminded me of my college sports days, wondering if I made the baseball team. Looking down the list of thirty-plus names, I spotted Sullivan with "jets" written beside it and number three, meaning I was third in the class. Then I went direct to Morely's name and he also had jets.

As I walked out of the auditorium Slick jumped me and I said, "You son of a bitch, I thought one of us didn't cut the mustard."

"Yeah, I know," he said. "I just wanted you to squirm a little longer while you waited."

There were only eight jet seats available, so we were pretty much assured of getting the same base location for our basic and advanced training. When we walked into the administration office, Lieutenant Jennifer Anderson, a tall, slender, good-looking blonde, was assigning the orders.

She was the assistant administrative officer and only dated officers who wore those coveted wings of gold, so the students could only look, drool, and if they wanted to find some cold comfort, enjoy her sweet personality.

As we approached the counter she bid us good morning and explained our options to us. "Gentlemen, have I got a deal for you!"

Oh boy, I thought, here it comes, the bat is about to be shoved up my ass. "Don't look so concerned," she said. "This *is* a good deal. The Navy has a new program in Pensacola which allows you to get your master's degree while going through flight training. When you receive your wings, you'll also receive your master's degree in aeronautical systems. Granted there will be more work involved, but what an opportunity!"

Slick abruptly asked, "What are our other options?"

"Your only other option is Kingsville, Texas."

Slick and I looked at each other and said, "We'll take the master's program in Pensacola."

"I think you've made an excellent choice, gentlemen. You'll be based at Sherman Field and attend the University of West Florida on a halfday basis."

"Lieutenant Anderson," I asked, "what else do we have to do?"

"Tomorrow I'd like you to check out with the ten people listed on this sheet. Once you've obtained a debrief from them, pick up your orders here and you're free to check out of VT-1. However, you must check into VT-4, which is your new squadron, before midnight on Wednesday. Friday morning you need to register at the university."

"Sounds good. Thank you for your help. See you tomorrow."

"Okay, and congratulations on being selected for jets and enrolling in the master's program," she replied as we left her office and headed to our rooms.

Once we got to our rooms and thought about what we were getting into, we knew that fun in the sun was over. I was no brain surgeon in college and Slick had been anything but a rocket scientist, but either of us would rather have had a sister in a whore-house than move to Kingsville, Texas.

The rest of the day was spent checking out and saying good-bye to friends and instructors. That evening we rented a small U-Haul trailer and hooked it up to the Blue Goose. We packed what few belongings we had and were ready for the forty-minute drive to NAS Sherman Field as soon as we checked out.

At two o'clock we picked up our orders and officially checked out of Saufley Field, drove to Sherman, and checked in at VT-4. As we entered the squadron spaces we noticed a big sign painted on the squadron's hangar—EXCELLENCE OUR STANDARD, PERFECTION OUR GOAL.

Being two of the fifty selected for the master's program, we were welcomed with enthusiasm and given the VIP check-in treatment. Once all the paperwork was turned in and we received our welcome-aboard packages, we checked into the BOQ. The rooms were like one-bedroom efficiencies and were brand new. We couldn't believe how nice they were.

There was no time to breathe. Thursday morning we were scheduled to meet with the squadron commanding officer, the training officer, and get fitted for our g-suits and oxygen masks. The afternoon would be dedicated to a pressure-chamber ride to a simulated forty thousand feet and a dynamic ejection-seat shot. The following day we had to register at West Florida.

By the time we got unpacked and settled in, it was almost midnight. The night was a restless one for me—a new bed, new surroundings, and a lot more responsibility to think about. When Slick and I met for breakfast, I learned that he, too, had a lot of apprehension and hadn't slept all that well. As we talked over our meal I wondered if we'd bitten off more than we could chew.

We were scheduled to see Commander Jim Wolfe, the commanding officer of VT-4, at 9:00 A.M. At 0845 we walked into his office. "Good morning," I said to his secretary, "I'm Ensign Sullivan and this Ensign Morely. We have a meeting with Commander Wolfe."

After checking the CO's appointment calendar, she said, "Please be seated and I'll tell him you're here."

Within a few minutes she returned and escorted us into his office. As we entered he got up from behind his desk, walked over, and shook our hands.

"Welcome to VT-4, gentlemen. Please have a seat."

Once we were comfortable, he said, "Congratulations on being selected for jets and enrolled in the new master's program."

"Thank you, sir," we replied in unison.

"How was your stay at Saufley?" he asked.

"It was a great experience," Slick said. "It was everything I expected and more."

"What about you, Ensign Sullivan? I understand you had some hair-raising moments."

"Yes, sir, I did. And I learned at a very early stage that you better be prepared for each flight."

"That's truer than you know, Ensign, because any given day your professionalism can be tested. We're pleased to have you aboard and I want you to know that what you are about to undertake will be most rewarding at the end of your stay with us. Remember to keep focused on your goals and don't get overwhelmed by the program. Look at this like a big elephant—take one bite at a time and eventually you'll eat the whole thing. Try to eat the elephant too fast and it'll overcome you. If you start to get behind, let someone know so we can help. Study hard, gentlemen, this is an opportunity of a lifetime. You may not think that a degree in aeronautical systems is worth much, but believe me, it will be important for your naval careers down the road. My door is always open, feel free to stop by if you need to talk. Do you have any questions for me at this time?"

Slick and I looked at each other, then looked back at Commander Wolfe, shaking our heads to indicate that we had no questions.

"Okay, then. It was nice to meet you and welcome again to VT-4."

"Thank you, sir," we said as he walked us to the door.

After leaving Wolfe's office, we met with Lieutenant Commander Hahn, the training officer in the training building. He briefed us on what to expect over the next nine months. Our first phase of flight training would be in the T-2C Buckeye, which would include transition, precision acrobatics, basic radio instruments, night flying, formation, air-to-air gunnery, and carrier qualification. After successful completion of basic flight training, we would progress to the TA-4, an advanced jet trainer. The syllabus followed the same stages as basic, with the exception of air-to-ground bombing.

"Your jet training, gentlemen, is completely different from the rest of the jet pipeline, due to the master's program. You will complete all of your ground school before you start flying the T-2. This will allow you to focus your energy in one area at a time. The nonmaster's students will have to work at their own pace and complete ground school while learning to master the T-2 flight characteristics. However, they won't have graduate studies to worry about, so it all works out in the long run."

Slick raised his hand and Lieutenant Commander Hahn acknowledged him. "Yes, Ensign, go ahead."

"What courses will we be required to take our first semester?"

"Right now it looks like you'll have aerodynamics, physics, and differential calculus."

"Boy, that's a heavy load," Slick replied. "What happens if we get behind the eight ball?"

"That's where I come in. I'll liaison with your school adviser, and if any of you should have scheduling problems or get behind, we'll work it out. Remember, we want this master's program to work and we'll do everything possible to assist you in your needs. But you have to do your part. You'll meet with your professors tomorrow at registration and they can answer most of your questions. Let's break for lunch now and we'll get you fitted for your 02 masks and g-suit after chow. We'll meet at the paraloft at 1300."

We drove to the officers' club for lunch and enjoyed a nice meal on the patio near the pool. The waitresses were all pleasant and you could tell that the club manager didn't do any hiring over the phone. After our action-packed morning and relaxing lunch, we went back to our rooms and changed into our zoom bags, which is what we called flight suits, grabbed our helmets, and headed for the paraloft. Once our class was assembled in the paraloft, the riggers measured us for our g-suits, MA-2 torso harness, and oxygen masks.

After everyone was fitted, we were escorted to the pressure chamber, a large cylinder that seated twelve and had the capability of simulating a climb to 40,000 feet. The device was used to see how students reacted to hypoxia, pressure breathing, and body-fluid expansion.

When we were all seated, the instructor briefed us on the use of the oxygen equipment and what we would be doing once we leveled off. After all questions were answered, the chamber safety officer closed the door and instructed us to hook up our oxygen masks and give a radio check when called upon. As soon as everyone acknowledged the safety officer's call, he instructed the controller to take us to 25,000 feet.

As I watched the altimeter climb through 10,000 feet, the pressure of the mask against my face made me feel a little claustrophobic. As we passed through 18,000 thousand feet the safety observer told us to look at the surgical glove tied to the ceiling. It had started to inflate like a balloon.

"Okay, gentlemen," he said, "what you see happening to that glove is happening to your insides. So if you feel uncomfortable, loosen your belt and expel some gas if needed. Don't worry, we're all on 100-percent oxygen and you won't offend anyone."

I chuckled a bit and forgot about my claustrophobia. Within several minutes we leveled off at 25,000 feet.

"Okay, is everyone all right?" asked the observer. After a thumbs-up from all, he instructed us to unhook one side of our oxygen masks and hold it to our faces until instructed to release it. Slick and I were instructed to play paddy cake until the onset of hypoxia; some of the others were told to play cards or draw pictures. When the word was given, we all released our masks and began our little games. For the first couple of minutes Slick and I didn't miss a beat.

Then hypoxia began to take effect and we couldn't coordinate our hands anymore. Shortly after that I had trouble seeing Slick's hands and he began to laugh uncontrollably. At that point the observer told us to put our masks back on. Within a minute or so we were back to normal. Some of the other students got so hypoxic that they couldn't get their masks back on by themselves and needed assistance from the observer. After everyone was back to normal, we went up to 40,000 feet to experience what it's like to pressure-breathe. This procedure was very uncomfortable because you had to force yourself to exhale before you got the next onrush of oxygen. After everyone got to experience this technique, we slowly descended back to sea level.

Once the demo ride was over and the door opened, I was the first out. As Slick and I walked to the classroom for our debrief, I said, "You know, Slick, I almost lost it up there."

"What do you mean?"

"The mask over my face and being closed in like that really made me uncomfortable."

"It bothered me, too, but we'll get used to it. Don't forget, Sweetwater, this is all new stuff for us. It'll become second nature once we do it every day."

"I hope, Slick, I hope."

Shortly after we were seated, the safety observer came in and debriefed us on the chamber ride. He showed us a videotape of our reactions. It was funny to see how each of us reacted, but it proved hypoxia could be deadly if not caught in time. Its effect on the human body gave us some knowledge of how to combat the problem if it was detected.

After the debrief we went back to the squadron where the ejection seat training was to be conducted. There were about ten of us who needed the dynamic shot for the T-2C LS-1A ejection seat. This device was a forty-foot vertical rail up which the seat would travel when the ejection sequence was activated. Each student would get two rides, one by activating the upper-face curtain handle and the second by pulling the lower ejection handle between his legs. The seat was propelled up the rails by a charge of dynamite. If the ride didn't get your attention, the explosion did, believe me.

I was number four in line, and when it was my turn I hopped into the seat and strapped in. After the rigger checked that my harness was hooked up correctly, I was lowered down to the bottom of the rail. I elected to use the upper ejection handle first. This was the primary method to use during an actual ejection. The handle was above my helmet, and when pulled down over my head, a face curtain would protect my face from the wind blast as I rode the seat up the rail.

When I felt comfortable, I gave the safety observer a thumbs-up, positioned my butt to the rear of the seat, made sure my back was straight, and pulled the upper handle down over my face. I was up the rail before I knew what had happened. The ride was more fun than an E ticket at Disneyland. But the scary part was, the shot was only an eighth of what a real ejection would feel like.

The secondary method of activating the ejection sequence was used in case you couldn't reach the upper handle due to excessive g-forces. Once I was in position, I put my right hand through the d-ring between my legs, then I took my left hand and grabbed my right wrist. With a sharp pull toward my chest the sequence was underway. The explosion and ride up the rail was much more dramatic without the face curtain. I could see what was happening and it made me realize how violent an ejection really was. Once back at the starting position, I unstrapped and Slick jumped into the seat for his two shots.

He actually got to do three, because his head and

torso were out of position on one and they made him do it over. After he qualified we hopped into the Silver Fox and drove back to the BOQ.

As we got close to home Slick said, "Take a swing by our old battalion and let's see what's cooking."

"Good idea." I bet things hadn't changed much and I was right. The DIs had a class of students out for marching drills, several were being disciplined off to one side, and the rest looked like a herd of cattle as they marched to the cadence of the drill instructor's voice. The picture was still very clear in my mind as the goose bumps rose on my arms and legs.

We didn't stay long for fear we might be asked to demonstrate the proper marching technique to the new class.

Registration day at West Florida was not your typical college experience. There were no lines to stand in and there were no crowds. The university and Navy both went all out to make our enrollment as pleasant as possible. We were escorted to a lounge where refreshments were provided while we met with the president and our class adviser. We registered and received our books without leaving the room. Everything was at our disposal and it was a professional welcome aboard.

Before lunch our class adviser showed us the campus and then took us to a special luncheon where we met our professors and their aides. After lunch we had a short question-and-answer period about the program and then we were free to go.

The weekend was a lazy one and I spent most of it getting caught up on correspondence to my family. Our schedule over the next several months would be brutal and there wouldn't be much time for letter writing. Starting Monday, we had ground school in the mornings for two weeks and graduate work in the afternoons. This would separate the men from the boys.

The first week was a killer. I had so many numbers running through my head, I couldn't keep my courses straight and I started to fall behind. After the second week at this bone-numbing pace, I began to settle into a routine that allowed me to catch up.

By the third week we started to fly and it was hard to imagine getting into an aircraft that had no visible means of propulsion. The gut-wrenching fear of getting into an airplane was back, just like with the T-34.

As I waited to meet my instructor I recalled the apprehension I felt at Saufley. The feeling of mastering the T-34 was gone. I was back to square one again. New machine, new instructor, new set of rules, and a lot more responsibility.

My brief was at nine, and when no one had called for me by quarter after, I started to get concerned. Just as I got up to ask the schedules officer if I had been canceled, I heard my name called from the back of the room.

"Sweetwater Sullivan, front and center, lad."

Oh boy, I thought, I've got a smart-ass for an instructor. When I turned around and focused on the voice, I was surprised at the image.

There, standing six-three, well built, and sporting

a perfectly groomed handlebar mustache, was my new flight instructor. As I walked toward him he extended his hand and introduced himself as Lieutenant Commander John "Hellcat" Ringer and immediately apologized for being late. "Let me get changed and I'll be right out," he said.

Within ten minutes he had changed into his flight suit and was just ready to start the brief when he was summoned to the phone. When Hellcat returned, he looked a little flustered and I asked him, "Is everything all right?"

"Oh, yeah, just a hectic start today. My wife delivered our second child this morning and I've been behind the power curve ever since."

"Are you all right to fly?" I asked.

"Sure am, or I wouldn't be sitting here."

"Well, doesn't the Navy give you time off when you become a new father?"

"They do, but I didn't request any. My in-laws are in town and they have things well in hand. Let's brief before something else comes up."

A half hour into the brief, I asked him how he knew my nickname. He smiled. "The students in the master's program were assigned to a specific set of instructors and we had to do a profile study on each and every one of you. When I was assigned to you, I acquired your training jacket and studied your progress to date. Sweetwater, I know your whole life history." He laughed.

I said, "I hope I didn't let you down."

"Not yet. Just know your procedures and I'll make you the ace of the base."

"You've got a deal, Commander."

"Call me John or Hellcat when we're together, it's less formal."

"Yes, sir," I replied.

The brief went on for another half hour and it was close to eleven before we headed down to the paraloft to pick up my LPA life vest, torso harness, g-suit, and mask. When we entered the space, Petty Officer Towers, a tall, well-groomed sailor, asked if he could be of any assistance and I said, "My name is Sullivan and I came to pick up my flight gear."

"Let me see," replied Towers, "oh yeah, Ensign Matt Sullivan 006-46-4781."

"That's me."

"Okay, sir, here you go. If you have any problems with your gear, bring it back and we'll fix her up for you."

"Thank you, Towers," I said as I headed to the locker room.

Hellcat was waiting. "I'll meet you in maintenance control after I suit up, Sweetwater."

"Okay," I said. The instructors had their own locker room, which was separate from the students.

The first item I donned was my g-suit. It looked like a pair of pants with its seat cut out. The upper segment wrapped around my midsection like a large corset and each leg was split by a zipper. When the leg sections were zipped together, they formed a tight fit.

The next item to put on was my torso harness. You got into the harness like you were putting on a parachute, only the chute was not attached. The webbing fit snugly around the groin and shoulders and was very uncomfortable when tight. This harness had four large connecting buckles—one on each shoulder and one on either side, just below the waist. These buckles connected to the ejection seat, where your parachute was housed.

After the torso harness was tightened down, an LPA life vest was put on and attached to the harness. This vest fit like a flack jacket around your upper torso and was secured at the chest and lower abdomen.

When I had put on all the equipment, I weighed an extra twenty-five pounds. As I waddled out of the locker room Petty Officer Towers, better known around the squadron as Charcoal Man, invited me to stop by the hangar for one of his famous charcoal-broiled burgers after my flight. He worked a grill outside the hangar during the noon hour for pilots and personnel around the squadron. Word had it that some of the troops put jp-4 jet fuel on his charcoal one day, and when he lit it off, he couldn't get the flames out. The fire was so hot it burned up his grill. From then on he was tagged with the nickname. I told him I would stop by if he was still open.

Within a couple of minutes Hellcat walked into maintenance control. I had the book out and was reviewing the discrepancies when he asked if I had any questions.

"No, sir," I replied, "everything seems to be in order."

"Good, let me take a look at the book when you're done and I'll sign us out."

The review of the log and checkout was almost exactly like Saufley's procedures, so it came easy. As we walked to the aircraft I felt like an astronaut with all the uncomfortable gear on.

"Listen, Sweetwater," Hellcat said, hardly able to control himself, "you don't have to tighten down your torso or buckle up your LPA until you're ready to climb aboard. It makes it a little more comfortable while you do your preflight."

"Thanks for the tip. I was wondering how I was going to bend down to inspect the underparts of this machine."

"You'll get used to the extra bulk after a few hops."

The preflight on a T-2 was a bit more involved than the T-34. The ejection seat and front cockpit alone had twenty-six items to check before you started on the exterior. The most important items on the seat preflight were to ensure the canopy actuator safety pin was removed and the three ejection-seat safety pins were pulled and stowed. The rest of the inspection in the cockpit was to make sure all switches and handles were in their proper positions and secure.

The exterior preflight had six areas that needed to be inspected. The equipment bay and fuselage area had eight items to look over, the nose section had nine items, the starboard equipment bay and fuselage area had another eight items, the starboard wheel well and wing had eight things to look at, the aft fuselage and empennage or tail section also had eight items, and the port wheel well and wing had ten items to inspect. The whole preflight took almost thirty minutes.

By the time the plane captain assisted me in strapping in, I was soaked with sweat and felt like a wet noodle. Thank God the instructor was going to demo everything like he did at Saufley. The start and pretaxi checklists were pretty straightforward and I had them down cold before the flight. The only two things that were really bothering me were the fact that I was sitting on an ejection seat that could fire me out of that cockpit in a split second and the claustrophobic feeling my oxygen mask was giving me.

Hellcat had me ride the controls with him for takeoff. Once we broke ground and the aircraft was in a positive rate of climb, he had me raise the gear and gave me control of the aircraft. What a thrill! It was actually easier to fly than the T-34. The nice thing about a jet is you don't have to worry about prop or mixture adjustment. Just a stick and throttles and try to keep ahead of the machine were my main concerns.

As we climbed up to 20,000 feet Hellcat took back control of the aircraft and told me to relax while he pointed out the training area. At that point I had a flashback about my accident and I started to get uncomfortable. I could feel my forehead bead up with sweat and I felt really claustrophobic. I told Hellcat I wasn't feeling good and he told me to take the controls. After I was flying for a few minutes, I settled down and we continued on with the hop.

We did some steep turns, slow flight, and stalls at altitude before going into the landing pattern at an outlying field. Because the T-2 was a much faster aircraft than the T-34, you had to stay ahead of the plane to avoid breaking through pattern altitudes or over-speeding the gear and flaps. The landings in a T-2 were much firmer than in the T-34, due to the jet's weight and approach speed. My first couple of landings were just short of controlled crashes. When we landed at Sherman Field, I thought my eyeteeth were about to fall out. We filled out the yellow sheet and went back to debrief.

"Well, Sweetwater, what did you think?" Hellcat asked.

"Things happened pretty fast," I replied.

"It's a normal reaction for you guys who just finished flying the T-34. You'll do fine, Sweetwater. Just continue to study your procedures and review your mistakes and think positive. Look at your last two landings—they were right on the money and your pattern work improved after each pass. This is the type of progress we look for on the first hop and you handled everything fine. Do you have any questions?"

"No, sir."

"Okay then, we'll see you in a couple of days."

"Thank you, sir, and good luck with that new baby."

"You bet. See you, Sweetwater."

Landing a jet is a little more involved than landing a T-34. You don't fly airspeeds in a tactical jet, you fly angle of attack, which is the acute angle between the direction of the relative wind and the chord of the airfoil. Once you get a good cross-check with your airspeed indicator and angle-of-attack indicator, you fly your approach using your angle-of-attack indicator and approach indexers.

The angle-of-attack indicator is located on the instrument panel in the upper left-hand corner in each cockpit and provides a visual indication of angle of attack by a pointer that moves over a scale graduated from zero to thirty units. The approach indexer is set at 15 units and stall warning is set for 17.5 units. The approach indexer is a small vertical rectangular box that sits on the instrument-panel shroud, adjacent to the wheels warning light.

If the approach angle of attack is too high, above fifteen units, which means your approach speed is too slow, the upper light will turn green. If you are on speed or fifteen units, the light will be amber, and if you are too fast or below fifteen units, the lower light will be red. It took me four landings to understand the sequence, and once I got the light show straight in my mind, I started flying a smooth on-speed pass. The flight had ended in a positive way and I knew what I had to do to correct my mistakes.

I hung my flight gear in my newly assigned locker and headed back to my room. After a shower I called to see if Slick was in, but there was no answer. I assumed he was still flying. While I waited for him to return I looked over our schedule for Tuesday and saw that we had to be at the university by 8:00 A.M. for our first class.

Within a half hour Slick was knocking on my door. "It's open, come on in," I shouted.

As he stepped into the room I said, "Morely, you look like shit. What happened?"

"Nothing, just getting back from a great flight."

"Do you want a beer?"

"Sounds good, Water. Have you got a cold one?"

"Is a pig's ass pork? Of course I've got a cold one. Do you want Bud or Coors?"

"A Bud sounds good."

"Coming right up. Tell me about your flight, Slick."

"Goddamn it, Water, that T-2 is a great machine. We did a little yanking and banking before we came home, and boy was that a thrill. How did your flight go?"

"Not bad. I got a little uncomfortable with all the gear on but had a good hop."

"Did you get a good instructor?"

"You bet. His name is Hellcat Ringer, and he said if I paid attention to his instruction, he'd make me the ace of the base. What's your instructor like, Slick?"

"He's a great guy and full of piss and vinegar. His name is Lieutenant Commander Tommy Steel, and he goes by the nickname Stainless."

"Sounds like a hard charger."

"He is. He just got back from Vietnam and can't wait to show me how it's done in the fleet."

"Sounds good. Go take a shower, Slick, and get out of that smelly goatskin. By the way, when was the last time you washed that son of a bitch?"

"Up yours," he replied as he headed out the door.

Slick and I had one more transition flight to acquaint us with the T-2 and then we would get eleven basic-instrument flights "under the bag." After our hooded, all-weather flying was completed, we had eleven more flights before our first solo. After we learned the basics of flying a jet, we had ten acrobatic flights, five dual, and five solo. Then we would get into radio instruments, where we learned how to navigate, fly airways, and instrument approaches.

After three months Slick and I were halfway through basic jets and were well into the master's program. For the first month or so I was overwhelmed with the math and needed some tutoring to keep my head above water. Slick adapted well and was burning up the program, both academically and aeronautically.

We didn't have much time to party and we only made it to Joe's and Molar Man's a few times during our first few months in basic. We made a couple of trips over to Mobile to see Sue and Jill, but they were out of our league. We couldn't afford their rich entertainment.

Our next big hurdle was the dreaded night flights. A lot of students have problems with this phase of training simply because they can't adapt to the environment. Both of our instructors told us to listen to what the "Prince of Darkness" preaches, because his word is gospel. Commander Bobby Brown got his nickname from teaching night flying. We only saw him around the squadron at night. He personally flies each student once before he lets him solo at night. If he feels you aren't catching on, he'll give you an extra hop. But if you can't hack it after that, you appear before a board to determine whether you should be retained or washed out.

Wednesday night at five, our class was scheduled

for our night-flying brief by the famous Prince of Darkness. At first when you heard about this officer, you kind of took it as a joke, but as you got close to the night-flying phase and heard some of the stories about this guy, you realized his legendary status was justified.

At 4:45 Slick and I entered the briefing room and it was dark, with the exception of one red light near the door. As we bumped into chairs, trying to get seated, I told Slick to turn on some lights.

"You can't," said a voice from somewhere in the room.

"What do you mean, we can't?" I blasted.

"There aren't any, we've tried."

By this time my eyes started to adapt to what little light there was in the room and I could see several figures already seated in front of us.

"What is this bullshit?" I asked.

"Sit down and relax. The fun is about to begin."

After ten minutes or so I was able to identify objects around the room.

On the hour, spooky Halloween music started playing and a voice, who identified himself as the Prince of Darkness, started to talk about dark adapting. He explained why we were sitting in a dark room with only a red light on and how the rods and cones in our eyes helped us see at night.

As he continued to talk Slick leaned over and said, "This fucking guy's elevator doesn't go all the way to the top." At that moment bright lights flashed on and what appeared to be a man in a Superman outfit, with a cape on his back, came swinging down from the ceiling in front of us on a trapeze.

Within a couple of seconds, the bright lights went out and we were all flash-blinded. We couldn't identify anything in the room. After a few minutes things began to appear again and the one object that really stood out was a man's figure standing in front of the class. After five minutes or so a voice said, "Cover your eyes, gentlemen, the white lights are coming on."

When the lights were turned on, the man in the Superman outfit was standing in front of us. He stood about six-three and looked like a middle linebacker for the Raiders. He was dressed in black tights with a silver silhouette of a half-moon on his chest. "Prince of Darkness" was written in silver letters above and below the moon. He had a silver cape on his back and was wearing black flight boots. When the disbelief left our faces, he told us to take a break and be back in ten minutes.

After we were all assembled in the room, Commander Brown made his second entrance, this time dressed in his flight suit. "Gentlemen," he said, "don't let that little show fool you, you'd be better off sandpapering a lion's ass in a phone booth than fucking with me. I'll be your worst enemy if you don't pay attention to what I have to say tonight. You four in the front row will fly tonight, the rest will fly tomorrow."

For an hour and a half all eyes were riveted on Commander Brown. Never had I seen intimidation used as effectively as this man had done. When the brief was over we had a solid idea of what night flying was all about and were prepared for the worst if something should go wrong. It was probably the most comprehensive brief I had seen to date. The fear that the Prince of Darkness had put into us at the beginning of the brief turned into respect for what we were about to undertake. By the time the brief ended, he had proved his point and done it very, very well.

As Slick and I walked to our lockers to change, I said, "I don't know about you, but I think I'd rather take my chances with that lion in the phone booth."

"You got that right, shipmate."

10

SHERMAN SCREAMER

After Slick and I changed into our flight gear, we walked to the briefing room and had a seat with the other two students. Commander Brown walked in shortly after we had taken our seats and asked, "Who wants to fly first?"

For a minute we all looked at one another. The pause was getting embarrassing, so I said, "I'll go first."

"Very well, Ensign Sullivan. You're it. I am going to brief you all at once, and when we land, whoever is flying second be ready to go. Each hop will be about an hour in length, and when you hear or see us in the landing pattern, be ready to hot-seat at the line. We'll shut down the port engine only. Look your seat over then climb aboard. I'll have to refuel after the second flight, so we'll do a hot pump crew switch on the third switch. Are there any questions about the sequence of events for tonight's evolutions?"

There were none, so Commander Brown started the brief.

The Prince of Darkness was a completely different person during the brief. He almost seemed compassionate. He knew we were uptight and he tried to make us feel comfortable with the mission. Some of the highlights he touched on were preflight inspection, dark adapting prior to going out on the flight line, and loss-plane procedures.

Flashlights have a red lens cover for preflighting at night. He reminded us that if we had a hydraulic leak we wouldn't be able to detect it with the red lens cover. Consequently in areas that needed to be checked for hydraulic leaks the reds lens had to be removed. We already knew about dark adapting from the brief, so he just reviewed the times it took to get completely adapted. The loss-plane procedures were a little more involved. He explained and reviewed the five Cs that we had learned at Saufley—confess, communicate, climb, conserve, and comply with enroute procedures.

Brown grew serious for a moment. "When students find themselves lost, they often won't admit it and they don't follow the five Cs, which just makes things worse. Of all the night flights I've conducted over the past three years, I've only had one student get lost and have to eject due to fuel starvation."

He paused to let that sink in, and I thought, I hope I'm not the second.

Satisfied that we were as impressed as he

wanted us to be, he asked, "Do any of you have any questions? Yes, in the back, go ahead."

"What happens if you lose your radios in the pattern, sir?"

"Remember what I told you earlier. Flash your landing light on and off three times, and we'll clear the pattern out and give you a green light from the tower. Once you see the light, you're cleared to land. Anyone else? Go ahead."

"About how many landings do we need, sir?"

"I'll be the judge of that. When I feel you can fly the pattern and land safely, we'll full-stop. Don't worry, I won't let you go until you're ready. Any other questions." There were none. "Okay then, the first four that I said would fly tonight, meet me in maintenance control after you suit up."

After we reviewed the plane's discrepancies list, Commander Brown took me to preflight our aircraft and his assistants showed the rest of the fellows a preflight while they waited their turn to fly. During the inspection Brown explained about the use of the red lens again and showed me how difficult it was to spot a hydraulic leak with it on. It was pretty amazing that you couldn't spot the leak. After the preflight I climbed in and went through my prestart checklist.

After I got the aircraft started, he took control of the plane and taxied us around the airfield, pointing out the different light colors and what they meant. White lights were for the active runway, blue lights were taxiways, and red lights meant stop. It was a whole different ball game at night and he had my full attention.

The takeoff and climb-out were uneventful. Once

we got to 15,000 feet, he turned the aircraft over to me and I flew a little round robin around the training area. He showed me different checkpoints and what to look for when we went out on our solo. After a short while he took the controls back and off to our starboard side was another T-2. I was amazed to see that it was within ten feet.

Commander Brown must have sensed my nervousness, because he said, "Don't worry, Matt, this is a planned part of the hop. Another instructor who works with me will demonstrate what it will look like when you're in trail of another aircraft. He'll make some turns to the left and right to familiarize you, then he'll climb and descend the aircraft."

It was amazing, and a little terrifying, how easy it was to misjudge what the other plane was doing. It took me a while to get acclimated.

After the demo was completed, we broke off and I flew us back to the field using radio-instrument procedures. I entered the landing pattern and made five touch-and-go's and full-stopped on my sixth pass. I taxied the Buckeye to the line and hot-seated with the next student. Commander Brown debriefed me as we taxied in. He felt I had a decent handle on things and complimented me on my landings. Feeling a little cocky, I climbed out of the seat, turned the plane over to the next student, and strutted toward the hangar.

I could see Slick standing by the line shack as I walked toward the hangar. "Well, how did it go?" he asked as I approached him.

"Great, but it sure is different at night. I thought I knew this airfield pretty well, but at night, everything seemed in the wrong place. When we were taxiing around, I thought we were headed for the weeds several times. Make sure you follow the blue taxi lights and take it slow. If you get confused, turn on your taxi light. It'll help guide you. Brown will try to make you go the wrong way, just to see if you know your light colors. It's a fun hop and he really knows what he's talking about, so listen to what he's telling you."

After my short debrief, I told Slick I'd see him in class the next morning. He gave me a thumbs-up as I walked to the locker room.

I didn't call Slick for breakfast because I figured he'd sleep until the last possible minute before he had to get ready for class. I was right—he not only waited to the last minute, he missed the first half hour of our review aero class. He looked pretty tired when he entered the classroom.

After class he debriefed me on his flight and it was almost identical to mine. After classes we went home and took a nap. Our brief was at 8:00 P.M. and our flight was at nine.

The hop was scheduled for three hours. We were to go on a short cross-country that took us over to Mobile, Alabama, then up to Montgomery and back to Pensacola. Upon our return we were to do two touch-and-go's and full-stop on our third pass. There would be an instructor in a chase plane to observe our flight and assist us if we got into trouble.

Slick and I had asked if we could fly our solos together and we got the green light. Lieutenant Commander Tom "Garters" Kistler was assigned as our chase pilot. He was a soft-spoken guy. Five-ten and slender, he had a nicely groomed mustache that gave him a distinguished look. He reminded me of British officers in those movies about India in the nineteenth century. He watched Slick and me map out our route and gave us some good pointers about filling out our DD-175 flight plan.

After we filed, we got our weather brief. The planned route was pretty good until we got near Montgomery. There was a line of isolated thunderstorms that went over to Columbus, Georgia, but shouldn't affect the flight. We planned to turn south and head toward Troy before we really got into the bad stuff, so we kept our original route.

The plan called for me to lead the flight up to Mobile, then pass the lead to Slick and he would fly us to Montgomery. Then he'd pass it back to me and I'd bring us home. The preflight, man-up, and takeoff went flawlessly. We got a good radio check and things were going smoothly. Our cruising altitude was 30,000 feet and it was a beautiful flight until we got near Letohatchee. Unexpectedly the weather had moved south of Montgomery and the ride began to get real bumpy. Within seconds there was a blinding flash and an incredible thump. It felt like I had been hit by lightning. We had flown right into an isolated thunderstorm.

By then, I was having problems seeing my instruments. I had been flash-blinded. Lieutenant Commander Kistler came up on tactical, a preset channel to talk to the flight, and told me to turn to a heading of 200 and Slick to turn to a heading of 150. Within a couple of minutes we were out of the squall line and back in clear weather. Garters told us to circle once we were in the clear. He coordinated with center and told them what happened. Center had us on radar and gave Slick a vector to Troy and told him to descend to 27,000.

Two minutes later they vectored me to Troy with an enroute descent. Kistler flew directly to Troy, circled over the navigational aid on the ground at 29,000. Within a few minutes Lieutenant Commander Kistler spotted Slick inbound to the fix. He told him to continue outbound, follow the flight planned route, and reduce his speed to two hundred indicated. When I hit the fix, he told me to speed up until I could see Slick. I was instructed to give two clicks on the mike switch once I spotted him. This was the signal to assume our regular speed.

Luckily our aircraft were not damaged and we got out of the heavy weather before we ran into hail or more lightning. That type of storm can rip a plane in half and Slick and I got an early lesson on the unpredictability of thunderstorms.

Once the bad weather was behind us, the rest of the flight went smoothly and we made it back to Sherman Field pretty much as planned. As I looked over my plane for damage Lieutenant Commander Kistler walked up to me and said, "Sweetwater, I want to commend you on your professionalism. Both you and Slick kept your heads and followed my instructions to a tee. If you had gone much further into that squall line, you could have run into some serious trouble. Good job."

"Thank you, sir. And thanks for getting us out of trouble."

"It's all teamwork, we had to work together."

"Have you seen Slick?"

"He just walked into maintenance control."

"Okay, I'll catch him there, thanks."

Slick and I went back to his room for a while. We were still nervous, and knew it would help to talk about our frightening experience. "You know, Slick," I said, "I couldn't see shit for ten or fifteen seconds after that lightning flash."

"I didn't get flash-blinded, but I had vertigo so bad I couldn't stay in level flight. We're lucky we didn't bust our asses, Sweetwater."

"You can say that again. It's a good thing Kistler was there to guide us."

We had the rest of the week off from flying to prepare for exams. Midweek we had a lecture on formation flying, and once our exams were completed, we would start our form hops. This phase of training would consist of nine two-plane flights, four solo two-plane flights, three four-plane hops, and two four-plane solo flights.

Slick and I and a couple other students spent the rest of the week studying and reviewing for the tests. It was important to get good grades during the first semester, because things did not get any easier as the university program progressed. By week's end Slick and I both felt comfortable with the material to be tested, so Sunday we treated ourselves to a night on the town.

We had an early dinner and relaxed at Molar Man's before heading home. This would probably be our last time at his place before he closed for the winter. As we were leaving we thanked him for his hospitality.

"We'll see you in the spring," I said. "And if we can manage it, we'll help get the place squared away for opening day like we did this year."

"You've got a deal," he replied. "Catch a few three-wires for me when you hit the boat this winter."

"Roger that," Slick said as we ducked out.

Our test schedule for the following week was math on Monday, aero on Wednesday, and physics on Friday. Thursday at the field we had our formation brief and the following Monday would be our first hop. We'd get a couple weeks off from school after exams and start our second semester midmonth. From then until Christmas break, the pace would be a real ballbuster.

The tests were like anything else: if you knew the material, it was straightforward. We both felt we did well on the exams and we'd receive our grades at the beginning of our second semester.

The formation brief was given by Lieutenant Commander Ken Roads, better known as "Dusty," the head instructor for this phase of flight training.

The eight of us going through the master's program were broken up into two flights of four. Slick and I were in the "Topcat" flight with Bobby Price and Freddy Sexton. The other four students were in the "Tigercat" flight. "Hellcat" was my form instructor, "Stainless" was Slick's, "Garters" was assigned to Bobby, and Lieutenant Thomas "Sundance" Karnes, he had the flaming mustache, was Freddy's instructor.

After the brief was over, we broke up into our flights. The senior instructor for each flight handed out baseball caps that had our flight's call sign embroidered over the bill. Our caps were orange and white and Lieutenant Commander Kistler was the senior instructor. Sundance was an assistant landing signal officer, and this phase of flight training promised to be real fun.

Most of the weekend was spent learning formation procedures. The first position we would be introduced to would be the parade position. The parade wing position is a fixed position on a forty-five-degree bearing from the leader with approximately seventy feet between corresponding parts of the aircraft. The proper safety clearances were nine feet nose to tail, ten feet wingtip distance, and four feet of stepdown. Some of the other flight positions that would be introduced on our first hop were the cruise position, breakup-and-rendezvous procedure, crossunder, and lead change. Probably the most difficult of all the procedures was the breakup-and-rendezvous phase.

During the breakup-and-rendezvous procedure, the lead aircraft "kisses off" his wingman, breaks left executing 60-to-90 degrees angle-of-bank for a 180-degree heading change. Once steady in the opposite direction for five seconds, the lead aircraft then rolls into thirty degrees angle-of-bank in either direction until his wingman catches up to him and is back aboard in the parade position.

Within three seconds after the lead breaks, the wingman goes after the leader by adjusting his airspeed and altitude. As the wingman closes on the leader's bearing line, he adjusts his closure rate until he is established on the outside of the leader's turn. The rendezvous is completed when the wingman stabilizes back in the parade position. Each student gets to fly several breakups, then a lead change is made and you repeat the maneuver again.

Slick and I were paired up for our two plane formation hops and we were burning up the syllabus by its completion. On our last two-plane form hops we overheard Ringer and Kistler talking about Lieutenant Commander Roads in the locker room. They were saying what a horse's ass he was and that he had turned into a full-blown screamer.

I leaned a little closer, trying to keep my presence a secret. This was juicy stuff.

Kistler said, "You know there are students who purposely get grounded so they won't have to fly with him."

"Maybe you should talk to him, Garters. He'll listen to you," Hellcat suggested.

"I have, but it doesn't work. But I have a plan to show Dusty what a real jerk he's turned into."

"Let me hear it."

"Later," Garters said. He was laughing like a madman, so I knew it had to be a good plan. I looked at Slick, and he just shrugged, then punched the air to show his disappointment. We tiptoed away before we got discovered.

We were concerned, because Dusty was scheduled to fly as our chase pilot on our four-plane solo flight. But we had a couple of flights to go before we had to deal with him. Even though he was the best in the business and was the formation department head, nobody, including the instructors, cared to be around him because of his lousy attitude. We figured he was burned out and needed a change of scenery.

Our four-plane hops started off a little roughly. It took a while for us to gain one another's confidence, but by the end of our dual instruction we were looking pretty good. Not as close as the Blue Angels, but almost. After a month and a half of yanking and banking, we began to feel like genuine naval aviators.

Monday was our four-plane solo flight with Dusty Roads. He would decide if we were ready to go into the final two phases of our basic training, guns and carrier qualification. Knowing that the instructors didn't particularly care for him made me concerned about his decision-making process. I had come this far without any major problems and I didn't want to have my record tarnished because he was having a bad day and wanted to take it out on someone.

We were scheduled for a nine o'clock brief with an eleven o'clock go. At ten after nine, Lieutenant Commander Roads had not yet shown. We were all hoping to get someone else, but no such luck. Shortly thereafter he walked into the brief and threw his briefcase down on the table in front of the chalkboard.

"You guys got your shit together?" he asked. "Because if you don't, your buck stops here."

It was a fine way to start a brief with four nervous students, I thought. He had to be a horse's ass. Ringer and Kistler were right: he'd lost it.

The brief was cut-and-dried. When he finished, he said, "I'll meet you out on the hold-short line for a radio check." Then he picked up his briefcase and stomped out. We looked at one another in disbelief.

After we suited up, we went to maintenance control to check out our machines and the shit hit the fan. To our surprise Hellcat, Garters, Stainless, and Sundance were waiting for us when we entered.

Kistler pulled us aside. "You fellows relax," he said, "and enjoy the show."

"What do you mean?" I asked. "We've got a four-plane hop to fly."

"Not anymore, Sweetwater. We're going to take your places and teach old Dusty a lesson."

"Holy shit!" I looked over at Slick.

"We're going to get our asses kicked," he said.

"Don't worry, men," Kistler said, with a shit-eating grin on his face. "The old man is in on the joke. We've been planning this for weeks. Now take off your gear and go up to the tower. Watch and listen to the 'Sherman Screamer' in action on channel five."

Channel five was the tactical frequency that formation hops used to talk on.

"Sherman Screamer," I said.

Kistler nodded. "Yeah, Lieutenant Commander Roads."

We ran back to the locker room, took off our gear, and headed over to the tower. By the time we got up in the tower, our instructors had completed their preflights and were starting their planes. They had arranged to have Dusty's plane parked way down on the end of the line so he couldn't see what was happening.

The flight disposition was: Hellcat in aircraft 310, Garters in 350, Stainless in 160, Sundance in 130, and Lieutenant Commander Roads in 300. The whole division was called "Topcat Flight." Dusty would follow in trail and tell the lead aircraft what he wanted to see. Whoever had the flight lead would execute the maneuver and the others would follow suit.

The aircraft were supposed to take off in two sections, then join up in a four-plane division once airborne. Prior to taking the runway, Dusty wanted to get a radio check. This is where the trouble began.

"Three-one, how do you read?" Dusty asked.

Hellcat replied, "Loud and clear, sir."

"Three-five, how do you read?"

Garters comes back, "Five by five, sir."

"One-six, how do you read?"

Nothing but silence from Stainless's aircraft.

"One-six, how do you read?"

No reply.

"One-six, do you read me?"

Again nothing. Five octaves higher, Dusty said, "One-six, if you read me, nod your head, nod your head."

Stainless starts nodding his head. Dusty comes back, "That's it. Okay sixteen, check all your connections."

Finally Stainless comes up, "16 to three hundred . . . how do you read?"

"Loud and clear, sixteen."

The four of us and the tower crew are laughing uncontrollably now.

"One-three, how do you hear?"

Sundance replies, "You're very weak but readable, sir."

"Okay, Topcats, take the runway and climb up to four thousand feet heading 270 degrees."

Each aircraft lined up on the runway in right echelon. The steplike formation from left to right was thirty-one, thirty-five, sixteen, and thirteen. When the first aircraft rolled, there was to be a six-second delay before the next plane took off and so on down the line. After thirty-one rolled, Garters waited until Hellcat got airborne before he started his roll. Stainless, who was in sixteen, started his roll two seconds after Garters rolled and they made a section takeoff.

Now we can hear Dusty in the background, yelling, "No! No! No!"

Sundance in thirteen takes off when the other two break ground. Dusty takes the duty and makes a roll-and-go takeoff without stopping to check his brakes. He was in a hurry to get airborne, trying to get everyone back together.

After they are all airborne, Topcat Flight comes up on channel five like a telephone party line, asking where each other is located so that they can join up.

Dusty goes nuts. "Knock that shit off, damn it!"

Everything goes silent at this point.

After ten minutes of flying, the flight finally gets into right-echelon balance flight. Dusty comes up on the radio and tells thirty-one, who has the lead, to make a thirty-degree left-hand turn. He then says, "If you read me, thirty-one, nod your head."

Thirty-one nods.

"Thirty-five, nod your head."

Thirty-five nods.

"Sixteen, nod your head."

Sixteen nods.

"Thirteen, nod your head. Thirteen, nod your head. That's it, Thirteen, really nod your head, that's it."

The next second, Hellcat rolls into a left sixty-degree angle of bank and descends to three thousand feet. Roads goes crazy and starts screaming, "Level out, level out, thirty-one, Topcat thirty-one, level out."

Now thirty-one and thirty-five go low, sixteen and thirteen can't react fast enough, so they fly over the top of thirty-one and thirty-five. Sixteen now has the lead and thirteen is off his right wing. When thirty-one and thirty-five level out, they climb back to four thousand feet and join on thirteen's wing.

The division is in right echelon, turning port. Dusty is screaming for sixteen to fly straight and level. Once he gets the flight straight and level, he tells them, "You assholes better start paying attention or we'll have a midair." They all start nodding their heads.

By now Roads has had it and tells sixteen to turn the flight to a heading of east and head back to Sherman. Stainless gives the free cruise signal to spread the aircraft out and enters a graveyard spin, which is a tight spiral with the nose of the aircraft pointed straight toward hell.

Dusty again starts screaming, "Pull out, sixteen, pull out! Sixteen, pull out!"

At 2,500 feet, sixteen levels out. At this point Dusty is screaming so loudly you can't understand him. Stainless climbs back up to the formation, which is heading back to the base. The flight disposition now has thirteen in the lead, thirty-one on his right wing, thirty-five on thirty-one's right wing, and sixteen on thirty-five's right wing.

Dusty comes up behind the flight and gets abeam sixteen's left side. He then tells sixteen to follow him home. Sixteen gives the carrier breakup-and-rendezvous signal to the rest of the flight.

Roads starts screaming, "No! No! No!" as he breaks left. Sixteen breaks into the echelon and the rest of the flight scatters, almost running into each other.

After fifteen minutes of circling and regrouping, the flight finally gets back into formation and is headed toward Sherman once more.

Dusty calls the tower. "Tower, I got four scared chickens in the air. Be ready to roll the crash crew."

As the Topcat Flight entered the break the first plane broke left, the second plane broke right, and the other two continued straight ahead. As the two planes approached the 180 neither of them had their gear down. The runway duty officer shoots his flare gun, signaling them to wave it off. They both added power and climbed out, passing each other at the ninety-degree position. It looked real scary, even though we knew that everything had been planned and they knew exactly what they were doing.

After all the aircraft landed safely, Dusty told the students to report to his office as soon as they stored their flight gear. The instructors hustled in and out of maintenance control before Dusty entered. As planned, the plane captain made sure Dusty was parked at the other end of the flight line. This gave the instructors time to get out of sight.

Twenty minutes later the four instructors walked into Dusty's office. As they all lined up in front of his desk, he said, "What do you guys want? I've got some downs to give to four of the worst form students I've ever seen."

"Say, Dusty," Garters said, "we're your four students."

"What do you mean, you're my students?"

"We four were flying."

"Bullshit!" he said. "I had . . ." Then it hit him. "Why you son of a bitch, Kistler, we could have all been killed out there. Get out of my office! Get out!"

The instructors filed out of his office and headed to the officers' club. Lieutenant John Myers, the air traffic control officer, had made a voice tape of the whole flight and we all reviewed it while having a few beers.

Dusty, though, went directly to the commanding officer and vented his frustration. The CO explained that he was getting a bad reputation for being a screamer and nobody wanted to fly with him. The skipper added, "When it was brought to your attention, you refused to accept the criticism. That's why I allowed this flight to happen. I felt if you heard what you sounded like in the air, you might take a good look at your instructional technique and clean up your act."

After an hour in the old man's office, Dusty still couldn't believe that he was labeled as a screamer and refused to accept the advice. The CO finally ordered Dusty to take three days leave. "Get your battery recharged before coming back to work," he said. Dusty left the skipper's office in a huff, vowing to get even with the bastard who set him up.

The following day we flew the four-plane hop without any problems. Garters Kistler ran the department and flew as our chase pilot while the "Sherman Screamer" took a few days off to cool his jets.

HEARTS AND DIAMONDS

After we finished our formation training, I began to feel like a real pilot. I felt I had gained the respect of my superiors and that they wanted me to be part of the team. But I realized that I still had some road left before I wore those wings of gold.

Slick and I each were several weeks into our second semester with a strong grade-point average. We had done exceptionally well during the first quarter and we wanted to continue enjoying that feeling. But our next two phases of training would really separate the men from the boys. Guns and carrier quals could end your aspirations of becoming a naval aviator in a heartbeat. These two stages of training were probably the most dangerous and difficult in our whole syllabus.

As for our previous phases, we had a thorough briefing on the T-2 weapon system. We would be using the LATAGS, which stands for laser air-to-air gunnery system, for guns. This system allows the pilot to shoot laser pulses at a retroreflective target. The device fires at a rate of 1,500 pulses per minute with the simulated machine-gun sound transmitted to your helmet headset. All pulses emitted are registered on counters in the front and rear cockpits. LATAGS does not simulate ballistics of real ordnance because of its instantaneous flat-line trajectory.

The system consists of three components: the gunsight, which has a transmitter\receiver in the front cockpit, an armament panel in the front cockpit, and a remote hit indicator located in the rear cockpit. The system is fired by depressing the trigger on the stick.

The gunnery syllabus consisted of ten flights, six with an instructor using the LATAGS system, and the last four, live-firing hops. I would be expected to maneuver my aircraft in harmony with three others at speeds up to three hundred knots, into a firing position on a towed banner. The "squirrel-cage" gunnery pattern may be compared to a circle. The four firing aircraft move around the periphery of this circle, ninety degrees apart. The circle moves along relative to the speed and direction of the towing aircraft.

After several trainers I got my procedures down and was ready to tackle the real McCoy. My first three flights were not pretty. I had problems getting into a firing position. After my fourth hop I suddenly got the picture and was hitting the target with every shot. Slick was a natural and was eating up the program. But he probably had the best instructor for the phase. Garters Kistler had won the air-to-air gunnery championship three years in a row and he passed his techniques on to those he instructed.

We were almost halfway through the syllabus when Slick started to get canceled a lot. We found out that Lieutenant Commander Kistler had received orders and was being transferred to the West Coast, and schedules was having difficulty finding an instructor to take over his student load. He had been due to rotate in six months, but it was rumored that a pilot had been killed and they needed a second tour pilot as soon as possible, so they'd accelerated his rotation date by five months.

Toward the end of the week Slick ran into Kistler at the exchange and chatted for a short while. Slick said Garters looked real tired and barely had time to talk.

"Well," I asked, "is he happy about the move?"

"Yeah, but he said he was having trouble selling his house. His realtor was bringing a client by to view the house and he was late, that's why he was in such a hurry."

"Boy, I hope I don't have to make a move that quick."

"Me, too. It wouldn't be so bad if the move were close by, but to have to move to the West Coast like yesterday, that's pretty tough."

"What's his family going to do?" I asked.

"I guess they'll rent here until his children finish school in the spring."

* * *

When I returned from my sixth gun hop, I checked the board for the next week's flights and noticed I wasn't flying Monday, then realized that it was a holiday. Slick had been assigned to Sundance and would remain his student until we finished hitting the boat. As I headed toward the locker room I noticed a flier on the door. It was an invite for instructors and students to say good-bye to Garters Monday at 1600. I noted the time and stored it in my computer. After I changed out of my flight gear, I headed back to the BOQ.

As I pulled into my assigned parking spot I could see Slick waving frantically at me from his window. Once I was out of the car, I could hear him yelling for me to get up to his room. Passing by my room, I dropped off my dirty flight gear and proceeded up to Slick's abode.

When I reached the door, I asked, "What in the hell is all the racket about?"

He said, "Water, we deserve a break today and I have the formula for the relief."

"Lay it on me," I replied.

"Let's head to Hot'lanta for the three-day weekend and chase some pelt."

"I like it," I said.

"We've got a place to stay and a couple of dates lined up if you want to rock-and-roll."

"Well, let's kick the tires and light the fires. Give me a few minutes to get packed and we'll roll. I'll drive and you can give me the details on the way."

"Roger that. I'll meet you at the Silver Fox in twenty minutes."

With spectacles, testicles, watch, and wallet aboard, we put the top down and were Atlanta bound within the hour. It was early afternoon and we had about a six-hour drive staring us in the face. Once we cleared the city limits and hit the interstate, I let the Fox purr. I briefed Slick on Tuesday's events, of which he was already aware, with the exception of Garters's farewell.

"We'll have to pick something up for him while we're in Atlanta," he said.

"Sounds good. Okay, now, Slick, let me hear the game plan and who we're staying with."

"First off, we're spending the weekend at my cousin's apartment in Peach Tree City. She's a landscape architect for a prominent Atlanta firm."

"How come we haven't visited her before now?" I asked.

"She just moved there, according to my parents. I gave her a call and asked her if she would like some company this weekend. She was all for it and said she had some friends that liked to party that we might enjoy meeting."

"What about her?" I asked.

"What do you mean?"

"What does she look like? Maybe I'll go after her."

"She's a plain Jane, about a strong five on the ten scale."

"Is she spoken for?"

"I think she's engaged."

The drive was scenic and interesting up to Montgomery, Alabama, then we ran into some weather outside of Auburn that continued all the way to LaGrange. This slowed our progress considerably, and we didn't arrive until a little after eight. The area where Slick's cousin lived was beautiful. The grounds were well manicured and it was a gated community.

When Corky, Slick's cousin, opened the door, I about dropped my eyeteeth. She was strikingly beautiful, with long strawberry-blond hair, and I knew Slick had suckered me in again. I was speechless when he introduced me to her. I could barely say hello. Once inside, she gave us the nickel tour and showed us where we could freshen up.

After she and Slick got caught up on all the family affairs and he brought her up to speed on his activities, she asked if we were up for a party.

Slick and I looked at each other and said, "Lead the way."

Corky said, "One of my colleagues is having a get-together in our party room and several of my single friends'll be there, so I'm sure you fellas can enjoy yourselves. Jim, my boyfriend, will be in town tomorrow, and if you'd like, we can take you to some of the hot spots around town."

"Sounds good, Corky," Slick said. "We just want to relax and unwind for a few days."

The party room was a couple of blocks away, and as we approached it I could tell things were under way by all the noise. Once inside, Corky introduced us to a couple of her friends and then turned us loose. The southern hospitality was warm and the women were gorgeous. Slick and I wasted no time picking out targets of opportunity.

As the night progressed we locked onto a couple of

girls but decided it was too late to put a full-court press on, so we set the stage for the next night's gala events. Both women worked for a marketing agency in Decatur, just north of Atlanta. We made plans to meet at eight at the Plantation, a well known nightclub near Stone Mountain.

The next day we picked Jim up at the airport. After he got cleaned up and changed, Corky and he showed us the sights around Atlanta. Jim was an executive for an advertising agency and had been in Boston negotiating a contract when we arrived in town. We had a late lunch at a restaurant in Atlanta's famed underground and were home by six.

Slick and I talked over our game plan before we left the house. Our main objective for the night was to get the girls to visit us in Pensacola, and if we got lucky, all the better. As I doused on some "sweetwater" Corky announced the bus was leaving, so we hopped in Jim's BMW and headed for the nightclub.

We arrived a little before eight and found a table almost in front of the dance floor. It was an ideal spot if you liked dancing and it was center stage for the band. Judy and Anna, the girls we had met the night before, arrived twenty minutes later and I made the introductions. I was interested in Judy and Slick liked Anna. As the night progressed I could see Judy was playing the cat-and-mouse game with me. She was analyzing my tactics, seeing if I was sincere or just out for a quick trip to the rack.

Being the gentleman I am, I played it like a true pro. Slick observed the same treatment, so it was easily perceived that the ladies had had a strategy session before show time. We partied until the wee hours of the morning, and when it was time to call it a night, we walked them to their car and said our good-nights. The ladies seemed to be impressed with our act, and when asked to visit us in Pensacola, they were more than happy to accept.

Tuesday was my first live-gun-firing hop and Slick was getting a back-in-the-saddle hop with his new instructor.

Lieutenant Commander Ringer gave me a lengthy brief and explained the differences between live-firing runs and LATAGS shots. We were in the air within two hours from the scheduled brief and I was lining up for my first run. I checked that my gun-firing switch was armed and started tracking the target, remembering to lead it and correct for wind. As I rolled in, a diamond image circumscribed the target and I depressed the trigger for a short burst then pulled off target. After several passes I began to feel more at ease.

Upon completion of the hop and debrief, I felt pretty good about my progress. I was looking forward to my next two hops, air-to-ground rocketry and bombing.

At 1530 we all gathered in our ready-room space to say good-bye to Garters. Most of the instructors and students were present, with the exception of Dusty. The instructors had a cake to present along with a few gifts and I would present him with a luggage set on behalf of our class.

As the ship's bell rang on the hour Garters entered the ready room to cheers and handclapping. There were numerous speeches made and gifts handed out before Garters himself was allowed to speak. After the last gift was presented, he walked to the front of the room. Just then, the ready-room door opened and the place went wild.

A half-naked girl, whose endowments were obvious, boogalooed across the floor, accompanied by stomping feet, whistles, and catcalls. She wiggled a little bit, shimmied up to Garters, and said, "I have a singing telegram for Lieutenant Commander Kistler."

Once the wolf whistles stopped, Garters, who was a pretty shade of pink by now, said, "Let's hear it."

"Roses are red, violets are blue, your orders have been canceled, and the joke is on you." As everyone stared she did a 180 and left.

No sooner was she out the door than Dusty Roads entered. The room went dead quiet, and he smiled as he said, "Your verbals and all this orders crap is bogus. I had it all made up. Maybe that'll teach you not to fuck with me again, asshole." He slammed the door on his way out.

"You've got to be shitting me," Garters said, over and over again. "Karen is going to cut my balls off. I sold our house, disrupted this squadron, and now I have no fleet squadron to go to. You've got to be shitting me."

At that point the rest of the instructors started to laugh, and before long everyone, including Garters, was laughing his ass off. When the noise subsided, Garters said, "I guess he got the last laugh."

Garters and Hellcat were talking after the crowd broke up and they figured out how Dusty managed to pull it off. He used to be a detailer in Washington, and since he knew how the system worked, it was an easy scam. Garters never figured the joke would go this far, but he made light of it and put the best face on things by saying, "I didn't like where I was living anyway. I only hope Karen has a good sense of humor."

We had a week off after we finished our weapons training and completed our tests before starting Field Carrier Landing Practice. We planned our mission around those events. After a few more confidence builders, I told Slick that I was going to call Judy and see if their schedule would coincide with ours. Slick thought it was a splendid idea, so I headed for the blower.

After a half-dozen rings Judy picked up and sounded pleasantly surprised to hear my voice. She was very receptive to the plan and would let us know once she checked with Anna. The rendezvous would occur in two weeks, if our schedule progressed as planned. I briefed Slick on the conversation and we went to dinner.

The rest of the week would be "shake-and-bake" hops for Slick and me, a term we used when shooting guns and dropping bombs. Slick would get back into the guns syllabus and I would start bombing training. Air-to-ground weapons delivery is much more dangerous than the air-to-air mission. Traditionally the air-to-ground mission produces a higher mishap rate due to target fixation, where the aircrew become so absorbed, they fly into the ground. A whole day's worth of briefings was devoted to target fixation and you can bet the briefer had my full attention.

The weapon systems that Slick and I would be dealing with in the fleet would be more sophisticated than the ones in the training command. But a complete understanding of this tactical phase was vital to our future if we were to qualify for fighters. The actual pattern while bombing was probably the most important. A good start will produce excellent target hits, whereas a poor start can cost you your ass. The dive angle, run-in-line, which is what we called the flight path to the target, and release altitude are a few areas that need to be exact to get optimum results.

The flight would consist of four planes, and each aircraft would be carrying six practice bombs weighing one hundred pounds each. Our brief lasted almost two hours, with movies showing correct and incorrect bombing patterns and aircraft models to demonstrate proper positioning. After having a good visual picture of what to look for, I felt more confident going into the actual flight.

Once we were all suited up, our instructors showed us what to look for when preflighting the bomb racks. They reviewed the hand signals the ordnancemen would be flashing at us during the arming of the bombs and went over the cockpit switch-ology.

The bombing pattern would be flown at 10,000 feet with the hard deck at five. This meant you couldn't fly below five thousand feet. This would prevent your aircraft from getting hit by its own frag pattern when

dropping live ordnance. We would each get two practice runs before rolling in hot.

After we took off and joined up as a flight of four, it
took twenty minutes to get to the range. Once set up
in the pattern, we commenced our practice runs. I
was number two in the division. The game plan was
to have one plane over target while the next aircraft
was rolling in. A nice tight pattern was the ultimate
goal. The instructors flew the first pass so we could
observe the proper checkpoints throughout the pattern, then we would fly a couple of passes to get the
feel of things before making our hot runs.

Hellcat gave me the aircraft when I was headed
downwind and abeam the drop zone. The target was a
large circle with three larger rings around the center
circle, each ring two hundred feet from the next. As I
approached the run-in-line I rolled 120 degrees to
pick up the track inbound. It wasn't as easy as it
looked. I rolled out left of the center line and my dive
angle was too steep, which would have made my
delivery land short of the target. My second practice
run was much better, and when it came time to put
bombs on the target, I was in the ball park.

The debrief was rather lengthy and we went over
each bombing run in detail. I knew where I had made
my mistakes and would correct them on my next hop.
I felt confident in my ability to put the aircraft where it
needed to be. I just needed the experience of flying
the air-to-ground pattern. Hellcat pointed out that on
one of my runs I got target fixation and flew through
the hard deck of five thousand feet. I knew exactly
which run he was talking about. I got so excited about

hitting the target one pass that I lost situational awareness on the next trying to follow one of my bombs to
the impact area. I quickly changed and headed back to
the BOQ to see if I had any messages from Judy. As I
approached my room I could see that there was no
note pinned to my door, so I slowed down. Once
inside, I sat down in my brown leather easy chair and
stared at my desk. It was covered with study material
for the upcoming tests. I felt like puking.

After I'd been veging out for an hour, Slick
knocked on the door.

"Want to go get something to eat?" he asked.

"No."

"Come on, Water, it'll do you good. You can't sit
here staring at the books all the time."

"You talked me into it."

He could see I was feeling sorry for myself. The
pressure of school was getting to me and I needed a
lift and Slick knew it.

While at dinner I said, "I'm tired of not being able
to get away from work."

"What do you mean, Water?"

"Well, we go to the squadron to fly, then we head
off to the university to study, then we come back to
the base to live in a one-room cell and study some
more. It seems like we never get away from our work.
I need a change of scenery and more living space.
Did you know most of our classmates live off base?"

"No, I didn't."

"What do you say we look for a place this weekend?"

"What do you have in mind?"

"We both like the beach, and with the winter coming, we might find a good deal. We get promoted next month, and with our pay raise we should be able to find something that will fit our budget."

It didn't take much to convince him, because he was almost as stir-crazy as I was. "It's worth a try," he agreed. "Let's take a look."

We kept the move quiet so as not to draw too much attention. Fortunately our flight grades and grade-point averages were high enough to allow us to move off the base.

By the middle of the week we were settled in. I couldn't believe what a psychological difference it made living off base. I felt like a new man. Sure, the drive to work took longer and we had to get up earlier, but just to hear the pounding surf at night and smell the salt air in the evening breeze made all the trouble worthwhile.

The week before the girls came to town was a busy one. We had two finals to take and a briefing on FCLPs. This would be our final phase in the T-2 before starting advanced training in the TA-4 Skyhawk jet. After we successfully completed carrier quals, we would start our final phase of training. It was hard to believe that in a few short weeks Slick and I would be landing on an aircraft carrier.

Judy and Anna were scheduled to arrive around four, so Slick and I spent most of the afternoon cleaning the house and stocking the refrigerator. We planned to invite the girls over for cocktails and show them the house before going to dinner.

The afternoon was warm, so we went bodysurfing after the house was squared away. It felt good not having to worry about school for the next couple of weeks, and the thought of being three quarters of the way through flight training was rewarding. But we had the Vietnam War facing us head-on, with the distinct possibility of both of us seeing combat within a year. We figured we'd have fun while we could.

We swam for almost an hour before calling it quits. While Slick got cleaned up I prepared some Gulf Coast shrimp for an appetizer and chilled the champagne. The house looked like a million bucks and the whole setup had the makings of a grand and glorious weekend. Just before I hopped into the shower, the phone rang and Slick picked it up. It was the girls. He talked to them while I showered.

Stepping out of the shower still dripping wet, I asked, "Did they say how the trip went?"

"They said they had a nice drive and were looking forward to a fun-filled weekend."

"What time did you tell them we'd pick them up?"

"About an hour. They wanted to get the road dust off and unwind a bit."

"Perfect. Shall we go together to get them?"

"I'll go. You relax and get dressed."

When Slick left to get the girls, I was going to start a fire in the fireplace, but it was so warm it wasn't necessary. I put the hors d'oeuvres on the living-room table and was opening the champagne when I heard Slick open the front door. I came out of the kitchen to welcome the girls and was pleasantly surprised by how charming they looked. The weekend was off to a

good start. After an hour or so of getting reac-
quainted, we left the house and went to dinner at the
Cove, a five-star restaurant overlooking the ocean. As
we finished dinner Judy leaned over to put her arms
around me and gave me a passionate kiss.

I was a little stunned.

"I'm having a wonderful time," she said.

I started to wonder what might be on her mind.
We went dancing for a couple of hours after dinner
then headed back to the beach. As we drove over the
Three-Mile Bridge Judy was all over me and we were
in a lather when we arrived at the house.

"You two better go for a walk on the beach and
cool off before you blow a fuse," Anna said.

While the girls freshened up, Slick made us some
drinks and I changed into my beach clothes. When
they came out of the bathroom, I knew they had a
game plan. I'd watched my three sisters operate over
the years, so I knew something was cooking. It
would be interesting to see how they were going to
execute it. After twenty minutes or so Judy suggested we go for a walk on the beach. Very clever, I
thought, I better look excited about the walk or she
may think I'm in a hurry to get her behind closed
doors. Of course, that's all I could focus on, but the
games must go on.

When we got back to the house, we made enough
noise to alert the neighborhood of our arrival, not
knowing what Slick and Anna might be up to.

When we entered, they were sitting on the couch
having some wine. After some small talk the girls
decided to call it a night and asked if we would take

them home. Slick and I looked at each other and I said, "Shall we walk or drive?"

Since we were only a few blocks away, we walked them to their room, said our good-nights, then headed home. As we walked back we compared notes and couldn't figure out what they were up to. They had about ripped our clothes off at one time or another during the evening, yet they wouldn't commit themselves to going all the way.

"I don't like it," I told Slick.

"You don't like what?"

"I don't like this cat-and-mouse play. We're all grown-ups, why are they pulling our chains like this? I'm so goddamn horny that the crack of dawn gets me excited. I've been working too hard. I need some loving, Slick."

"It's that southern-belle mentality, Water. They like to be pampered and courted, you know what I mean?"

"Yeah, but while we're playing games, I'm about to explode."

"You're not the only one. If you could have seen the tag match we had while you two were on the beach, you'd have thought I had been laid ten times over. These gals are just playing hard to get. Let's get some sleep and tackle the challenge tomorrow."

By noon the next day we were up and ready to party. The day was warm, so we decided to spend the afternoon at the beach. While waiting for the women to show, Slick made some snacks and I brewed up some fishhouse punch, a perfect drink for a warm afternoon.

We took our picnic basket and beach chairs to the

water's edge and set up camp. As we baked in the sun and enjoyed the water, I became uneasy with Judy's appearance. Don't get me wrong, she was a knockout in her swimsuit. It was her legs that turned me off. She hadn't shaved them for a while and the hair wasn't very becoming. I didn't say anything until we were about to leave and I couldn't keep my mouth shut any longer.

While we were deciding what we were going to do that evening, I interrupted the conversation and said, "We're not going anywhere until Judy shaves those wheels."

"Well, Matt," she said, "if they bother you that much, you shave them."

"You've got a deal, my dear."

Slick rolled his eyes in disbelief. "I've got to witness this one. It has to be a first."

She had called my bluff, but I would be goddamned if I was going to let her off the hook. When we got back to the house, I told her to get out of her wet suit and put something dry on. Slick and Anna waited in awe, thinking I had no idea what I was up to.

Within a few minutes Judy came out of the bathroom with a towel wrapped around her and in a smart-ass tone said, "I'm at your service, sir."

At that point I took the floor. "Now," I said, "I want you to sit down and relax on the sofa and imagine that you're in an exclusive beauty salon in Beverly Hills. Sweetwater's House of Beauty."

While they were getting situated I opened a bottle of champagne and served each of them a glass. "Please enjoy," I said, playing the part of the owner with a French accent. "Madame Judy, I believe you're next."

I escorted her to my bathroom. I helped her get seated on the counter near the sink and had her raise her right leg. She was starting to look a little nervous.

"Judy, I want you to sit back, relax, and enjoy the music while sipping champagne, and leave the rest to me."

"You won't cut me, will you?"

"Why, heavens no, my dear," I replied. "I've been doing this for years without a cut or scratch." I could hear Slick and Anna chuckling in the background.

With the bathroom radio tuned to some soft music and the red heat lamp activated, the atmosphere was set for Sweetwater's first leg shave. Continuing with the accent, I said, "Judy, I will now prepare your right leg for a most sensuous and soothing shave. Would you like the summer rate or winter rate?"

"What might the difference be?"

"The winter rate is a shave just above the knee and the summer rate is higher to accommodate the swim-suit look."

"Oh, I see," she said. "Why don't you give me the winter rate on my right leg and the summer rate on my left leg?"

"Very well," I said, knowing that I had her full attention.

At this point I turned on the hot water and waited until it was steaming. Then I took a washcloth and saturated it with the hot water, rinsed it off, and placed it just above the kneecap. She jumped a bit, but in a soft voice I said, "Relax! Enjoy!"

I moved the hot towel slowly up and down her leg. Once the leg was nicely massaged, I applied shaving cream. I could see Judy was really getting into the mood. Her eyes were closed and she was seductively grooving to the music.

Slick and Anna were watching from the doorway when Anna said, "I want to be next."

After an afternoon of drinking, and feeling no pain at this point, I knew I had to be careful not to cut her. I took my Trac II razor and shaved her leg as smooth as a newborn baby's bottom. After checking around the kneecap and ankle, I again turned on the hot water and rubbed her leg down, removing the unused shaving cream. Then I got some Vaseline Intensive Care lotion and applied it all over her leg.

I thought she was going to have an orgasm. The sexual excitement was so overwhelming she grabbed me and started kissing me uncontrollably. No slouch in the observation department, Slick said he was going to walk Anna back to the motel so she could get cleaned up for dinner.

I broke away from Judy and said, "We'll be over shortly."

"Not until you finish my other leg, buster," Judy commanded.

Once Slick and Anna were out the door, Judy jumped down and repositioned herself back up on the counter. She pulled me close and rubbed her breasts into my bare chest.

"If you keep this up," I said, "I won't be able to perform my job, madame."

"I doubt that," she replied.

As I started to put the hot cloth on her leg, she had positioned the towel so that I could see her bush, and she knew it. Trying not to stare, I started to apply the shaving cream again.

"Do you do hearts and diamonds?" she asked.

A bit confused, I said, "I beg your pardon?"

"Do you do design work—you know, hearts and diamonds?"

It finally hit me. I said, "Sure, what's your fancy?"

She dropped the towel and said, "I prefer hearts to diamonds."

I was trying to keep my composure while rising again to the occasion as she ceremoniously removed my clothes.

"Then, madame," I said, "hearts it will be. Just let me finish this leg before I fulfill your desire."

Having trouble concentrating on the leg, I completed the shave without a scratch while we embraced on the bathroom floor.

Coming up for air, I asked, "Are you serious about that design work?"

"You bet I am," she said, pulling me closer.

Before the night was over, Judy's bush had been shaped into a lovely heart.

We never did make it to dinner.

12

MEATBALL
LINEUP AOA

Now that our morale was boosted and our white count was back to normal, Slick and I were ready to experience the ultimate achievement of a naval aviator— landing 13,000 pounds of aircraft on the moving deck of an aircraft carrier. We were to start our field-carrier landing practice Monday morning. At 7:45 Slick, I, and six others sat in our ready room waiting for Lieutenant Sandy Mapleford. He was the training command's head landing signal officer and would brief us on events to come. The atmosphere in the room was tense, and you could feel the anxiety among the students.

A few minutes past the hour the lights dimmed and the projection screen automatically unrolled to begin a sound-on-sound slide presentation on carrier qualification. The slide show lasted twenty minutes. After the presentation the lights were turned back on and Lieutenant Mapleford, better known as M-plus-9, introduced himself.

"Gentlemen, welcome to the final phase of your basic flight training. I'm sure you'll find this the most rewarding of all your syllabus flights. In a few short weeks you'll join an elite group of aviators, those who have trapped aboard an aircraft carrier. But if you don't listen to me, you'll never see the flight deck of the *Lady Lex*."

Lieutenant Mapleford was a slenderly built man, with a beachboy image. But the word around the squadron was "Don't let his boyish looks fool you." He was a tough customer when it came to discipline around the boat, and rightfully so. One mistake and you get killed or kill someone else. When you're landing on a carrier deck, there's no room for error.

"You'll be divided into two flights," he said. "The first group of four will fly the planes over to Wolfe Field, which will be the practice field we use, and the second group will bus over. The second group will fly the birds home while the first group buses back to the base.

"Before going to the boat, gentlemen, you will have to pass a comprehensive exam on carrier procedures and get a thumbs-up from me, which you will have to earn. An instructor will lead you out to the ship, circle overhead until each of you gets six arrested landings, and then will escort you home. If you qualify, you'll start advanced training the following week. If you're disqualified, you will have a field evaluation board, to see if you will be allowed to continue in stage.

"If you get a thumbs-up, you go through the whole FCLP process again." He paused here for effect, before adding, "And if you get a thumbs-down, you will be washed out of the flight program. Understood?"

After the syllabus was laid out, Lieutenant Mapleford discussed the techniques of flying the optical landing system, better known as the "meatball" or lens. Although we had been using this system since we started flying navy aircraft, there had never been a real sound brief on its functions, especially for shipboard landings. Sandy took care of that.

"Think of the meatball as a cross. When the orange-ball image is in the middle, you are flying a correct approach. The meatball is set up for a three-and-a-half-degree glide slope to the deck, and if you keep the ball in the center of the cross, you should hook the three wire. There are four arresting cables on the carrier deck. The first wire is about 120 feet from the fantail and the other wires are about 40 feet apart. If you hook the one wire, you probably flew a low pass. If you catch a two or three wire, you were on glide path, and if you hook the four wire, you probably saw a high meatball all the way to touchdown."

He waited to see if there were any questions, then continued. "The ball will move up and down on five vertical square lenses depending on where you fly your aircraft. If you get too low, the ball falls to the bottom of the cross and starts to turn red. If your pass is unsafe or the deck has a problem, the airboss or LSO can wave you off by hitting the pickle switch.

This activates a set of red flashing lights in the center of the so-called cross, and it's a mandatory wave-off when these lights are activated."

Mapleford then explained the proper pattern at the ship. "Gentlemen, at three miles behind the carrier I want your aircraft at eight hundred feet, hook down, and 250 knots. At a quarter of a mile I want you to be at three to four hundred feet starboard of the island at eight hundred feet of altitude. When you're ten seconds past the bow, break left and descend to six hundred feet. On the downwind leg, lower your gear and flaps, establish fifteen units AOA—that's angle of attack for those of you who slept through the lecture—and complete your landing checklist. At the ninety-degree position you should be at four hundred feet and 15 units AOA. As you roll on final you want to intercept the glide path, working for a centered meatball. Your lineup should be straight down the center line of the landing area and AOA at fifteen units. Remember, gentlemen, a good start will result in a good pass. Your scan once on final should be—check the meatball, look at your lineup, check your AOA. This should continue until you are in close, then all attention should go to the meatball. Once the lens passes you by on the left, shift your scan straight ahead. If everything was done correctly, you should catch the two or three wire. Once you hit the deck, advance your throttles to full power, and when you feel the plane stop, go to idle."

He paused again, looking at our faces to make sure all this information was sinking in. "Once safely on deck, you now belong to the yellow shirts. They are the flight-deck directors and they will taxi you clear of the wires and get you lined up for your catapult shot. Watch their signals and follow their directions. But if at any time you feel uncomfortable, stop the aircraft and talk to the tower. At times they may try to rush you, so don't set yourself up for complacency. Remember you have checklist to complete before going to the catapult. Am I making myself clear?"

The flurry of heads nodding in unison told him he was. "After your cat shot climb straight ahead. When comfortable or when the airboss tells you, turn downwind and do your landing checklist. Once you've completed your sixth landing and you're catapulted off, you'll hear the airboss call, 'Gear up. Your signal is bingo.' At that point climb straight ahead until clear of the pattern, then join your instructor overhead the ship. After all students have joined back up, your instructor will escort you back to the base.

"Let's break for lunch and continue at 1300. Does anyone have any questions so far?"

By 12:50 we were all back from lunch and waiting for the next lecture. At 1:00 P.M. the lights dimmed, the screen automatically unrolled, and a film started. The movie lasted ten minutes: it was about aircraft crashes at the ship. When the lights were turned back on, you could hear a pin drop. Lieutenant Mapleford really had our attention now.

"Gentlemen, this film was not meant to be a scare tactic. It was shown to make you aware of what can happen at the ship, and believe me, I will not let you go to the boat if I feel you're not ready.

"I'm going to pass out the CV NATOPS, which is the carrier naval air-training and operating-procedures standardization manual. You must know this forward and backward before you go to the ship. You'll keep your same call signs. The Tigercats will fly first and the Topcats will bus over. There will be ten FCLP periods, your first and seventh hop will be with an instructor, and the rest of your flights will be solo. Your eleventh hop will be to the ship. Are there any questions?"

Again no one raised a hand. "Very well then, I'll see you in the pattern at Wolfe Field tomorrow. Tigercats brief at eight and I want to see the first aircraft on final at nine-fifteen. Topcats, your bus will leave from here at 8:30."

At eight the next morning Slick and I sat in on the Tigercats brief. We were pissed that we didn't get to fly first, but it worked out for the best. At 8:30 the bus picked us up and drove over to Wolfe Field.

The trip took forty minutes and the planes were coming into the break as we got off the bus. Watching the flight of four T-2s hit the break sent chills up my spine. I couldn't believe I was only a few flights away from my first carrier landing. As we watched the Tigercats bounce, our instructors pointed out certain mistakes they were making—for example, flying too close abeam, poor starts at the 180, and not flying the meatball to touchdown. The pointers made up for the bus trip over. Most of these mistakes were common for the first bounce period.

Within the hour I was strapping into my T-2 and Hellcat was in my backseat. I took off and climbed to six hundred feet above ground level then turned downwind. At that point Hellcat said he had the aircraft and showed me what a good pattern looked like. After two passes he gave the plane back to me.

"Okay, Sweetwater, show me what you've got," he said.

There were several voice reports that had to be made and the most significant call was to the LSO at the ninety-degree position. At this point I had to call, "Three hundred, Topcat, ball, 3.2, Sullivan."

This told the LSO the side number of the aircraft, what group was entering the pattern, and that I could see the meatball on the lens. The 3.2 was the amount of fuel I had in thousands of pounds and the pilot's last name was given on the first pass. If I couldn't see the meatball as I passed through the ninety-degree position, I would say, "Three hundred, Topcat, 3.2, clara," which alerted the LSO that I was either high or low coming through the ninety. With his trained eye, he would have me adjust my altitude accordingly.

My first pass looked like I had never flown a T-2 before. I was all over the sky and my ball control on the glide slope looked like a roller coaster. Hellcat told me to relax and not worry so much about getting the voice report out. He started making the calls for me and I began to fly a better pattern.

The left side of the runway at Wolfe Field was painted like a carrier deck and you had to land the plane in the designated carrier box. There were no wires, of course, but the LSO could tell what wire you would have caught if they were in battery. You were graded on each approach and these grades would determine if you could hack it at the ship. If you flew a 4.0 pass, you were graded with an okay underlined; if you flew between a 3.9 and 3.7, you received an okay grade; if you flew between a 3.6 and 3.0, you received a fair grade; and if you flew anything below a 3.0 pass, you got a no grade.

My first FCLP period was not a pretty sight. I had a lot of no-grades, several fairs, and a couple of okay gifts.

After my last pass M-plus-9 said, "Gear up signal delta."

This meant for me to climb to five thousand feet over the field and circle counterclockwise at two hundred knots. As the other airplanes completed their bounce period they would also climb to five thousand feet and join on me. Once all planes were aboard, I was to lead them back to NAS Sherman Field. This was called the "Wolfe Rendezvous" and whoever completed first would lead the formation back home.

At twelve o'clock we were to meet Lieutenant Mapleford for a debrief in the officers' club. We all gathered around several large tables for lunch, and after we ate, Sandy made his rounds, debriefing each of us in turn. Everyone was pretty humbled after the first FCLP period, but it was to be expected. Slick and I went home after the massacre at the O club, and laid out the FCLP pattern with tape in our living room. We walked around the pattern as though we were flying it, reciting our procedures and reviewing our mistakes. Within an hour or so we felt we had it wired.

The next day our flight got to fly first and we were

on our own. Stainless gave us our brief before we manned up and reviewed some of the common mistakes. All in all this was the best stage of flight training. We were treated with a little more respect and the student image wasn't so prominent.

Ensign Bobby Price led us over to Wolfe and I was number four in the formation. We had all flown together in the formation stage, so we were pretty confident of one another's capabilities. We kept the formation loose on our way over, but as we approached the initial for our straight-in, we tightened it up.

As we approached the numbers for the break we looked like the Blue Angels. Bobby broke at midfield and the rest of us each took an eight-second interval on the plane in front of us before we broke.

My homework had paid off. My first pass was right on. I hit every checkpoint and flew a rails pass to touchdown. As I climbed out after my first pass M-plus-9 came up on tactical and said, "Nice pass, 304."

This got me pumped and for the first time in the T-2, I began to feel in control of the situation. But by the end of my period my performance had deteriorated considerably.

Mine was the last aircraft to land in our group, and taxied up to the fuel pits and shut down. While the planes were being refueled for the next group, M-plus-9 debriefed us on our performance. I had a pretty good idea where I made my mistakes and Sandy confirmed my suspicions. But I felt good because I knew I could correct the problems. The hop was much better than my first and the trend was upward. After we received our debriefs we loaded into a van and headed toward NAS Pensacola. Slick, Freddy, and Bobby also did a nice job, so the atmosphere on the ride home was pleasant. It was great to see and feel the enthusiasm in our group.

We had a different driver from the one who drove us over the day before. This guy was older than dirt and we weren't sure he was going to make it home. Things were pretty quiet for the first several miles then the old boy piped up, "You fly-boys want to stop and have a beer at the Hit the Silk Tavern?"

We looked at each other uncertainly, not sure if it was legal or not. "Hell," he said, "I've been driving you college boys back and forth to Wolfe Field for fifteen years and there hasn't been a group of ya yet that turned me down."

Sitting in the front seat next to the driver, I turned to the rest of the guys and said, "We're done flying. Why not?"

They all said, "Let's hit it."

Toby, the driver, said, "Don't let Big Bertha intimidate you college boys. She's the owner and she tips the scales about three fifty." Without cracking a smile, he added, "I used to poke her back in my younger years, but she got so goddamn big that it took a hydraulic winch to get her off me."

We all looked at one another and started to laugh.

Toby continued, "I bet you fly-boys don't know how Bertha named this place."

Being the spokesman for the group, I said, "Nope, can't say we do."

"About twenty years ago some young fly-boy had to send his machine back to the taxpayers and bail out. Bertha and Claude, her ex-husband, were putting the finishing touches on their new establishment when this fly-boy came sailing through the front plate-glass window. To their surprise, he only had some minor cuts and bruises. They offered him a drink while he waited for the crash crew to pick him up, and named the tavern after that incident. As a matter of fact, Bertha still has some of his chute hanging behind the bar."

As we pulled into the dirt parking lot of the Hit the Silk, we weren't sure if old Toby was pulling our legs or not. He entered first and we followed. The place was a real dive, but it had character. The bar was straight in from the doorway, and there were two pool tables to the left of the bar. A shuffleboard table and dart board were set up in the back right corner. Pickle barrels were used for chairs at the bar and there was an old parachute draped on the back wall.

Bertha was working the bar when we entered. When she saw Toby, she came out from behind the bar and gave him a big bear hug and lifted him off the floor.

"Easy, Bertha," he said, "you're going to crush me."

"Ah, you old buzzard, you used to give me a run for my money a few years back."

"That's right, but you weren't the size of a tank then."

"Fuck you, you old bastard." She gave him another hug. "Say, are these the new fly-boys in town?"

"You've got it. They go to the boat at the end of the month."

"Did you tell them about Hector?"

"Not yet. I wanted them to get a few beers under their belts before I brought up the subject."

I looked at Slick and the rest of the guys with concern.

"All right, fellas, come on up to the bar," Bertha said. "The first drinks are on me."

After we all had a drink in our hands I asked Toby about Hector.

"Hector is a very, very large shark that follows the *Lady Lex* and eats its garbage as the crew throws it overboard," Toby explained. "He's been following that carrier for years and must weigh close to 1500 pounds now. He occasionally gets to eat a juicy young aviator every now and then!"

Freddy Sexton piped up. "Let's change the subject. We've got to tackle that carrier in a couple of weeks and I don't need to hear about a shark waiting to eat me."

Bertha and Toby got a good laugh out of his concern, but the rest of us had sheepish smiles.

With a wink I told Slick, "Grab your beer, sport. Time to get your butt wiped in a game of shuffleboard."

After a few games Toby said, "Come on, fly-boys, it's time to go."

We wrapped things up, paid our bill, and left. As we drove onto the base we could see the flight of four returning from Wolfe. Pretty good timing, I thought. We hopped out of the van, told Toby we would see him on the next cycle, got into the Blue Goose, and headed to the beach.

On the way home we compared notes on our performance in the pattern and also came to the conclusion that Toby and Bertha were probably married.

The little show they put on was a front to sidetrack us from their little scam. Scam or not, it was fun to stop and mingle with the locals. It kind of reminded me of some of the bars and people in New England.

As we got closer to the boat date I was beginning to feel confident about my progress. By the end of my sixth FCLP period, I was flying some good passes. Our seventh flight was with an instructor, who would be checking to see if we had developed any bad habits, and might throw in simulated emergencies to see how we handled them.

My check ride went well, but I didn't perform to my highest potential. Slick had a good flight, as did Freddy, but Bobby had some problems. He wasn't responding to the LSO's calls and Lieutenant Mapleford was on him most of the flight. Being up on the same frequency, we could all hear the debriefs he was giving to Bobby after each pass.

When we got back to the squadron, Bobby was down and his confidence was shattered. We all went up to him and tried to make him feel better by telling him that we all had bad days and not to worry about it, but it didn't seem to help.

Our eighth flight was canceled due to weather, so we had to fly on a Saturday to make it up. It was our turn to ride the van over, so we tried to pump Bobby's confidence up during the trip. His attitude was good and he seemed more confident. The Tigercats were finishing up their period as we arrived. While the planes were being refueled Lieutenant Mapleford came in from the field and gave us a little pep talk.

"Okay, Topcats, you've only got a couple more

periods before we go to the ship. I want you to work hard out there today and listen to what I'm telling you. Remember, I can't work you if you don't listen to my calls." He was looking directly at Bobby.

After M-plus-9 left, we reinforced Bobby and told him to kick some ass. As we walked to our planes the weather started to come in and the ceilings were dropping. We let Bobby take off first so he could be the first down the chute. His first pass was right on and Mapleford let him know it. That's all it took for him to get back in the groove and get his confidence back.

As the period came to a close the weather was so bad that we couldn't rendezvous at five thousand, so Sandy ordered us to join up in twos and head home. Slick was behind Bobby, so he joined on him and Freddy joined on me. Bobby was in a left-hand circle at 1,200 feet above the field when Slick lifted off from his last touch-and-go.

Tuesday was our final FCLP period and my pattern work was real good, but my lineup and ball control were weak. I didn't feel real pumped after my runs. Slick and the rest of my squadron mates did real well and they were on a natural high.

There were a lot of stories floating around about students who peaked early and fell apart at the boat. I couldn't get the possibility that I might be one of them out of my head. Slick tried to fire me up by telling me that it was good that I got the bullshit out of my system before I went to the boat. After a while I began to believe him and started to think positively.

Thursday was a big day for everyone. Not only did we have a major event in our lives, but our squadron, VT-4, was having her change of command. Normally they don't schedule a change of command during carrier qualifications, but the boat schedule had changed at the last minute and it was too late to rearrange the ceremony.

Our new commanding officer had been our executive officer for over a year and would take over the squadron in a couple of days. He was a squeaky-clean fighter pilot whose call sign was "Gunny," short for gunnery sergeant. Commander Tom "Gunny" Leonard, Sr., was a perfectionist and he ran the show with that attitude. A lot of the guys didn't care for his style, but I liked it, because you always knew where you stood with him. There were no games. He was firm but fair, and told it like it was. His son Pete "Gunny" Leonard was in his senior year at the naval academy and was scheduled to start flight training in the fall.

Like father like son, they both had the same MO, so naturally the son got the same call sign as his dad.

Wednesday we checked all of our equipment and made sure it was in top working order. Neither Slick nor I got much sleep. We met each other in the living room several times throughout the night. Our overhead time at the ship was eleven o'clock. This meant that we had to be circling over the ship at eleven o'clock, and when the group in front of us finished, the airboss would call us down to enter the pattern.

My alarm went off at seven and I wasn't too excited

about getting out of bed, because I had just fallen into a deep sleep. Slick came into my room and said, "Hey, Water, it's not pretty outside. The weather is dogshit."

"Let's see," I said.

Slick opened the blinds and he was right: it was wet and foggy. Just then the phone rang. Slick answered, and reported that it was the squadron duty officer. Our overhead time had been changed to one. This meant we didn't have to go in until ten.

We left the house at nine and arrived at the squadron by quarter to ten. The change of command was being held at wing headquarters so that the jet noise wouldn't disrupt the ceremony.

We went up to the ready room and got an update on the weather. Freddy and Bobby arrived all suited up in their flight gear.

"The only way you guys will get to use that gear today is in a simulator," Slick said.

"Is the weather that bad?" Bobby asked.

"The ship just reported the weather is down to the deck and it doesn't look like it's going to clear. They're going to make a decision within the hour."

We sat around for forty-five minutes before Lieutenant Commander Kistler walked in and gave us the cut sign under his chin. "Not today, men. Flight ops have been canceled. Be here tomorrow at five. Your overhead is at eight and I'll be flying you out to the ship."

The next morning the weather was the same. We sat around the ready room until ten and then the word came for the Topcats to man them up. The ready room went from peace and tranquillity to general quarters. Garters came in and gave us instructions, everyone made a last-minute head call, and we wished each other good luck before going to maintenance control. After we checked the flight logs, we walked to our airplanes simultaneously.

The *Lady Lex* was about fifty miles offshore, where the weather was clear. We were to take off individually then join up once we were on top of the overcast. Everything went like clockwork as we entered holding over the ship at 15,000 feet.

Then the voice of authority called. "Aircraft 301 and 303, signal charlie." This meant for those two planes to descend and enter the break. Unfortunately, it was Slick and Bobby who got the call to come on down first.

I could see some other aircraft in the pattern, so I assumed that's why only two were called down. Slick and Bobby tightened up their formation as they came into the break. I was envious as I watched them peel off at the bow. Slick was the lead aircraft, so he was the first to see the back end of the ship.

As he passed through the ninety-degree position he gave the required call, "Three-oh-one, Topcat, ball 3.6, Morely."

"Okay, Slick," called M-plus-9, "you're looking good. Keep her coming."

Slick touched down in wires, added power, and climbed straight ahead until the airboss cleared him downwind for his second touch-and-go. Bobby was a little close abeam and overshot his first pass. Sandy had him wave it off. As he climbed back up to pattern altitude M-plus-9 told him what he did wrong.

Slick had a nice second pass and M-plus-9 barked, "Slick, drop your hook as you turn downwind."

Bobby's pattern was better and he got a good start on his second approach. "Okay, Bobby," Sandy said, "you're a little high, ease it down. Easy with your power, come left a bit, watch your attitude . . . power! Power, damn it!"

Bobby started to sink in close and probably would have caught a one wire. Slick was off the ninety when Bobby climbed back up for his second touch-and-go. "Okay, Slick, you're low and to the right. Work the ball back to the center, check your lineup."

With only a few seconds to correct, Slick got the ball in the center, checked his lineup, and flew his first arrested landing to a two wire. The arresting drove him forward in his straps and he was at full power for several seconds before he realized he was aboard. Looking straight ahead for the yellow shirt, he saw the hookup signal, followed by the taxi ahead directions.

As he cleared the wires and was lining up for his first catapult shot, he heard M-plus-9 yelling, "Power! Power! Power!"

He looked to his left and saw Bobby's plane way left of center line and just slightly airborne in front of the lens.

Quickly he focused back on the director and got lined up for his shot. While Slick waited for the steam pressure to build, he heard Mapleford talking rather sternly to Bobby.

"Settle down, Bobby. Fly the goddamned airplane and stop letting it fly you." He wanted Bobby to try another touch-and-go before he had him drop his hook. I couldn't hear all that was taking place because I was switching back and forth on the frequencies.

Slick saw the catapult officer put his aircraft into tension and give him the turn-up signal. Going into tension on the catapult was like cocking the hammer of a gun. Slick went through his prelaunch procedures, and when he was satisfied everything was up and up, he saluted the cat officer, letting him know he was ready for launch. The cat officer then touched the deck with his right hand, signaling the firing officer to launch Slick's aircraft. Within a second Slick was on his way down the cat track going from zero to 160 knots in 2.5 seconds.

At the end of the stroke, Slick eased the stick back and climbed out to pattern altitude. By this time Bobby was lined up for his third pass. Everything looked much better and M-plus-9 didn't have much to say. After Bobby touched down and was back in the air, M-plus-9 said, "Nice pass, hook down."

My heart started to pound, because the big voice in the sky said, "Three-ten and three-oh-six, signal charlie." Garters came up on the frequency and said, "Show them what you've got."

Freddy and I started down, and as we were passing through eight thousand feet we got the call, "Signal delta, signal delta! We've got a plane in the water, plane in the water!"

My heart skipped a beat as we leveled off at seven thousand feet and started to orbit. Then we heard, "Topcats, return to base, switch to tactical."

As we switched onto tactical Garters came up. His

voice was calm as he told us to climb to 10,000 feet and join on him. We flew back to the base and landed.

The plane captain taxied me into spot and I raced through my shutdown procedures, unstrapped, and sprinted for the ready room. By the time I got up there the place was a madhouse. Our new skipper was talking to Lieutenant Commander Kistler and Freddy and I were looking on with fear in our eyes.

While everyone was waiting for more information to come in, Garters came over and told us what he had learned. "We have a plane over the side and two men in the water."

"Is it Slick or Bobby?" I asked.

"No confirmation yet to who's in the water."

"Son of a bitch," I said, slamming my fist into the palm of my other hand. Freddy and I went to the back of the ready room and sat down.

Within an hour Garters came to the back of the room. I could tell that he didn't really want to say anything, but didn't know how not to. He took a deep breath and looked away. "Bobby's dead," he said. "He ejected, got tangled up in his chute, and drowned before the frogmen could get to him."

"Oh Jesus," I said. The tears ran down my cheeks. "Where's Slick?"

"He's okay and will remain on the ship overnight."

"What happened, sir?" Freddy asked.

"Evidently Bobby got into a right-to-left drift in close and didn't respond to the wave-off call. He hit the deck hard and the plane took the optical landing system out as it went over the side. Bobby punched out, got a good chute, but got tangled in his shroud lines, and they pulled him under. The helo was on station within a minute and a swimmer went in the water to help, but it was too late. Bobby's body was about fifteen feet under when they cut him loose. They couldn't revive him."

"Who was the other person in the water?" I asked.

"I think they said it was the LSO."

"What?"

"Yeah. When the plane started coming at them, they jumped into the escape net and one of them missed the net and went over the side. They picked him up within minutes and his pride was the only thing hurt."

"What do we do now?" Freddy asked.

"They've sent a team out to repair the optical landing system, and if all goes well, you'll be out there tomorrow finishing up." His voice broke just once, but he took a deep breath, nodded, and pushed on.

"I know how you men feel, but you've got to put this behind you. This is an unforgiving business you're in and it's unfortunate you lost a classmate at such an early stage. But I can guarantee this won't be the last mishap you'll witness. Go home and try to get some rest, you've got a big day ahead of you. And don't forget Bobby in your prayers tonight. The squadron duty officer will call you later this evening and give you your overhead time."

FINAL
COUNTDOWN

After Lieutenant Commander Kistler finished talking with us, I went to my locker and changed into my uniform. As I left the locker room I decided to stop by the CO's office to see if I could be of any help. The skipper was just leaving when I got to his door.

"Good afternoon, sir," I said.

"Matt, how are you doing?"

"I'm okay, sir. I was wondering if I can be of any help—Bobby was in my class and I'd like to assist in any way possible."

"That's kind of you, Matt. Talk with Lieutenant Karnes, he'll be handling the funeral arrangements." He was kind of subdued, and when he changed the subject, I knew he was trying to keep a lid on things. "Did you get any traps today?"

"No, sir. Freddy and I had just been cleared out of holding to start our descent to the ship when the accident happened."

"Put it behind you, son. You've got a job ahead of you tomorrow. I'll be leading you to the boat in the morning if this weather clears."

"Yes, sir. Have a good evening."

As I walked away from the skipper I headed down the passageway to the standardization office, where Sundance worked. The only person in his office was his secretary. I left a message with her and told her how to get in touch with me. As I left the office the shock of losing a classmate really began to hit me, and I didn't want to go home knowing I'd be alone.

At 8:00 P.M. I received a call from the squadron duty officer. The SDO informed me that our overhead was scheduled for ten and our brief time was at seven. I tried to stay up late to tire myself out so I could get some sleep, but the accident still weighed heavily on my mind. I tossed and turned all night. At times I awoke gasping for air, as though I were drowning, and others times I was thrashing in bed trying to get untangled from the shroud lines of the parachute pulling me to my death.

The alarm went off at 5:30, and when I sat up to turn it off, I felt like a bulldozer had run over me. I hadn't slept soundly for several nights and the pressure was starting to take its toll. I said a little prayer to help me get through the day safely, then jumped into the shower.

As I drove to work I went over my procedures, especially survival guidelines. The weather was clear and there was no doubt that I would get my six arrested landings that day. The squadron was back to business as usual. I went directly to the locker room and changed into my green, flame-resistant flight suit.

Freddy was already seated when I entered the briefing room. I took a seat next to him.

"How you doing?" I asked.

"Didn't get much sleep last night."

"You weren't alone."

Freddy was much closer to Bobby than I had been, and I could see he was still hurting. Then the skipper walked in and we jumped to our feet.

"Seats," he said, "seats. Good morning, gentlemen. Are you ready to do it?"

"Yes, sir!"

"What happened yesterday is gone, but not forgotten. You must compartmentalize your thoughts and press on with your lives. If this accident has upset you to the point where you can't perform today, speak up. Otherwise I'll assume you're ready, both mentally and physically, to hit the boat."

There was no response, so Commander Leonard said, "Good! Okay, this is the game plan—we'll go out as a flight of three and I plan on getting several traps myself. Once I complete, I'll climb to 15,000 overhead the ship and wait until you've finished. Check your gas on your last trap, and if you're below 2.2, hotpump before your last cat shot. The ship is only twenty miles out and we'll be the first to arrive. Ensign Morely is finishing up his traps as we speak, and we should have a clear deck upon arrival. You've been through this brief before—do you have any questions?"

"No, sir!"

"Then let's do it!"

We checked the maintenance logs for our aircraft and walked to our machines. As I was going through my after-start checks I saw two T-2s coming into the break. The first plane broke at the numbers and the second plane broke three seconds later.

As we taxied from our line I could see that it was Slick and Garters. Garters evidently flew to the ship, bagged a few traps, and escorted Slick home. Slick had his white silk scarf wrapped around his neck like a World War II fighter pilot and was giving me a big thumbs-up as he taxied into his spot.

When cleared onto the active runway, all three of us positioned ourselves in right echelon. Skipper was the lead, Freddy was to his right, and I was to Freddy's right. The tower cleared us for takeoff, the skipper gave the turn-up signal, and we all went to military. After looking each other's aircraft over, the skipper released his brakes and started his takeoff roll. Four seconds later Freddy rolled and I followed suit.

Passing three thousand feet at 250 knots, we were all joined up. Departure cleared us to 10,000 feet and switched us to strike, the controlling agency on the ship. As we leveled at ten the skipper called strike. "Strike . . . Topcat flight checking in, angels ten."

"Roger, Topcat flight, signal charlie upon arrival."

As we approached ten miles the skipper spotted the ship and gave the descent signal.

My heart started to pound and I could feel the sweat dripping under my arms. As we hit three miles the skipper said, "Tighten it up, Topcats! Let's look sharp going into the break."

As we passed down the right side of the ship, Gunny with his hook down, gave Freddy the kiss-off signal and broke at the fantail, a maneuver only a seasoned pilot would do. We continued upwind for ten seconds, then Freddy kissed me off and broke and I continued upwind for another ten seconds before I broke.

The skipper trapped aboard on his first pass. Freddy and I had to do two touch-and-go's before we made our first arrested landing. As I flew downwind I went over my landing checklist and worked on my pattern. When I passed through the 180-degree position, Freddy was just lifting off. I gave my required call and flew what I felt was a perfect pass to my first touch-and-go.

Climbing out and passing four hundred feet, M-plus-9 said, "Topcats, lower your hooks. Three-oh-eight, I'll call you downwind."

"Roger."

I climbed straight ahead and leveled off at six hundred feet.

As Freddy turned off the 180 I got the call to turn downwind. Double-checking to ensure my hook was down and my landing checklist was complete, I worked for a good abeam position. I started my turn off the 180, and I saw Freddy trap aboard. Not watching my altitude caused me to be high when I rolled out on final. Like a good student should, I was calling out my scan to myself as I came down the shoot.

"Meatball, lineup, AOA," M-plus-9 warned, "you're high, 308. Ease it down."

To myself I said, "I know it, goddamn it!" I worked to get the ball back in the center. Crossing the ramp, the ball started to fall off the bottom, so I added power to catch it. As I slammed aboard, catching the two wire, I drove my head into the front glareshield and jammed the stick into my stomach. I had forgotten to check whether my harness was locked. It wasn't, which allowed me to lurch forward.

Stunned by the impact, I was slow getting out of the wires, which caused my CO to wave off his second pass. As I taxied clear M-plus-9 came up on the radio and said, "I guess we'll check to see if that harness is locked next time, won't we, 308?"

I was embarrassed and pissed off, but said nothing as I taxied to the catapult.

Before I knew it, I was being hurled into the sky and lining up for my second pass. That one went better, and the third was better still. I was starting to get into it, and before I realized it, I had completed my six landings and it was time to climb up to join on the skipper. As I passed 12,000 feet I spotted Freddy making a run on the skipper at my nine o'clock position. I accelerated and joined on them within minutes. Once we were aboard, the skipper said, "Good show, gents. Let's head home."

Feeling like the ace of the base, I reached down to the lower left pocket of my g-suit and pulled out my white silk scarf and wrapped it around my neck. It was tradition to wear your silk scarf when flying back from the ship for the first time. All the way home I thanked my lucky stars that everything went well. I couldn't wait to call home and tell everyone that I had made my first carrier landings. Then I thought about Bobby and the excitement died.

After we landed and pulled off the duty runway, we taxied back to our line in formation. Our plane captains parked us and we shut down in unison. We each did a postlanding inspection of our planes, then we met on the ramp and the skipper congratulated us. As we walked toward the hangar I could see Slick waiting to greet us. He had a table set up inside the hangar with some champagne and snacks to celebrate the occasion. It wasn't much, but it was more than he had received when he'd returned. Slick had a camera and we got pictures of the gala event.

Once the excitement of our return simmered down, we got cleaned up, turned in all our T-2 training materials, and checked into advanced. Basic and advanced training were combined in VT-4, so we didn't have far to go to check in. The south side of the hangar was used for T-2 training and the north side was dedicated to TA-4s.

The squadron duty officer was waiting for us when we checked in and presented us with a welcome-aboard packet. We would get a syllabus brief on Monday morning and meet our instructors. That afternoon we would start our final phase of the master's program. If everything went well, we'd get our wings and graduate in October. We were beginning to see the light at the end of the tunnel.

The memorial service for Bobby was scheduled for ten o'clock Tuesday morning. Slick and I were asked to be ushers. In his will, Bobby had requested that he be cremated and his ashes distributed in the Gulf of Mexico. I could tell this was going to be a very traumatic time for me. As a young boy I'd lost a close friend, who had been mistakenly shot by a hunter. The emotional pain from that accident had taken weeks to get over.

On our drive home I asked Slick, "What in the world happened out there?"

Slick filled me in on the details. "Bobby was having problems right off the bat with lineup, but seemed to settle down after a couple of passes. Lieutenant Mapleford felt he was ready to come aboard and had him drop his hook. The next pass he got a hellish right-to-left drift started and had to be waved off in close. Evidently he didn't respond to the LSO's calls and tried to set her down. I was on the catapult ready to be shot off when I saw men running. I looked to my left and saw his plane going over the side and Bobby ejecting."

"Jesus Christ," I said, "did he get a chute?"

"I saw it blossom, but he only got one swing before he hit the water. They pulled me off the cat at that point and sidelined me. I saw the rescue swimmer jump from the helo and that was it until they brought Bobby back aboard. By that time I had shut down and was told I would be spending the night aboard. I went up to the control tower to watch the rescue. They had Bobby back on deck within ten minutes and the medical team tried to revive him, but he was gone. Sweetwater, I couldn't sleep all night. I paced up and down the passageways wondering what went wrong. One flight-deck crewman said he saw Bobby waving once he was in the water, then the next thing he knew, he was gone."

"The poor bastard never had a chance."

That night Slick and I stayed close to home and went to bed early. We were exhausted from the stress of car quals and the loss of a friend. After eight hours of sleep I felt much better.

I called home after breakfast and had a nice chat with my folks. I gave them a detailed description of each landing at the ship, but I didn't mention anything about the accident. I knew my mother; she worried enough for all of us, and probably wore out her rosary beads praying.

The weekend went by fast and Monday was on us before we knew it. The morning was spent getting our study materials and meeting our new instructors. Commander Leonard, our CO, gave us an inspiring welcome-aboard speech, which set the tone for our final phase of training.

Slick's instructor was the marine captain Jim Lott, whom we had run into at Dirty Joe's back at Saufley. He had been the one trying to make time with Mary out in the parking lot one Wednesday night. My instructor was Lieutenant John Macdonald, "Johnny-mac" for short.

Lott didn't remember us, thank God, because we had ridden him about his high and tight squirrel-cut hairdo. Johnny-mac was laid-back and seemed like a straight shooter.

The afternoon wasn't much fun. We received our new class assignments and the bullshit started up again. But with only three classes to complete before we got our degrees, we could put up with just about anything.

Slick and I had to be at the church by nine in our service dress blues, with medals and white gloves. The programs that we were to pass out had Bobby's picture on the front with his biography and a schedule of events listed on the inside. When I looked at the program, tears filled my eyes. Slick saw that I was getting choked up and tried to soothe me, but it only made things worse.

By quarter to ten the base chapel was filled. Bobby's mother, father, and sister were the last to be seated. Freddy escorted Bobby's mother to her seat and I assisted his sister. Bobby had requested in his will that in the case of his untimely death, no one in his family was to wear black and mourn his death. He stated that he was doing what he always wanted to do, and if he was to die doing it, so be it. Accordingly his mother and sister were dressed in bright colors and each carried a red rose. Mr. Price was wearing a light tan suit and also carried a red rose.

The memorial service lasted about forty-five minutes and there wasn't a dry eye in the place when it concluded. Commander Leonard's speech was very touching and he read Psalm 23, which I have never forgotten. It goes like this.

> *The Lord is my constant companion*
> *there is no need that he cannot fulfil.*
> *Whether his course for me points*
> *to the mountaintops of glorious ecstasy*
> *or to the valleys of human sufferings,*
> *He is by my side.*
> *He is ever present with me.*
> *He is close beside me*
> *when I tread the dark streets of danger.*
> *And even when I flirt with death itself,*
> *He will not leave me.*
> *When pain is severe,*
> *He is near to comfort.*
> *When the burden is heavy,*
> *He is there to lean upon.*
> *When depression darkens my soul,*
> *He touches me with eternal joy.*

When I feel empty and alone,
  He fills the aching vacuum with his power.
My security is in his promise
  to be near to me always,
  and in the knowledge
  that he will never let me go.

After the psalm, Commander Leonard described Bobby's life-style and summed it up with a quote from Robert Herrick: "That man lives twice who lives the first life well." Sitting through the memorial service made me stop and realize that you must live a good life each day, because in our business, there may not be a tomorrow.

After the service a motorcade drove from the chapel to the flight line, where a helo would fly Bobby to his final rest. Freddy, Slick, and I were asked to spread his ashes over the Gulf. As we stood at attention beside the helo his parents walked toward us with the urn. They handed Bobby's remains over and it took all of our strength to keep from breaking down. His mother gave each of us a hug before we flew off.

All three of us sat in the rear of the helo. The air crewman hooked safety belts around us as we sat near the open door. We flew to the mouth of Pensacola Bay, and while the helo hovered at fifty feet we spread Bobby's ashes into the Gulf. The flight took ten minutes, and upon our return, we handed the urn to Bobby's family and went home, feeling as empty as the urn.

14

SPIES IN
THE SKY

As I sat in ground school, learning about the two-place, lightweight, high-performance, delta-wing TA-4, I suddenly realized that this was my final stage of flight training and I had better burn up the syllabus if I wanted fighters. All of my classmates were doing well to this point and the competition for fighters was stiff.

Other than the addition of night formation and air-combat maneuvering, the TA-4 syllabus was laid out pretty much like the T-2 training. Ground school was scheduled to take two weeks and would cover all the systems and aerodynamic characteristics of the TA-4 Skyhawk. After ground school we would start our transition syllabus, which included five familiarization flights followed by two solo hops.

The two weeks went by fast. Learning about the aerodynamics of wing slats and how they improve air-flow characteristics over wing surfaces at high angles of attack during approach and landing was fascinating. The wing slats open and close independently and automatically as the aerodynamic loading on them dictates.

Because so many variables such as airspeed, gross weight, and applied load factor affect the operation of the wing slats, no fixed airspeeds can be established as the points as which the slats begin to open or close. In general, they begin to open below two hundred knots, and are fully opened at stalling speed. The aerodynamic structure of the TA-4 Skyhawk was a lot less forgiving than that of the T-2 Buckeye.

Flight training has lots of emotional highs and lows. As you become familiar with one airplane you move on to a new one, and just when you feel comfortable in your new environment, you move again.

We finished ground school at noon on Friday, so we decided to have a cookout at the house and invite our classmates. Slick and I started the party early with a six-pack of Coors that we had flown in for special occasions. By seven o'clock we had over fifty people at our house. Someone had spread the word that we were throwing a party and the floodgates opened. Most of the people who showed up brought their own food and booze and we provided the barbecue and paper dishes.

The party went on until the wee hours. By the next morning we had bodies all over our property. People were dancing in the driveway while others enjoyed conversation with old friends. Slick and I were kept busy with barbecuing and entertaining. This was our first party and we'd been overdue for a blowout.

Despite the party, at 0630 Monday morning, Slick and I were in our ready room waiting for Lieutenant Macdonald and Captain Lott to show. Lott showed up first and took Slick to one of the four briefing booths and I anxiously awaited Johnny-mac's arrival. Within a few minutes the squadron duty phone rang and the watch officer answered it. After he hung up, he told me Johnny-mac was in the Seaweed Deli, a small grill in the hangar, getting a bite to eat, and he wanted me to join him.

As I walked through the deli doors he waved me toward his table. "Morning, Sweetwater, how're you doing?"

"Fine, sir," I said.

"Knock that 'sir' shit off, Water. You're in a real squadron now."

I nodded my head, acknowledging his request. "You're my superior, and it's hard for me not to call you sir."

"When we're together like this or in the air, don't worry about the protocol, I want you to start feeling like a fleet aviator. Now let's go over some course rules and squadron policies before we brief."

The brief and preflight followed the same scenario as the other phase-one briefs, long and precise. I was slow on my after-start checks, but got into the swing of things once we pulled the chocks. Unlike the instructors for my previous intros, Johnny-mac made me do everything myself once we lit the fire.

When cleared to take off, I taxied into position and checked my flaps to one half, then advanced the throttle to military, released the brakes, and started my takeoff roll. At two thousand feet I checked my line speed for 126 knots, and at 153 knots I was airborne. At three thousand feet I raised the gear, and passing through 170 knots, I raised my flaps and accelerated to my climb speed of 200 knots. We climbed up to 15,000 feet and got a general feel for the aircraft, with the gear and flaps in both the up and down configurations.

After a tour of the operating area, I did some stalls and confidence maneuvers then hit the landing pattern for multiple landings. I really had to stay on top of this machine or it would get away from me. The Skyhawk was faster and more maneuverable than the Buckeye.

My fourth and fifth hops were spins and out-of-control flight. No one liked them because they were violent and dangerous. But we had to experience these flight characteristics in case we found ourselves in a departure or spin situation. A departure from controlled flight can occur as a result of nose-high, low–airspeed conditions or asymmetric slat extension. Lieutenant Macdonald demonstrated the first departure by pulling the aircraft to eighty degrees nose-high and decelerated to near zero airspeed. As the aircraft started to slow I clutched the side canopy rails, awaiting the ride of my life.

Without much warning, the aircraft went into an uncommanded nosedown pitch, followed by a random poststall gyration in the roll and yaw axes. My head was snapped from side to side, bouncing off the canopy as my body was pinned in the safety harness up against it. After two hops practicing these maneuvers, I was pretty beat up when I returned to the flight line. My head was pounding and my whole body ached from the g-forces.

Slick and I carpooled most of the time and we had the Silver Fox today, so I was driving. It was close to nine o'clock at night and the fog was as thick as pea soup. The trip across the three-mile-bay bridge was slow due to the fog, and when we got to Gulf Breeze, a small beach town before Santa Rosa Island, all traffic had stopped. We sat for two hours before we got onto the island and home.

Tired and out of conversation, we hit the hay as soon as we got home. While making breakfast the next morning, I heard some shocking news on the radio. The owner of a local company that built cigarette boats in Panama City had been murdered the previous night on Santa Rosa Island. According to the police, he had been assassinated in a Mafia-style execution, then hung over the Santa Rosa Bridge by his ankles. So that's why the traffic was backed up for so long, I thought. When Slick got out of the shower and sat down for breakfast, I told him the story. He couldn't believe it. He knew of the guy, because he followed ocean racing.

"Probably drugs involved," he said.

"Yeah, I suppose."

I slept in on Sunday morning and took it easy for the first time in months. It sure felt good just to relax and enjoy the quiet time. Slick was out working on his car when I came alive and ventured outside. After I got cleaned up, we went for a bike ride around the neighborhood.

We proceeded down the beach to the water tower and to our amazement we saw activity around Molar Man's bar and grill. We pedaled up to the restaurant and saw Melon working out back. He wasn't due to return until next week, so we quietly approached him and Slick made a sound like rippling machine-gun bullets and I said, "Check your six, Molar Man."

Not expecting anyone, he jumped about three feet in the air. "Goddamn it," he said, "I knew it had to be you two. How's things going?"

"Great," I said, "only a few more months to go before we complete. I thought you weren't supposed to be here until next weekend."

"I wrapped things up early and Nancy kicked me out the door with my golf clubs. She'll be down next week."

"Well, what do you want us to do?" Slick asked.

"Are you sure you want to help?"

"We wouldn't have offered if we didn't."

"Well, you can start by taking off those wooden shutters and setting the tables up outside. I want to take it easy this year and do a little each day. Last year I tried to do everything in one weekend and it took me a week to recover from the strain. I planned it better this year. Work in the mornings and play golf in the afternoons."

"Sounds like a winner to me," I said. We worked until four and then started to party. Before we knew it, it was way past our bedtime and we both had a first- go solo flight in the morning.

My alarm went off at 5:00 A.M. I reached over, turned it off, then promptly fell back asleep. When Slick realized I wasn't up, he came to my rescue and got my motor started, but it was too late. I was behind the power curve and things just got worse.

Slick headed for the squadron after he got me up and I made a mad dash to the shower. After two cups of coffee and a drag race to the squadron, I was only thirty minutes late. Luckily the weather wasn't the greatest and the first launches had been delayed. Still playing catch-up as I finished strapping into the plane, I saw Slick take off.

Realizing my state of mind, I knew I had to pay particular attention to detail or I might lose situational awareness and get into trouble. It was easy to do with the A-4. Once I got the aircraft started, I began to settle down and got my priorities in line. My after-start checks, taxi and takeoff went well, but there was something in the back of my mind that I had forgotten to do.

At 20,000 feet at the top of my first loop, I suddenly realized what it was I had forgotten. The black cups of coffee had taken effect. I had to go to the bathroom and I mean *now*. The cramps were so severe that I doubled over in the cockpit. Knowing I couldn't make it back to the base before the explosion took place, I did the only thing a pilot could do.

I lowered my seat, trimmed the aircraft up to straight and level flight, loosened my g-suit and boots, tucked the bottoms of my flight suit into my boots, tied them as tight as I could, and let it rip. Luckily I was on oxygen and didn't realize how bad it was until I returned to base.

When I called to return to base, the tower asked if I was experiencing any difficulty. I told them that I wasn't feeling well and would be landing shortly. I was met at the flight line by a medic, and when he climbed up the ladder to see if I was all right, he knew what had happened. It wasn't long before the whole squadron knew that I had shit in my flight suit. I was afraid my call sign would be changed to Swampwater.

Since I had only completed a third of my flight, I had to fly again once I got cleaned up. Everyone around the squadron tried to be professional when they saw me. But when I looked at them, they would break out laughing, so I joined in. While I looked over the aircraft logbook in maintenance control, the maintenance chief informed me that there was an important all-officers' meeting at 1500. What I thought was going to be a light day had suddenly turned into a marathon.

The second half of my flight went without incident. My landings and confidence maneuvers were executed with certainty and the flight ended on a positive note. I filled out the yellow sheet and went to the locker room to change.

As I approached my locker some smart-ass had a large bottle of Kaopectate taped to the door with a note attached, which read. *When without, flush it out.* It got a little laugh from me, but I was still feeling the embarrassment.

Once showered and changed into my uniform, I headed for the ready room. When I entered, most of the squadron was already seated and I could feel all eyes staring at me. The tension started to build. All the seats were taken, so I headed to the back of the room and found a spot to stand where I could see what was going on.

At 1500, Commander Leonard entered the ready room with two men dressed in dark suits. "Attention on deck!" was called by the executive officer and we all came to attention.

"Seats, gentlemen," the skipper announced, and everyone who could sat down.

"Gentlemen, the shooting of José de la Barbolla on Friday night, which I'm sure you've heard about, was the result of a very large drug deal that went bad. These men to my right are DEA Special Agents Winterer and Wagner. We've been asked to assist them and the Coast Guard in the search for Manuel Salvador Ortega, a Colombian drug kingpin, who they feel is behind it. I will now turn the brief over to Special Agent Winterer."

"Thank you, Skipper. Good afternoon, gentlemen. I'm Special Agent Bob Winterer and this is my partner, Steve Wagner. The DEA is working with local authorities and federal agencies to locate Ortega. He's wanted in six states and we believe he was the man who murdered Mr. Barbolla Friday night.

"You men are going to be our spies in the skies. As you fly around the Gulf Coast area we want you to be on the lookout for unmarked aircraft which will land almost anywhere to transfer their drugs and for fishing boats that look like this one in the photo Special Agent Wagner is holding up. If you see anything that resembles either, please notify us immediately. We'll be passing out kneeboard cards with code names and radio frequencies to help you alert us if something comes up."

The ready room was buzzing, and Winterer waited for the noise to die down before continuing. "Drug trafficking along the Gulf Coast has increased 200 percent in the last year, and we really need your help. This brief is classified, so don't be discussing this out in town or around individuals who do not have a need to know. We'll be in touch as things develop. Are there any questions?"

Captain Lott raised his hand and was acknowledged. "Yes, sir. A couple of weeks ago I spotted a small twin-engine airplane at Wolfe Field while I was on a weather hop. There was a truck near it, and when I came by for a better look, he was on the roll and disappeared in the overcast."

"That's the kind of information we're looking for. I can guarantee you that it was a drug deal going down."

"Why didn't you report it, Captain?" the skipper asked.

"I thought it was one of our flying-club planes out doing touch-and-go's."

"Has anyone else seen this type of activity in and around the Gulf Coast?" There were no more replies.

"Okay, gents," Winterer said, "thank you for your time and let us know if you spot anything. Remember, you'll probably see more when the weather is bad, early in the morning, and just before dark."

The XO called us to attention and the skipper and special agents departed, then he dismissed the group.

As we walked out of the ready room I felt the pressure lift a bit, knowing that this assignment probably took the heat off me, for a while anyway.

In the security of my home and away from the humiliation at the squadron, I told Slick the whole story blow by blow. Although it sounded funny, it could have turned into a real dangerous situation if I had become incapacitated in the cockpit. Slick had experienced a similar gastric emergency while at

Saufley and he could sympathize with me. People don't realize how painful this is at high altitude.

After all the details of my unpleasant experience were aired, Slick and I went over the kneeboard cards the DEA agents handed out.

"Do you really think we can help these guys?" Slick asked.

"I don't know, but if what Captain Lott told us is true, there may have been a lot of drug trafficking going on and we just weren't aware of it. I think we can play a role, now that we know what to look for. What's on our schedule next?" I asked.

"We start formation flying Wednesday with four day hops and four night flights. Then we start our weapons phase."

"Have they decided where we're going on our weapons detachment yet?"

"Nope, it'll either be California or New Orleans, depending on range availability."

"I hope we go west. I've never been out there, and they say it's a different world on the West Coast. All the guys I've talked to who went to San Diego had a blast. You know we've got a test in structural engineering on Friday, don't you?"

"Please don't remind me. I just can't seem to get fired up about this course. Milt makes it interesting, and his labs are fun, but I must be getting burned out."

"Burned out, my ass, Slick. You've only got the highest grade in the course, what are you complaining about?"

"I guess I'm tired of all this studying."

"You got that right, but we've only got a few months left."

* * *

My first form hop didn't go all that well. I couldn't quite get the hang of it and I got frustrated as the hop progressed. My in-close parade position was very sloppy, due to poor power control, and the harder I tried, the worse I got. My second flight was better, but not up to my best, although during the tall-chase phase I did well. By the end of my first four-plane hop I was back in the groove and my confidence reestablished.

Friday was a no-fly day, due to classes at the university. Monday would be my final day-formation flight before I started night training. This is where the master's program hindered my performance in the air. Not flying Friday and having two days off over the weekend caused me to get rusty and it would take me half of my next hop to get back up to speed. Luckily the instructors took all of this into consideration when and if you had a poor hop.

Monday's four-plane was average and I wasn't feeling as confident as I should have, going into the night phase. Flying formation at night was a whole different ball game. Relative motion was harder to detect and figuring out the light show on the other aircraft was going to be a real challenge.

Slick and I were scheduled for our first night form hops on Wednesday. We would get four. One instructional two-plane flight with one solo hop and one instructional four-plane with a solo flight. We would brief at 5:00 P.M. and launch at seven for all evolutions. Wednesday was spent studying our procedures and night-communication signals by use of a flashlight. All communications during day formation flights are done by hand signals, but at night it's necessary to use the flashlight. The only time the radio is used during formation flying is in the case of emergency or if something appears unsafe.

We were suited up and ready to brief at the appointed time. Lieutenant Macdonald would fly with me and Captain Lott would be in Slick's aircraft. Johnny-mac gave the brief, which lasted almost an hour. With the use of TA-4 models and slides, we got a pretty good picture of what to expect on our first flight. The starlit night was clear, with a half-moon to boot.

Our flight would work up in the northwest corner of the training area, near Bay Minette. This was the designated training area for night formation hops. The instructors would demonstrate the section take-off utilizing their flashlights for all hand signals. Once Captain Lott was comfortably airborne and in parade formation, the instructors turned the aircraft over to us and we began our training.

With five feet of stepdown and five feet of wingtip lateral clearance, we practiced parade formation in right and left echelon, making turns away from and into the section. Then we did some crossunders. Upon receipt of the crossunder signal from the lead aircraft, I commenced an arcing crossunder by reducing power, dropping my nose, and sliding aft to clear the leader's tailpipe and jet wash.

As the nose passed below and aft of the leader's tail, I smoothly added power and completed the crossunder by sliding up and forward to the proper wing position on the opposite side. After doing this several times, I went to a free cruise position. This position provides better lookout capabilities and maximum freedom of movement for the leader and my aircraft.

The instructors demonstrated the first rendezvous before we were permitted to try one. Turning on the top anticollision light indicated the start of the maneuver. In right echelon, the lead aircraft would break left, then three seconds later the wingman would break and follow. When a quarter of a mile in trail, he would click his mike button twice and the lead aircraft would roll his wings straight and level. Once in level flight, the lead aircraft would roll into a thirty-degree angle of bank left or right at 250 knots and remain in this turn at the altitude at which the maneuver was started until his wingman got back aboard.

Once the wingman saw the lead aircraft turn, he would roll his aircraft inside the lead's radius of turn and descend two hundred feet, then position the cluster of lights from the lead aircraft on the upper right windscreen and fly that sight picture down the bearing line at 250 to 270 knots. By adjusting your closure rate with your throttle and radius of turn, you make a smooth rendezvous to the port parade position, then cross under to the right and set up for another breakup and rendezvous.

Slick and I each got to do four before we swapped the lead and let the other complete his. My last two rendezvous were not very good. I had trouble getting back aboard. When I started to get in close, I had the feeling that I was rolling inverted and coming down on top of the lead aircraft. When this sensation hit me, I would decrease my roll angle and I could never join up. What I had was a bad case of vertigo.

After Slick completed his four, Johnny-mac wanted me to try a couple more. He felt I was turning my head too much in the cockpit, causing me to get dizzy. He suggested that I slow my head movements down and see if that didn't help. My rendezvous was better and I got aboard, but I still had vertigo.

After all the maneuvers were completed and the instructors were satisfied that we were safe for solo, we headed home. Slick had the lead and would take us into the break at home field. As we passed over the small town of Loxley, Johnny-mac came up on the radio and told Slick to put the flight into a left-hand turn. He wanted to check something out.

As we circled, Captain Lott came on, "What's up, Johnny-mac?"

"I thought I saw lights at Silverdale Airfield."

Joining the conversation, I said, "I didn't know Silverdale had lights."

"They don't," Johnny-mac answered. "That's what caught my eye. And boy, it sure looks like lights down there. Jimbo, continue to circle overhead Silverdale, I'm going down for a look."

"Roger," Lott replied.

"Sweetwater," Johnny-mac said, "I've got the aircraft."

"You've got it," I said.

Once clear of the lead aircraft, Johnny-mac made a dive run on Silverdale. As I got my bearings I could see the lights he was referring to as we made a low pass over the field. The silhouetted landing strip was lit by smudge pots. It had to be a drug drop.

By the time we got back around for another run, half the lights had been extinguished. Johnny-mac dialed in the frequency the DEA agents requested and reported the sighting. We then climbed back up and he did a running rendezvous on Slick's plane. Once back into position, he turned the controls over to me and I flew on Slick's wing back home.

The ready room was buzzing with phone calls by the time we checked in. The duty officer wanted Lieutenant Macdonald to call Special Agent Winterer and brief him on the sighting. Evidently our call had activated the Coast Guard from Mobile, and local DEA agents had launched their Blackhawk helicopter to the scene.

After the four of us debriefed the mission, we broke up and discussed each maneuver individually. Lieutenant Macdonald felt that I had done a good job for the most part, and the problem I had experienced was not uncommon. "Your semicircular canals got out of whack with all the head turning, Water. Especially in the breakup and rendezvous. The starlight didn't help matters, either. I don't think you're unsafe, and I'm going to clear you for solo flight with Slick tomorrow night."

On our way home Slick admitted to having some problems of his own. "My closure rate and bearing line control were dogshit."

I had the feeling that it was going to be exciting for the next couple of nights. One thing that saved us both from getting a down was that we were not unsafe and we made the right corrections to get back on track.

We had classes on Tuesday and were scheduled for our solo flight on Wednesday. Freddy and his new flying partner, Tommy Boyd, would fly the night before, and we would have our first four-plane hop on Friday.

When we checked in to brief on Wednesday night, the CO gave us an "Atta boy!" for spotting the drug runners. Apparently the drop had not been made because we had put a spike in the operation. At least that's what Winterer told us. This made Commander Leonard's squadron look good in the eyes of his superiors and made us all feel like part of the team. As the skipper was leaving he said, "Hey, Sweetwater, don't be drinking any coffee before you fly tonight."

"Don't worry, sir, I won't." I tried to sound cool, but my face turned beet red.

15

PRESUMED
DEAD

After my face returned to its normal color I sat down for the brief. Slick was the flight lead for the night's mission, so he did the briefing for the hop. Captain Lott would fly as safety observer and chase pilot. The mission was the same as the night before so the brief was short. We all knew what the sequence of events would be and what had to be accomplished.

I was still concerned about the vertigo and hoped slowing my head movement in the turns would reduce the disorientation. By now Slick and I had flown together enough that we knew each other's moves pretty well and each felt confident about the other's capabilities. Slick would run through all the maneuvers first then pass the lead to me.

The takeoff and join-up went very smoothly and I felt comfortable by the time we got to the training area and started our series of maneuvers. Captain Lott circled a thousand feet above us to watch. The parade turns and crossunders went well, but Slick got a little too aggressive on the tail chase and spit me out a couple of times.

I knew the breakup and rendezvous were next and I could feel my blood pressure start to rise. Once set up and comfortable, Slick hit his top anticollision light and broke. It was show time. I had reviewed the maneuver a dozen times and knew what I had to do. I got set up on the bearing line and started my closure on Slick. I checked to make sure I was two hundred feet below his aircraft, looked at my airspeed, and positioned his lights on my windscreen.

Everything was tracking well and I couldn't believe how smoothly the rendezvous was going. As I got closer I started to make out the silhouette of his plane and slid into the proper parade position. Once comfortable, I crossed under and setup for another.

Both rendezvous went well and slowing my head movement eliminated the vertigo. I felt good when Slick passed me the lead. Now I just had to fly a smooth platform for Slick and we'd be done. The maneuvers went like clockwork, and as we headed home Captain Lott commented over the tactical frequency, "That was one of the finest night form hops I've seen in a long time."

We were on the deck by 9:30 and riding high. We knew we'd flown a shit-hot hop and were ready to tell anyone who wanted to listen. Since it was Wednesday night and things were just starting at Dirty Joe's, we headed for the beach.

Joe's was rockin'-and-rollin' by the time we arrived and we wasted no time getting some fuel aboard. We'd been around long enough to establish a reputation among the locals as part of the beach crowd that could do no wrong. Standing back in the corner to catch my breath, I observed several students who had that familiar bewildered look on their faces. I knew they had to have just checked into Saufley and were starting the flight program.

When the night turned into the early morning, Slick and I headed home. The next day wasn't pretty, but it was worth the headache. Classes never seemed to end and the day was long. We hadn't lit our hair on fire for months, but it sure felt good.

Sunday afternoon Slick and I received a call from the duty officer, who informed us that we had a weapons brief at 0900 Monday in the ready room. We couldn't figure out why we were having our brief so soon. We weren't supposed to start for another week.

When we walked into the ready room on Monday morning, we knew something was cooking. All the students and instructors in our class were present. At 0905 the commanding officer entered and we all came to attention. He asked us to be seated and began his brief.

"Gentlemen, we've had some major changes which will affect your training and that's why I've gathered you here today. The *Lexington* blew a boiler yesterday and has to go into the yards for several months, for repairs. We're working with the Atlantic Fleet to get another carrier for your qualification, but in the meantime we have to accelerate your weapons detachment.

"Next Monday you'll be sent to NAS New Orleans for a month of weapons training. The rest of the week will be devoted to your classes at the university. Lieutenant Commander Tim Gosma will be the detachment officer-in-charge while you're in New Orleans. I know a lot of you had your hearts set on going out west, but that's the breaks of naval air. Your orders and advance travel pay will be ready for pickup at the duty desk on Thursday. This will be your first set of travel orders, so get your affairs squared away before you leave. Remember, you'll be representing the U.S. Navy and I don't want to hear of any trouble while you're on det. Read my lips! No trouble! Are there any questions?"

I raised my hand and, when I was acknowledged, asked, "What about our night four-plane formation hops?"

The skipper said, "All form hops not completed prior to departure will be done while on det."

There were no more questions and the CO turned the brief over to Lieutenant Commander Gosma.

The OIC passed out some more detailed information and told us he would distribute the orders on Thursday at 1300. After the brief Slick and I headed home to get our seabags and affairs in order for the trip. On Sunday afternoon a DC-9 would airlift all the excess luggage and support personnel to NAS New Orleans. The students and instructors would fly the TA-4s to New Orleans on Monday morning.

Sunday morning we were up bright and early and drove to the base to drop off our baggage for the airlift.

Baggage in the TA-4 is normally stowed in the nose cone and in the forward engine compartment. Due to the limited space we could only take an overnight bag, so the rest of our gear had to go on the DC-9.

By the time Sunday night rolled around, Slick and I were beat. Getting the house closed up and taking care of our personal affairs for several weeks was a major task. I couldn't imagine what it was going to be like when I had to put everything in storage for eight months while on deployment. Oh well, I thought, I guess I won't be the first junior officer to do it.

During our departing brief on Monday, the CO entered the ready room with Special Agents Winterer and Wagner. They gave us an updated intel brief on the drug lord Ortega. They'd gotten a tip that Ortega was going to make a run for Colombia.

Winterer went on, "All airports from Pensacola to Port Arthur, Texas, will be on the lookout for anyone filing a flight plan to Colombia. Ortega was spotted in New Orleans last week and a plane was seized at the airport trying to smuggle him out."

That got our attention, because the room went deathly quiet.

"Gentlemen," the DEA man continued, "we have strong evidence indicating that Ortega is going to make a run for the twelve-mile coastal limit sometime in the next few days. A small ocean freighter is the pickup boat, and if he makes it into international waters, we can't touch him. That's where you'll be able to help us. We want you to keep an eye out for a large black-and-gold Fountain called the *Jazz Singer* while you're working the Marsh Island range."

Already I was starting to have visions of what it might be like.

Winterer, confident that we were hanging on his every word, went on, "Remember that boat builder who was murdered a few weeks ago on Pensacola Beach? Well, he made these Fountain forty-two-foot Lightning boats and the smugglers are using them to run drugs from outside the twelve-mile limit to the mainland."

Winterer studied our faces for a few moments while he let that news sink in. "Last night Ortega conversed via scrambled phone with his headquarters in the Cauca Valley in Colombia. His headquarters has dispatched a banana freighter laden with cocaine which is headed for the western Gulf of Mexico. Once the drugs have been off-loaded, we feel Ortega is going to make a run for it."

Slick's hand shot up. When Winterer nodded to him, he asked, "Where do we come in, sir?"

"The DEA has made arrangements to modify the local loran transmitters so that the freighter will sail inside the twelve-mile limit, thinking he is still in international waters. If we succeed in baiting the freighter, we will seize her with Ortega aboard and kill two birds with one stone."

Slick interjected, "But why do you need us? Your Blackhawk can outrun that Fountain forty-two."

It was Wagner's turn. He stood to address the question. "Not as easy as you would think, Ensign Morely. Interdiction boats are my specialty and this Fountain is not your ordinary racing machine. It's been modified with two GE T58-GE-16 turboshaft jet engines. The high-speed shafts are connected to a mix box that drives two outboard Arneson surface drives. The engines are rated at 1,775 horsepower each. Gentlemen, this boat is capable of 140-plus knots, almost as fast as the Blackhawk."

Slick whistled then sat down as Wagner continued. "Through intelligence we found out that the hull has a double layer of wetsuit rubber laminated to its surface. The rubber has a thin layer of tinfoil inside it which deflects all known surface search radars. We call it the 'Stealth Boat from Hell.' This boat can make it to the twelve-mile limit in about five minutes, onload the drugs, and be back in someone's backwater estate or marina in less than twenty minutes. It's almost foolproof. They send out decoy boats to distract our patrols long enough for the banzai run. We just don't have the high-speed support to catch or track them. That's where you will come in."

We were all zeroed in on him now, and he knew it. "If you spot the *Jazz Singer* or the banana freighter, track the vessel and report its position to 'drug-runner control' on 355.5. We will then activate operation 'Texas Tea.' A coast-guard vessel will close in on the freighter and we'll track and disable the Fountain if necessary. Now, unless there are questions, that concludes our brief."

There were none, so the skipper then briefed us on safety and personal conduct while we were on the road. After his speech he wished us well and escorted the special agents out.

By the end of the DEA's brief, I had heard enough about Ortega and operation 'Texas Tea.' My main concern was to do well while on this weapons det, and if I could be of help when things went down, so be it. Lieutenant Commander Gosma gave us our launch sequence and let us go. Slick and I were in the third wave. We launched in sections instead of two divisions.

The trip down was uneventful and we were checked into the BOQ by 4:00 P.M. We were scheduled to fly twice a day, weather permitting. The first week would be devoted to air-combat maneuvering and night formation. Once these flights were out of the way, we would start bombing, and finish up with guns and rockets.

The ACM—air-combat manuvering—hops were wild and really the high point of our TA-4 training so far. But carrier qualification was always the cat's pajamas. During the ACM phase you put all of your talent and aggressiveness on the line to master your machine against the doggedness and skills of your opponent. You learn to be cunning and farsighted as you conceptualize the three-dimensional, fast-moving dynamics of planes in ever-changing attitudes and relative positions. Going straight up and down at speeds below stall to the shaking threshold of supersonic was what it was all about.

We refer to ACM as "hassling." It's much like the World War II and Korean War dogfight movies. But you're traveling at speeds three times as fast. The key to hassling is to keep your bogey in sight at all times. The first one to lose sight dies. To get to this level of expertise, you have to practice all the fundamental maneuvers.

We started with the yo-yo, a simple but very effective vertical maneuver involving keeping a speed advantage on the bogey while maintaining position behind him by pitching straight up then down on his radius of turn. This allows you to maintain nose-to-tail separation on him while you track your missile or gun-aiming system on his aircraft.

Graduating from the yo-yo, we learned elusive aerobatic tactics like hammerhead reversals, high-speed pitch-backs, blow-throughs and high-"g" barrel rolls. Always remembering that speed is life and a tally-ho is a kill.

Challenge, challenge, challenge, drill, drill, drill, press, press, press was the credo our instructors tried to instill in us during this phase. Each hop called for a little more, and very soon we were going against the best instructors, who had fleet experience and many combat missions in their flight logs. To say personalities don't get into this business is pure bullshit. Even the best of instructors couldn't keep their pride out of the cockpit. This comes with the territory.

Teaching us was their goal, but not getting shot runs in your blood, and they let us know it. Demonstrating how to lose a fight was an unnatural act. They always taught us how to win, and if we ever had to fight, we were trained to win, believe me.

The night four-plane hops went well, but they weren't as much fun as the two-plane. We had to fly eight breakup and rendezvous, and by the end of the hop I was beat.

By the end of the week, we got word that a coast-guard C-130 had spotted the banana freighter about three hundred miles south of Pensacola. And he was targeting the coastline somewhere close to New Orleans. DEA agents had located the *Jazz Singer* in a private boat house at Port Eads, near the Mississippi delta, and were keeping it under surveillance. Things were falling into place, and once the freighter got near the twelve-mile limit, we would start our alert flights.

Sunday and Monday Slick and I got our first two bombing hops, and what an eye-opener. It was a good thing we had our instructors aboard. The Marsh Island range had it all, from moving land targets, to sea targets, to fixed bombing rings. They even had aerial targets to shoot at. Our first two hops were on the fixed-ring targets. The dive angle and speed really took some getting used to. The pulling g-forces off target were awesome and I got target fixation on a few runs and went below the hard deck of five thousand feet. By Monday, though, I was moving some dirt around inside the hundred-yard raked target ring and Johnny-mac lost a few beers due to my accuracy.

By Monday night, the banana freighter had moved within twenty miles of the international limit. The Coast Guard launched her 110-foot cutter from its Blue Buck Point station and she would head southeast until called in to make her catch on the Colombian freighter. The trap was set, the loran was indicating twelve miles, but was actually 2.2 miles short of the twelve-mile limit. Now it was up to Ortega and the *Jazz Singer* to move.

The freighter sailed within the twelve-mile limit between Pensacola and Mobile for a couple of days before it started to move west toward New Orleans. The Coast Guard allowed several drug runs to and from the banana freighter, to avoid tipping anyone off that they were being watched.

Wednesday was our first four-plane solo bombing hop and I was appointed the lead. We were the Topcat flight and would use this call sign to identify ourselves. Being the flight lead, I had to make all the radio calls for the division.

I taxied the division to the red label area to get our bombs armed by our ordnance crew, then to the end of the taxiway or hold-short line. Armed and ready for takeoff, I switched the flight to the tower. "New Orleans tower, Topcat flight ready for release, VFR departure to Marsh Island, live ordnance aboard."

"Roger, Topcat flight, position and hold runway 27."

"Roger. Position hold, Topcats," I repeated back. I taxied the division onto the active runway and took the left side, "Everyone line up on me in right echelon."

"Topcat flight, winds 260 at five knots, cleared for takeoff."

"Roger, cleared for takeoff," I replied.

Once cleared, I gave the turn-up signal with two fingers and it was passed down the line. When all aircraft were at military power, I made a circular motion with the control stick to check all the control surfaces, then moved my rudders forward and aft to ensure there was no binding, and looked at my gauges for proper indications. Once satisfied my machine was ready to fly, I gave my wingman a thumbs-up. After my wingman checked me over for any leaks or loose panels, he did the same procedures in the cockpit as I did, and when he was satisfied, he passed a thumbs-up to his wingman and so on down the line.

When all aircraft signaled they were up, I released my brakes and started my roll. Two seconds later my wingman started moving and so on until we were all airborne. When the last bird had wheels in the well, he gave two clicks on his mike button and that alerted me that everyone was safely in the air.

At that point I called the tower. "Tower, Topcat flight airborne."

"Roger, Topcat flight. Switch to departure and have a good one."

"Roger. Thank you, switching," I replied.

Waiting a few seconds so that everyone could switch to departure, I then made the call to check-in. "New Orleans departure, Topcat flight checking in, passing 1.2 for five thousand feet, direct Marsh Island."

"Roger, Topcat flight, radar contact, turn left to 190 and climb to one-five thousand."

"Roger, Topcat flight turning to 190, climbing to one-five thousand."

With everyone monitoring the same frequency, they were anticipating my signal for the turn to the left, followed by a hand signal to continue climbing to our cruising altitude of 15,000 feet. It felt pretty good running the show, but you had to know what was going on because you were responsible for the whole flight.

By the time we reached fifteen thousand feet, we were out over the water and departure control called. "Topcat flight, cleared direct Marsh Island, switch to range control, have a nice flight."

"Roger. Switching," I replied. Again, giving everyone time to switch up range control, I made the call. "Range control, Topcat flight inbound with sixteen live mk eighty-two bombs."

"Good morning, Topcat flight. The range is cold, you're clear to the delta target, call when in hot."

"Roger."

"Topcats, say altimeter setting."

"Altimeter is 29.97."

"Roger. Niner-niner-seven," I replied.

Resetting my altimeter, as I had hoped everyone else was doing, I led the flight down to 10,000 feet. As I lined the division up for the target, I stepped our speed up to three hundred knots. Passing over the target, I kissed off my wingman and broke hard left. Seven seconds later he did the same to his wingman until we all had a good separation.

Each of us made one cold pass before we started our live runs. As I pulled off target and was heading downwind, I reviewed my dive-bomb checklist. Function-selector switch—bombs and gm armed. Station-select switches—station two selected. Master-armament switch—on. Bomb-release button—waiting.

Approaching the run-in line, I rolled my TA-4 120 degrees onto her back, picked up the run-in line, rolled wings level, and called in hot. At a thirty-degree dive angle and four hundred knots, I hit my bomb-release button as I approached five thousand feet and pulled off the target. Pulling four and a half Gs as I climbed to ten grand, I looked over my left shoulder to see that I had a respectable hit.

Freddy Sexton was dash two, Slick was dash three, and Tommy Boyd was dash four. My second pass wasn't very good. I was too high on my run-in and the bomb overshot the target, but Freddy and Slick looked like they were having good runs. I couldn't pay much attention to Tommy's run because I was out of position to see his hits.

As I lined up for my third run everything felt right. I was on speed, my altitude was perfect, and things lined up nicely as I rolled wings level. Approaching the hard deck, I released the bombs, pickled them as we called it, pulled, and started my climbing left turn. As I passed through five grand I looked over my left shoulder and saw a bull's-eye hit. It couldn't have been prettier. I even got a bull's-eye call from the target observer.

Now that I had the proper sight picture, I wanted to drop six more. Unfortunately I only had one mk eighty-two left. By my fourth run I had my ground checkpoints in line and I wanted to see if I could nail that bull's-eye one more time. As I hit my roll in point everything looked good and I snapped my aircraft on her back, picked up the run-in line, and was six seconds from release when radio silence was broken.

"Topcats, Topcats, this is Blackhawk 01. Activate Texas Tea! I say again, activate Texas Tea."

I immediately went to safe on my armament switch, called off target cold, and climbed up to 10,000 feet. I got established in a left-hand turn and told my division to save all armament and join on me. While everyone was rendezvousing I checked in with drug-runner control on 355.5.

"Control, this is Topcats, how do you read?"

"Topcats, this is control. I read you loud and clear. Texas Tea is in operation. Target of interest is making run for mother at this time. Request two of you anchor over Marsh Island and two anchor over Blue Buck Point and wait for instructions."

"Roger," I replied.

By the time I had our instructions, everyone was aboard. I told Slick to circle over Marsh Island at 15,000 and I would take Freddy down to Blue Buck Point. At this point Slick was the lead for his section and was responsible for its flight safety. As Freddy and I broke off I told Slick, "Watch your fuel."

The coast-guard cutter started moving in on the banana freighter who thought he was safe in international waters. Blackhawk was following the *Jazz Singer*, which had already started its run down the coast toward Marsh Island.

Blackhawk called for the Marsh Island aircraft to assist on the chase. By the time Blackhawk got involved, he couldn't keep up and was losing the speedy Fountain boat. Listening to the net as we circled over our checkpoint, I thought, That lucky Slick is going to see some action.

Within twenty minutes things began to happen quickly. The coast-guard cutter intercepted the freighter and was in the process of boarding her when Slick and Tommy spotted the *Jazz Singer*. The boat was approaching Point au Fer and there was no mistaking it.

Slick started the flight down and I heard him tell Tommy to pick up a combat spread. This gave them a little separation and some room to maneuver if necessary. They rolled in behind the boat at two miles, descended to 150 feet, and slowed to two-hundred knots. When they got abeam the *Jazz Singer*, they couldn't believe their eyes. The boat was dead in the water and was full of women flashing their tits up at them as they flew by.

It was a decoy, and Ortega was still on the loose.

Slick and Tommy circled around the boat until Blackhawk came on the scene. Once they confirmed that Ortega was not aboard, they were released and sent back to anchor at Marsh Island. Checking their fuel, Slick figured they had forty minutes left on station before they had to head home.

While the coast-guard cutter was seizing the freighter, its crew spotted a white Fountain boat that appeared to be the kingpin's ride to safety. When the racing boat got close enough to see what was going on, it turned and headed west. The Coast Guard called control with an approximate heading and control gave us a vector to the area they wanted us to investigate.

I put Freddy into a combat spread as we started down. When we passed 10,000 feet, Freddy came up on tactical.

"My oil pressure's high."

"Did your 20-percent oil light illuminate?" I asked.

"Roger that. It's just come on."

This was bad news. He needed to get his bird on the ground ASAP.

"Okay, Fred, listen up. Call Lake Charles Airport, declare an emergency, and follow your low-oil-pressure procedures. I'm going to track this boat and I'll come pick you up once I turn the problem over to the DEA boys. Remember, fly the plane. I'll see you soon."

Freddy broke off and I continued on the vector. As I searched for the boat I thought, We're only students. How in the world did we get tied up in this mission? I wasn't sure where Slick was, I had Freddy inbound to a civilian airfield with an emergency, and I was getting low on fuel. I could see Grandpa Pettibone's headlines in next month's issue of *Approach*—A WHOLE DAY RUINED.

I figured I had twenty minutes left before I had to head to Lake Charles to refuel. After searching for five minutes or so, I spotted a target that fit the description of Ortega's escape boat. I tried to contact Blackhawk but was too low at that point.

In desperation, I descended to five hundred feet and made a recce pass to confirm my sighting. Not only was it Ortega's boat, but the sons of bitches were shooting at me. As I started to pull up and away from them, I heard a loud pop behlnd my head. Looking over my shoulder as I climbed to 10,000 feet, I could see a hole in the rear canopy and I couldn't believe what was happening to me.

After I leveled off, I contacted control. "Have located the escape boat. Am under fire. Running out of fuel and have to depart in ten minutes."

"Any ordnance aboard?"

"One mk eighty-two."

After three minutes or so, control came back and gave me the order to disable the racing boat any way I could before leaving station. I rogered my orders and got my weapons system set up for a no-shit bombing run.

All sorts of things started to race through my head. I had never practiced hitting a moving target on the ground, but I knew from my air-to-air guns that I had to lead my target. Kind of like when I was deer hunting in Maine with my dad. If he could only see the shit I was involved with now.

Running out of time and fuel, I flew over the speeding boat as I did the target on the delta range. After flying upwind for fifteen seconds, I broke left. As I passed abeam the target I rolled in hot, picking up the boat's wake as my run-in line. Using only a twenty degree dive angle, I figured it would place my bomb in the ball park and the frag would do the rest.

As I released my weapon and started to pull off target, all hell broke loose in the cockpit. The airplane became almost uncontrollable. When I looked at the instrument panel, I could see that both the utility hydraulics and flight-control hydraulic warning lights were flashing. I grabbed the stick with both hands and tried to level the wings and stop the rolling climb to the right. The controls were stiff and I knew I had some major problems.

As I passed through five thousand feet the cockpit started to fill with smoke, and terror raced through my body like an electric shock. Trying to control the plane with one hand and key the mike for my Mayday report with the other hand was almost impossible. Then it happened—the plane pitched over into a thirty-degree nosedive and I was out of control.

I grabbed for the lower ejection handle and pulled like hell. For an instant I saw my life history flash in front of me in slow motion. It's true, I thought. It really does happen like they say. Then the explosion of the canopy separating from the plane brought me back to reality. As the rocket motor fired, my egress from the plane was like a space-shuttle shot, and the wind blast just about ripped my head off. That was my last conscious thought.

I didn't know it, but the next time somebody mentioned my name, it would be to report that Ensign Matt "Sweetwater" Sullivan was listed as missing at sea and presumed dead.

16

WINGS
OF GOLD

Much of what happened next didn't happen to me. Instead it happened without me and I was only able to piece it together later on.

They searched for me for a week. Every day the planes went out, and every day they came back without having found anything. At the end of the week, reluctantly, a decision was made to call off the search. A memorial service was scheduled, and even Slick admitted that there was no reasonable alternative.

Commander Leonard was the escort for my parents when they came to Pensacola for the memorial service. The detachment flew back from NAS New Orleans and my uncle the Reverend Father David Duffy, said the mass. It was a very emotional event and the church was filled to capacity. Like my former classmate, Bobby Price, I didn't want anyone dressing in black and mourning my death. I had made it clear in my will that I was doing what I loved to do, and if an untimely death occurred, so be it.

After the service everyone gathered outside the base chapel to express their condolences to my family, without knowing what had been planned. Within five minutes, Captain Jim Lott made a solo low flyby in a TA-4. As he approached the gathered crowd at one hundred feet, he stood the plane on her tail and climbed straight up, doing victory rolls until he was almost out of sight, then a flight of four more TA-4s flew over, with one aircraft peeling off to symbolize the missing man. As far as the attendees were concerned, it put a final end to my short but rewarding experience.

The members of my family were having a rough time maintaining their composure in the reception line. I had been the only son, so the Sullivan family name came to an end. When Slick Morely approached the family, he broke down and cried, telling my mother how sorry he was and how close I had been to him. My mother brought Slick close to her and whispered to him, "He's free of all pain now and he's enjoying the ecstasies of paradise, which are beyond our human understanding."

Slick gave her a hug and then walked to the parking lot, where he stood and looked into the sky for several minutes. He and the rest of the detachment that flew in for the memorial service would head back to New Orleans the following Sunday to complete the remaining week or so of their weapons det. Slick stayed in the BOQ at Sherman rather than going to the house on the beach. He couldn't face looking at my belongings this soon. He and another officer planned to inventory all of my personal items when they returned and forward them to my parents.

The trip back to New Orleans was uneventful, and after all the planes were on deck, Lieutenant Commander Gosma got everyone together and pointed out that I was gone and it was time to press on. But he told them that if anyone still felt uneasy by Monday morning, he would arrange counseling.

On the tenth day after my ejection, I began to recall some of the events that had led up to the explosive acceleration that launched me into the hostile environment of space. Yes, I was still alive, but I had some memory loss and couldn't put the puzzle together.

Lying on my back, I opened my eyes and focused on what was the most beautiful set of legs I had seen in a long time. In a heavy Cajun accent, a voice asked, "How are you feeling today?"

I replied, "What do you mean, how am I feeling today? Where am I? Who are you? What's going on here?"

"Hah, you feel better you, no?"

Sitting up on a mattress on the floor in a crude-looking room, I faced the woman who had literally saved my life.

"Who are you?" I asked again.

"I'm Kimberly Benetton. I found you floating in the water a week ago and I brought you to my house to help you get better."

"A week ago? You mean to tell me I've been here a week?"

"That's right, mister. You were unconscious for almost a day, and when you came to, you were incoherent and confused. I fixed that nasty cut over your lip the best I could and nursed you back to health. You need to see a real doctor when you get back to where you belong. I had to sew that cut shut with fishing line to keep it from bleeding."

"You found me in the water?"

"That's right. You were wedged between two cypress trees near my fishing route and were about to be eaten by several gators when I pulled you into my skiff."

A chill ran up my spine at the thought.

"You're a big boy. I had a hell of a time getting you into my boat, me. My uncle helped get you up into my flat."

"What do you do?" I asked.

"I fish and run moonshine for my uncle, who sells to fishing camps along the bayou. What was all that gear you had on, you?" Kimberly asked.

"I fly jets for the Navy, and I had to eject due to a malfunction. God, I need to get back to New Orleans—how far are we from there?"

"By boat two days, by land one—that is, if you can get a ride."

"I really need to get back, my squadron thinks I'm missing."

"Missing, hell, they think you're dead."

"Dead, how do you know?"

"Heard it on the radio. They looked all over this area for a week, but I kept you safe."

"Why didn't you bring them to me?"

"Couldn't . . ."

"Why?"

"Scared to. I was afraid they would put me in jail."

"Jail, my ass, they would have made a hero out of you."

"Nope, they've been trying to get me and my uncle for years for running 'shine and fishin' without papers. I'd gone to jail for sure, me. Plus I . . ."

"You what?"

"Oh, never mind."

Things started to fall in place now, and I knew I had to get back to civilization. I had heard some wild stories about Cajun people and what goes on in the bayou. I was thankful that this good-looking Cajun woman found me first. Who knows what could have happened, I thought.

"Can you take me to a road so I can hitch a ride?" I asked.

"Tomorrow Happy Anderson will be returning to New Orleans from his week at sea. I'll get you on his shrimp boat. I supply him with fresh fish and 'shine and he brings me supplies I need from New Orleans. It works out well. We've been trading this way for years. Happy is dependable and he'll get you to New Orleans safely."

It wasn't long before the sun went down and the night sounds of the bayou came alive. This was the first time that I had any real awareness of what was going on around me. As Kimberly fixed some gator steaks and fish I started to think about my family and what they must be going through. What a nightmare it must be, I thought.

I started to get out from under the covers and realized I didn't have any clothes on. I hopped back under the sheets and Kimberly laughed. "Don't you worry, Matt, I've seen you naked for a week now. You can walk around if you like."

"How do you know my name?" I asked.

"Saw it on your green suit. And it was all over the news."

"Oh," I said.

"Why you called Sweetwater, you?" She laughed.

"It's a long story," I said.

"I bet. You got a lot of stories, you. I bet that, too."

"Don't be funny."

"Here's your underwear, if you want."

Feeling more than a little embarrassed, I slipped it on before getting up to walk around her one-room house.

Looking outside, I was amazed to see that the structure was up on stilts. Several stairs led down to a boarded pier where a boat was tied up.

"Kimberly," I said, "I have to go to the bathroom. Where is it?"

"Out the door and 'round back. You'll see a little house—that's it."

Taking the lantern that Kimberly gave me, I worked my way down the steps and around back to a two-hole outhouse.

Later, as we sat around the table eating some crawfish gumbo, I asked Kimberly, "How long have you been living this way?"

"About eight years," she said.

"Where're your parents?"

Her face grew cloudy for a moment before she

said, "Dead. Killed in a car wreck. Uncle Lotus took me in and taught me how to survive in the swamps."

"What about school?"

"Quit after the tenth grade, me."

"Do you ever want to get out of here?"

"I did at first, but I had nowhere to go, so I made the best of it and I'm doing all right for myself now."

"What about men?" I asked. I suddenly realized that I was staring at her rather large and shapely breasts. I felt myself blushing, but pressed on. "Did you ever think about getting married?"

"I was raped by some swamprats a few years back and haven't had much use for men since."

"Why didn't you get out then?"

"I couldn't."

She seemed reluctant to continue, but I had the feeling I shouldn't let her back away from whatever it was that seemed to be bothering her. "Why?" I asked.

"I kill one of those bastards that raped me."

"Is that what you wanted to tell me earlier?"

"Yes, I'm afraid the game wardens are still after me."

"Do they know you did it?"

"Can't say for sure, but I ain't about to find out."

Kimberly gave me a glass of clear liquid with my soup and asked me to take a swig. I took a drink, didn't get much reaction at first, and was about to tell her so, when it hit me like a team of mules. "What is that shit?" I asked.

"It's some of Uncle Lotus's shine. What do you think?"

"Boy, that's some strong stuff."

"Not really. Just sip it and it will go down nice and smooth."

* * *

By twelve the next day, I had gathered my belongings and helped Kimberly load the fish and booze, then we headed for the rendezvous point. At times I didn't think the old skiff was going to get us there. We had about twenty minutes before Happy steamed into view.

As I was climbing onto the shrimp boat Kimberly gave me an address where I could write to her. Happy would pick up her mail once a week and bring it, along with the supplies she needed.

As I hugged and kissed her good-bye, I told her I would never forget what she had done for me, and that I would always keep in touch. I also told her that if she ever needed my help, I would come to her rescue.

As Happy pulled alongside Kimberly's skiff I realized that his shrimp boat wasn't exactly state-of-the-art and I had some doubts it would make it back to New Orleans. Kimberly boarded and asked me to wait until she explained to Happy what I was all about. After ten minutes or so, Happy and his crew of two came out to welcome me. He and his crew members looked like they had come from the movie *Deliverance,* especially Happy himself. He looked a lot like the banjo player. After the introductions were out of the way, I helped Kimberly load her goods aboard and we got under way.

Happy and his crew weren't very friendly at first. I spent most of the day lying on fishing nets wondering what the future had in store for me. I tried to help the crew with some chores, but they insisted I relax.

That evening things lightened up a bit and we got into some moonshine, which helped break the ice.

The reason everyone's jaws were so tight was the fact that I was an outsider and they were concerned about the secrecy of their operation. Once I gained their trust, life was more pleasant. Still not real comfortable around the crew, I didn't get much sleep that night.

The next day Happy treated me like I was part of the crew. He showed me how the shrimp operation worked and let me steer the boat for a while. I expressed my concern for Kimberly's well-being and that I wanted to repay her for saving my life. He said he took her into New Orleans a couple times a year to socialize, but she could never wait to get back to the swamp. "It's in her blood, son," he said, "and she'll probably die there."

"If I wanted to give her something, Happy, how would I go about getting it to her?"

"If it's a letter or a package, just mail it to that address she gave you and I'll see she gets it."

"What if it's much bigger?"

"What do you mean?"

"I want to buy her a new boat and motor. That hole-ridden skiff she's got now isn't safe. Could you find a suitable boat and motor for her?"

"You bet I can. I know just the place."

"What kind of money we talking, Happy?"

"I can get a used flat-bottom boat and motor that would be perfect for under a thousand."

"Good, when I get back I'll send you a check, and if you could make that happen, I'd appreciate it."

"Consider it done."

As night started to fall we steamed passed Port

Sulphur, on the Mississippi, which was about an hour from Happy's slip and New Orleans. I started to get butterflies in my stomach, because I knew once I stepped on that base, all hell would break loose. I was torn as to whether I should call my parents and let them know I was all right or let the Navy do it. I was afraid the shock might be too overwhelming if I called.

About ten minutes out, Happy gave me all the info on how to contact him and what I could and couldn't discuss about his operation. I reassured him that I would only talk about my rescue and return to safety. Happy's slip was at a large commercial fishing pier just on the outskirts of New Orleans. There were plenty of taxis available, so I wouldn't have a problem getting a lift. Happy lent me some money to hold me over. At first I hadn't been sure about Happy and his crew; now I knew why Kimberly thought so highly of him. He was a hardworking soul, and once you had gained his confidence, you were a friend for life.

As I stepped onto the pier I said good-bye and waved to his crew. "Thanks for the lift. I'll be in touch within a week."

As I walked off the pier and up the stairs to the street, I got a lot of stares due to my torn-up flight suit and the flight gear I was carrying. As I crossed the street to get a taxi, I spotted a line of phone booths and I couldn't keep from calling home. I didn't have the correct change, so I had to call collect. I couldn't imagine what would happen when my folks answered.

I dialed zero and got a New Orleans operator. "Ma'am, my name is Ensign Matt Sullivan and I'd like to make a collect call to my parents in Dexter, Maine, but before you connect me, I need to explain something to you."

I told her what had happened and she was more than willing to dial the number and not go through the normal spiel of saying, "Will you except a collect call from Matt Sullivan?"

When the phone rang, my heart was in my mouth. An eternity later the receiver was lifted, a man's voice said, "Yes, good evening . . ."

I said, "Dad, Dad, it's me, Matt. I'm alive and well."

"Oh my God," he said, "Matt, Matt, my son . . ." He started to cry. Within a few seconds my mother was on the extension and she was hysterical. After the initial shock had subsided and I could talk, I explained what had happened.

Before I could continue, the New Orleans operator interrupted. "South Central Bell will be paying for this call, and we all wish you the best."

I thanked her for her generosity and continued my story. "Mom, Dad, the Navy doesn't know I'm alive yet, so you'll probably be getting another call. After I hang up, I'll go to the base and check in with the command duty officer. At that point all hell will break loose, so just sit tight and wait for the call."

"Shall we tell them we've already talked with you?" my mother asked.

"Sure, tell them I called as soon as I got off the shrimp boat."

"Should we fly down?" Dad asked.

"You'd better wait and see what develops. I suspect I'll have to be hospitalized for several days while they run tests. Let's wait until I get this behind me.

Maybe I can take some leave and come home."

"Okay, son, take care and let us know where you'll be once you check in. Don't worry about the time, we won't be able to sleep anyway."

After I hung up, it felt as though the world had fallen off my shoulders. What a relief! I was glad I'd talked to my parents first, rather than have the Navy break the news. I walked over to the taxi stand and got a cab.

As we drove to the base the cabdriver was very interested in my story, and when he dropped me off at the front gate, he wouldn't let me pay. Come to find out he was a maintenance chief working after hours to help make ends meet. I thanked him for the lift and checked in with the gate sentry.

Having lost my ID card in the accident, I had only my dog tags for identification. The sentry called the duty office and had the duty driver escort me to the duty office. Once I was inside the duty office, things began to happen very quickly. The command duty officer was called, and when he got to the office, he made things happen.

I was taken directly to the dispensary and within an hour I was transported to the local hospital for tests and observation. The military chain of command was activated and everyone was notified that I was alive and well.

The next day I was transferred to the aerospace medical center at NAS Pensacola. There I would undergo extensive tests and a complete evaluation. It was like a hero's welcome when I got off the plane. Commander Leonard and a lot of the squadron personnel were waiting to greet me, along with several reporters from the Pensacola area. After a brief statement I was escorted into an ambulance and taken to the hospital.

After a series of tests I was hooked up to several IVs and put in a private room. Thinking I would get some peace and quiet, I started to fall asleep when suddenly the door opened and in came five members of the accident board. The interrogation went on for several hours and I was totally exhausted when they left.

Even though I was in pretty good shape physically, the doctors wanted to do some brain scans to make sure nothing had been damaged. They gave me a mild sedative so that I could get a good night's sleep.

At ten the next morning I was scheduled for an EEG then some aeronautical maneuvers in the centrifuge. These tests would determine whether I would remain in the flight program or be washed out.

By the afternoon's end I was pretty tired and began to realize I was not in the best of health. My body fluids and blood chemistry were out of whack and I needed rest and proper nourishment to get back on track. That evening my doctor let me have a few visitors.

Slick was my first caller, and it was great to see his smiling face. "You son of a bitch, Water, I knew you were too tough to die. It's great to have you back."

We gave each other a big hug and Slick brought me up to speed on the latest news.

"Your bombing run was a great success," he said. "The boat was disabled to the point where it almost sank. The DEA and Coast Guard caught Ortega and seized the Colombian freighter."

He told me there was a lot of media coverage and newspaper articles on the operation and that the Navy got a big plug for our efforts. "I have all the articles at home," he added, "in case you want to read about your little exploit."

Then he got serious. "Tell me what happened, Sweetwater. We looked for you for a week and came up with nothing."

I told him the whole story from the time I pulled the ejection handle until I got to the base. When I finished, Slick said, "I'd better go. I'll be in touch to see if you need anything." As he walked out Commander and Mrs. Leonard walked in.

"Hi, Skipper," I said. "How are you, Mrs. Leonard?"

"I'm fine, Matt. How are you feeling?"

"Not bad, considering all the testing I've been through. Have you heard any word, Skipper, as to my condition?"

"Not yet, but we'll know in a few days. Matt, after you're released from here, I want you to take ten days convalescent leave and go home and visit with your family. I've been updating them each day on your progress and they can't wait to see you. The doctors feel you'll be ready to go home in a few days."

"How about my training? I want to graduate with my class."

"Matt, don't worry about that now. Let me handle it. That's what they pay me the big bucks for! You just relax and get yourself back in shape. If there's anything you need, please feel free to contact me."

"Thank you, sir."

"Take care of yourself, and get some rest now. Good night."

"Good night, and thanks for stopping by."

As the days rolled by, I began to feel stronger, and stronger and by the fifth day I got the green light to go home. I'll never, ever forget that day. Captain Jim Giefer, my flight surgeon, entered my room at seven sharp on the tenth of June and said, "Ensign Sullivan, we can't find a bloody thing wrong with you. You are to report to your commanding officer, in a full flight status, and finish your flight training."

I let out a yell that must have been heard around the world. Or, at least, down the hall. I got on the blower, called Slick, and told him, "Get your ass down here to take me home."

"You mean it?" he asked.

"Bet your sweet ass, I mean it. Get a move on, partner."

Within an hour I was checked out and on my way to the beach house. When I got home, Slick had welcome-home signs and posters from friends hanging all over the place.

After the excitement of getting home died down, I called Happy to find out if he'd found a boat. He told me he'd located the perfect boat for Klmberly. The cost was 950 bucks, and I told him a check would be in the mail that day. He'd deliver it on Monday, on his way out to sea. When I sat down to write out the check, I decided to throw in an extra hundred for Happy himself.

As I walked out and sat down at the kitchen table, Slick threw a white envelope on the table in front of me. "What's this?" I asked.

"Open it and find out."

I broke the seal and dumped the contents on the table. My leave papers, a plane ticket my squadron mates had chipped in for, and an invitation to a party in my honor lay in front of me. I was speechless. Tears came to my eyes.

"Welcome home, Sweetwater," he said, "from all your friends. By the way, Molar Man is throwing the party for you," he said. "It'll be a long time before you forget this one. It starts at three tomorrow and will go on until we put you on the plane Sunday morning. You'd better pack now, because you won't have enough brain cells left to think with, come Sunday."

The trip home was a long one and I arrived at Bangor airport at 5:00 P.M. When I walked up the jetway and saw the crowd, I thought my parents had brought half the town with them. After all the crying and hugs subsided, we left for Dexter.

During the week at home I spent some prime time with my family and did some fishing with my dad. By the end of my leave, I was ready to get back to Pensacola and get on with the final stages of flight training. My main concern was to finish with my class, with whom I had trained for almost two years.

When I reported off leave Sunday night, the duty officer informed me the CO wanted to see me at eight sharp Monday morning.

Monday morning I was standing in the Skipper's reception room. At eight on the nose he asked me into his office and told me to be seated. "Matt," he said,

"I'll be your instructor and we'll get you completed in time so you can graduate with your class. It's not going to be easy, though. You may be flying two or three times a day when we get down to the wire."

"That's okay, sir," I said. "I'll do whatever it takes."

"Tomorrow we'll fly a back-in-the-saddle hop just to get you back in the air. If things go well, we'll fly a couple of form hops and do some acrobatics the rest of the week. Then we'll get back into the bombing patterns and finish up what you missed down in New Orleans. Your classmates have already started their field-carrier landing practice for an August boat. I've talked to Captain Frank Duffy, the CO of the *America*, and he's going to let you carrier qualify on his ship in September when the fleet comes out to get refreshed. We'll work out of NAS Norfolk and Lieutenant Mapleford will work you up and wave you at the ship."

"Sounds good, Skipper. I'm ready to go."

"Great. See you tomorrow morning at nine. Oh, before I forget, your class adviser needs to see you at the university to get things back on track so you can finish with your class."

"Thank you, sir. I'll give him a call and set up a meeting."

This was one thorn in my side that I didn't need right now, but I had gone this far, so I'd better see it through. I called Bob Barr, my class adviser, and arranged an afternoon meeting. When I left his office, I was pleasantly surprised at his willingness to complete me on time. The university bent over backward to meet my needs. This was all I needed for motivation. The guidelines were set, the plans were laid, now I just had to execute.

My first few flights were a little rusty, but I was back in the groove after my third one. It was kind of like riding a bike—you never forget how, it just takes a while to get back in step. I wasn't the least bit apprehensive about strapping that TA-4 to my butt and getting back into the air. Everything felt natural and Commander Leonard was pleased with my progress.

My bombing and rocket hops weren't as realistic as rolling in on the drug runners' boat, but I did have one advantage—the targets didn't shoot back.

After finishing my weapons phase, I had a couple of weeks before I started FCLPs. I used the time to catch up on my studies and work on my thesis.

The next month was a ballbuster and I didn't see much of Slick or the outside world. Most of my time was spent at the library or in an airplane getting ready to hit the boat. The one thing I didn't want was a poor performance at the ship, where the fleet pilots would be watching.

By the end of my practice carrier landing periods, Lieutenant Mapleford felt I was ready and had no qualms about sending me to the ship. Saturday afternoon we left for Norfolk and flew up as a flight of two. Lieutenant Mapleford walked aboard the ship Sunday evening and she got under way Monday morning.

The overhead message came in Monday evening and I was scheduled for a nine o'clock bounce period. This meant I had to be over the ship ready to land at 9:00 A.M. The skipper would lead me out and circle overhead until I completed my six traps, then he would drop down and get a couple of landings himself. After we fueled, he would pick up Lieutenant Mapleford and fly back to the beach.

Although I was confident about going to the boat, I didn't get much sleep and watched the hours tick off until it was time to get up. We briefed at six and I was turning and burning at 0820. The flight to the ship only took twenty minutes since it was working sixty miles out from Virginia Beach. As we anchored overhead I said a prayer that everything would go all right.

At five after nine the airboss said, "Sweetwater, the deck is yours. Come on down!"

I kissed off the skipper and made a diving left turn to set up for the break. The skipper said, "Give 'em hell, Water," as I peeled off.

At eight hundred feet and three hundred knots I came smokin' into the break and smartly broke at the bow.

My first two passes would be touch-and-go's, and if everything looked good, my third pass would be an arrestment. The setup and start for my first pass couldn't have been better. I flew an okay pass to the deck, added power, and climbed back to pattern altitude for my next pass. Abeam the LSO's platform, Lieutenant Mapleford said, "Water, drop your hook."

Within ninety seconds I was aboard with my first trap in the Skyhawk. The catshot was a little more aggressive then in the T-2 but nothing I couldn't handle.

After my sixth arrestment I was supposed to spin off and get some fuel while the skipper got his landings. I didn't say anything and the yellow shirt taxied me to the cat. Before I knew it, I was airborne and turning downwind for my seventh trap. If this wasn't the "cat's meow," I don't know what was!

Before it was over, I had bagged an extra five traps and was pretty proud. As I sat on the foul line, just abeam the landing area, the purple shirts gassed me up. The skipper of the ship came up on the radio and said, "Sweetwater, those extra traps were for that bull's-eye on the drug boat. Good show and good luck in the fleet."

I came back with a "Thank you, sir," and got ready to blast off with my skipper.

The game plan was for Skipper Leonard to launch on cat one, and me on cat two, with a five-second delay. Once safely airborne, I would join on him and we'd fly back to the beach. After I was aboard, the Skipper made a left turn and we did a low flyby of the ship as we departed.

After we landed and shut down at NAS Norfolk, the Skipper and Lieutenant Mapleford came over and congratulated me. I was riding pretty high, because I knew I'd flown some good passes and hadn't let anyone down. That evening we hit town to celebrate.

The flight back to Pensacola was uneventful and the following week I would be designated a naval aviator. As I got into the Silver Fox I couldn't believe that my dream was finally going to come true.

The winging ceremony was scheduled for Friday morning, so my parents and sisters would arrive Wednesday afternoon. Slick and I were scheduled to give our final dissertations on Monday and we would receive our degrees on Friday during the winging ceremony.

Slick's parents were scheduled to arrive on

Thursday, so we set up a dinner party for both our families at the officers' club for that evening. Slick had met my family during the memorial service, but I had not met his. It would be a nice way to spend the last evening before the big day.

The whole week prior to getting our wings was packed solid with wrapping up loose ends. Logbooks had to be verified, checkout procedures had to be completed, tests and final reports had to be given, and reservations and transportation had to be arranged for our families. The atmosphere around our house was like the week before a major household move—parties, business transactions, and emotional strain. By Thursday night's end, I couldn't wait until it was all over.

Friday morning was like suiting up for the big game. We had not shifted to our winter uniforms yet, so the uniform of the day was service dress whites with medals. We made sure we looked sharp, as though we were going to a personnel inspection. Our families met us at the house and we drove as a group to the base.

The ceremony was being held in the base auditorium and we had to be seated by 9:00 A.M. On the hour, Vice Admiral Ray Turk, Chief of Naval Training, walked out onto the stage with Captain George Powell, Commanding Officer Naval Aviation Schools Command, Captain Jim Morris, CO Naval Air Station Pensacola, Commander Tom Leonard, CO VT-4, and Dr. Abraham Blumberg, President of the University of West Florida. The assembled crowd came to its feet and the school's command band played our national anthem.

Vice Admiral Turk was the guest speaker and he addressed the graduating class. He talked about the history of naval aviation and what an elite group we were about to join. His speech was not long, but he made it very clear that we had reached the hallmark of naval aviation and were about to become members of an exclusive fraternity, one that was qualified to operate from a ship at sea as well as from land.

After the opening remarks, Captain Powell began the winging ceremony. The families of the students receiving their wings were asked in turn to join the officers on stage. It was naval tradition for the mother to pin the coveted wings of gold on her son's chest. Once the wings were in place, we were presented our master's degrees by Dr. Blumberg, then proceeded through a receiving line to be congratulated by the top brass as we left the stage.

The students went in alphabetical order. But when Captain Powell skipped over my name and went to the next student, my heart skipped a beat and I felt a sinking feeling in my stomach. Slick looked at me and I looked back with a blank stare.

After all my peers had received their wings, Captain Powell turned the podium over to Vice Admiral Turk. He started off by saying, "Ladies and gentlemen, as you have probably noticed, we have omitted one officer, not because we've forgotten him, but because we have something special to present to him. Ensign Matt 'Sweetwater' Sullivan, front and center."

I got up from my seat, walked directly to the podium, and squared off in front. "Reporting as ordered, sir."

At that point the admiral read the following: "The president of the United States takes pleasure in presenting the Distinguished Flying Cross and Purple Heart to Ensign Matthew Howard Sullivan, United States Navy, for services set forth in the following citation." He then reviewed the sequence of events that had occurred when I disabled the drug boat and was shot down.

After he pinned the medals on, he requested my family's presence up on the stage. Once they were in position, Captain Powell handed my mother a set of wings and Admiral Turk said, "Mrs. Sullivan, would you please pin those wings of gold on your son?"

As the tears poured down her cheeks her trembling hands pinned the wings above my chest. The admiral continued, "Ensign Sullivan, your road to gold will go down in naval history as one of the greatest achievements ever by a student naval aviator. We will never forget you. And before Dr. Blumberg presents you with your master's degree, I would like to give you your orders to VF-124, the Fighting Gunslingers, at NAS Miramar, Fighter Town USA."

The crowd came to its feet and gave me a standing ovation.

 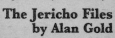